Annie's World: Jake's Legacy

Daniel Lance Wright

Annie's World: Jake's Legacy
Copyright © 2012 by Daniel Lance Wright

This is a work of fiction. Any resemblance to actual persons, living or dead, is purely coincidental.

ISBN: 978-0-9850066-2-4

Library of Congress Control Number: 2012934024

Cover Design by All Things That Matter Press

Published in 2012 by All Things That Matter Press

CHAPTER ONE
JUST WHEN LIFE SEEMS POINTLESS...

Foot pain interrupted Jake Henderson's rambling thoughts on the world as it was. Boots pulled off a corpse a few miles back to replace the ones he wore had little sole remaining, but more than on the ones he now called his own. This pair wasn't much better. Add the reshaping process and he wondered if it was an improvement at all. Foraging for food must wait while he rested. A fallen tree made a convenient place to rest. He used the time to rub circulation into his hot, tired feet while yearning for a cool breeze.

Dropping the frayed knapsack slung over his shoulder to the ground, he sat heavily on the log. As his butt touched, he grunted and sighed. It was such a welcome relief to simply sit. While wrestling a boot off, he looked to the remnants of a nearby building sheathed in rusted corrugated metal—a barn once upon a time. It must be less than a hundred years old, given its condition. "Humph." *Probably built when some farmer thought things would get better.* He pulled the other boot off and looked at wiggling toes, and then propped a foot on his knee to rub it as his eyes drifted back to the barn.

Suddenly, a locust slashed across his view in a darting flight for its life from a mockingbird. "Don't let it get away, pal," he muttered to the bird.

The gray bird deftly plucked the insect from the air.

"Yeah!" He winked and nodded approval. "That's how it's done." Jake felt kinship with the bird; he spent most waking hours in search of food, too.

Pushing shoulder length sandy blonde hair back from a beard the same color, a sudden streamer of air, a cool breeze, on his now-exposed sweaty neck eased his anxieties for a moment. The sky appeared pristine blue, but scarcely worth a glance. The morning spring in his step had become an afternoon plod. The day wore down—so did he. Ill-fitting boots only compounded an existing problem.

With an analytical eye, he looked again at the ramshackle building. It seemed structurally sound in the front, a broad entryway centered. If doors had ever existed, they were long gone; the back wall and roof, sometime in the distant past, had collapsed. He wondered what use it might serve. Shelter for the night perhaps. As quickly as the idea hit, it was dismissed—too much daylight remained for foraging, regardless of fatigue. Food trumped all. Nevertheless, he considered its potential usefulness. He might pass this way again.

Judging by the odor, a thorough foot airing was overdue. He

switched feet and propped the other ankle over a knee and gave it equal treatment. He moaned, enjoying the sensation.

The guttural sound of pleasure stopped abruptly when he noticed movement at the back corner of the collapsed building.

A form appeared.

He sat still and made no sound.

At first it appeared apelike, but as it cleared the brush between trees he saw it was a man. The scraggly beard, long hair, deteriorating clothes and grimy face indicated he had been victimized by this world, too. The man had not noticed him and Jake wanted it to remain that way. Something held the guy's attention inside the portion of the structure still standing. Jake was leery of people, and more so of ones who skulked about and didn't announce their presence.

As the world regressed, continuing a downward slide that began some two hundred years earlier, there was no law enforcement and no doctors. No one remained alive he depended on: no family, no friends. The walls of the solitary prison Jake lived in were mortared with distrust. If the man he watched happened to be up to something nefarious, the outcome could not be good. Toward whom he didn't know; nor why and didn't care, but he was curious. All the while he continued rubbing the aching foot.

Whatever was inside the building continued to hold the man's attention. He sneaked to a rusted-out hole in one of the corrugated metal panels and watched for a time.

Jake wondered what in God's name he was so intently staring at.

The man pulled away and searched the ground, snatching up a jagged shard, possibly a piece of the metallic skin off the old barn.

Jake finally got a good look at the stranger's face. The man smirked, rotating the rusting metal in his hand, feeling for the better grip, then turned and glided high on his toes, disappearing from sight around the back corner of the dilapidated structure.

Jake heard an angry male voice coming from inside but nothing he understood. Suddenly, he was immensely curious and had to know what was going on inside that old barn.

He pulled his boots on, then sprang to his feet. He ran to the same rusted hole the man had used, but stopped to the side of it. He moved laterally until he could see the goings-on inside.

The man had confronted a pretty wisp of a woman with long blonde hair, about twenty-five, he guessed. There was nothing about her appearance that indicated she could protect herself.

"I'm not tellin' ya again. Give me the sack," the man bellowed, brandishing the metal shard menacingly.

The woman didn't seem the slightest unnerved. "I can't do that," she said in a friendly tone. "It's all the food I have, but I'll share with you." She smiled.

Although calm of voice, her stance was defensive, legs spread and arms crossed over her chest, blocking his view of the cloth bag on the ground behind her. Clearly, this wasn't the first time she had been challenged.

How can she be so calm? That guy has crazy eyes, Jake thought. People get killed for less every day.

She was smooth-skinned and feminine and certainly did not convey the appearance of a fighter. The man stood more than a head taller.

"What's your name," she asked.

"Last chance, gimme the sack."

"Sorry, I can't do that."

He lunged, the jagged piece of metal leading the way to her abdomen.

She spun sideways, stabbing a boot heel into the wrist of the weapon-holding hand.

His fingers sprang apart and the strip of metal slammed, clanking, into the wall. He roared and grabbed his wrist.

Resuming an at-ease posture, she let her arms fall limp and then held her hands out in a show of acceptance. "Look, I don't want to hurt you. I don't even want to fight you. Believe me when I tell you there's nothing in that sack worth your life or mine. Let's try this again. What's your name?" she said, almost pleading.

From between hair-covered lips, the man bared crooked yellow teeth, snarled, and charged.

With uncanny speed she leapt nearly six feet off the ground and locked her legs around his head before twirling to the ground. His spinning body followed, hitting the ground in an explosion of dust.

The woman rose and dusted the brown denim vest she wore over a loose-fitting, lighter brown shirt. "Now look what you've done. My clothes are dirty. I just washed them yesterday." She clucked her tongue. "For heaven's sake," she said, eerily nonchalant, still slapping dust from her pants.

Jake looked on, surprised and awed by what he witnessed. She was marvelous. A fine-boned woman incapacitated a much larger man with speed that boggled his mind. Now the wretch lay on his side, semiconscious.

She squatted next to the man, arms over the points of her knees. Jake was enamored. Her hair caught afternoon rays through the wide doorway, glistening wisps dancing over her cheeks in the breeze. Such femininity, grace and beauty just didn't match up to the extraordinary display of fighting skill or her present calmness. She was neither angry nor scared.

Examining the man from head to toe, she drew a breath then released it in a nasal snort. In lackadaisical fashion, she shoved him onto his back.

He moaned and reached for his head.

"I sure would like to be your friend." She patted his stomach, then rubbed tiny circles on it almost as if she petted a puppy. "But we can't even begin until I know your name. So, what's it gonna be? Do I get your name and we get chummy or shall we dance again?" She patted his stomach a final time.

He rolled over onto his side then onto his stomach and pushed up onto hands and knees. He fell sideways to a sitting position. Powdery dust drifted away from him. "Baker," he said, then grimaced and grunted. "Hiram Baker." He held his drooping head in both hands.

"Do you always force your intentions on people, Hiram Baker?"

"A man has to eat."

"True. But there's plenty to be foraged in the countryside. By chance you've had a bad day, a person, as myself, might share with you. We all have those days."

She stared at him for a second longer, then stood. "Oh, well." She sauntered to the cloth bag that had started it all. "If you insist on acting like a lunatic, you're going to be a high maintenance friend for sure." She snickered. "We have to do something about that nasty temper, Hiram Baker." The young woman looked at him and smiled as if he were a pal from way back. She then turned away. The warmth of her smile and glint in her eyes indicated she already knew they would become friends.

She knelt and sat on her heels in front of the sack, flipped back the flap and produced a small handful of berries, what appeared to be a piece of dried meat, and a few mushrooms.

The man came to his feet. Without taking his eyes from her, he retrieved the metal shard and, in one giant step, approached from behind as she remained down on her knees looking through the bag.

Jake's breath hitched as he prepared to scream a warning. His face distorted into what should have been a yell but, suddenly, he was conflicted. Survival instinct kicked in and prevented him from warning her. His head overrode his heart and he made no sound.

Back presented to him, she continued rummaging through the sack. "I think I have plenty to keep you going until you can find something on your own and, if you like, I can help—"

The man grabbed the hair at the front of her head and yanked, flipping her chin up and ramming the pointed piece of jagged metal into her neck. Blood gushed in spurts from the jugular wound. Still holding her hair, he dragged her away from the sack, then tossed all she had removed back inside. His disregard for the woman was absolute.

She writhed in the spreading dark red pool, strength fading.

Jake stood, mouth open, paralyzed.

A young girl leaped from a darkened corner, ran to the squirming woman and dropped to her knees. It was clear the injured woman was losing the battle for life as she pathetically grabbed at her throat. The youngster wore pants too short under a threadbare top too large. Her shoes didn't match, and her light brown hair blended with the color of her face.

The man took his prize and marched to the space created by the missing panel at the rear of the building where he'd entered. The brute looked over his shoulder and snarled, "Bitch." Then he was gone.

Jake stepped through the doorway at the front of the building. The woman arched her back, then collapsed. She moved no more, eyes fixed and vacant. Limp fingers draped the end of the makeshift weapon protruding from her neck. The young girl cried. Jake heard no sound other than a raspy push of air from the youngster's throat.

Stepping around the grieving girl, he looked into the woman's lifeless eyes, and then sank to one knee. I'm no better than that guy. I should've warned her, he thought.

The youngster ignored his presence.

Jake didn't speak to nor touch the child. He let her mourn. The woman was likely her mother, or, given her youthful appearance, an older sister perhaps. Regardless, the woman had been the girl's caregiver and now she was gone.

He rose and walked outside.

Still the girl ignored him.

He continued on to the log where he'd rested. With an exhausted thud, he collapsed onto it. Shame and guilt tired him more than the day's work had. The face of the little girl burned an indelible image in his mind. He wondered if he should help her. After a time and several conjured points of view, he concluded it was best not to get involved. Safer. Vigorously rubbing his face, he washed his conscience of complicity.

He rested his elbows on his knees. Loathsome thoughts about how the world had gotten into this mess swarmed him. Four generations had passed since the decline began; the passing of the fifth lay in the near future. Four generations of Texans in his family had come and gone since that fateful decade almost two hundred years ago. 'Texan' was an empty label. Texas had not been a state or member of any union in over a century, just a name for the place he lived. There had not been a United States of America in many decades. Nowhere in the known world existed a stable government. Texas had reverted to what it had been before given the name.

Dissolution of central governments worldwide brought economic evolution to a halt in a single generation some eighteen decades ago. World economies collapsed, followed closely by governments—a domino effect, simple and pure, leaving in its wake the world as it was: chaotic and primitive.

Now, coming out of a cold winter, he welcomed the warm spring of 2208, but it only marked another season of surviving. The after effects of that drunken orgy of excess those many years ago worsened with time.

Jake harbored no delusions of his insignificance: an irrelevant cog in a broken gear. Still, he fanned flickering hope that an answer lay waiting to be discovered. Maybe there was a way to piece it all back together—how and by whom yet to be decided. The savage death of the young woman took a sizeable chunk from hope; just another vile cruelty, the likes of which seemed to be at every turn. What he'd just witnessed stood as proof. People died every day over small bits of food. Life had become cheap, and its devaluation continued.

He glanced again at the collapsing corrugated metal building and wondered a final time about the young girl. But selfishness ruled. He had to fend for himself. So would she. He looked skyward, taking his thoughts to their inevitable conclusion: The world is about survival, nothing more.

Slapping his knees, he came to his feet and adjusted his knapsack while silently vowing to not forget the name Hiram Baker. He resumed his journey.

After walking for a time, he began a gentle descent. Trees increased in number as he swished through lush spring grass. A river lay somewhere just ahead. It can't be more than a mile, he thought.

Although he had made the decision and made it firm, guilt simmered as he wondered about the wisdom of leaving a helpless child alone—a death sentence for sure. Non-action made him the executioner. Rampant cruelty, which he abhorred about the world, he realized, was as deeply ingrained in him as it was in Hiram Baker.

Bubbling remorse finally boiled over. The weight of conscience won out. He threw his hands into the air and shouted, "Damn it all!"

His walk slowed to a shuffle and, finally, a full stop. He dropped his head, frustrated by the inability to harden his heart, and turned to go back. There, barely a hundred feet behind him was the young girl. *Well, I'll be ...* His face relaxed into a faint smile as he thought, Okay, kid, I'll let you follow me, but you'd better stay out of my way.

After half an hour over uneven terrain and increasing brush to dodge, Jake stopped to mop sweat from his brow.

The little girl had begun to close the gap. She stopped walking when he did, maintaining a safe buffer between them. She continued to cry, rubbing a tiny fist into her eye.

Jake stood on a knoll and looked away from the expected river to a valley that gently sloped to the crumbling remains of some nameless city in the distance, inhabited by cannibals. Stories were common that all large cities suffered the same fate. He didn't care to find out if it was true. Open countryside was the safer choice, even with people like Hiram Baker lurking about.

From that crumbling skyline, he looked at other remnants of technology littering the landscape. The wide trail he walked had been a thoroughfare once paved in black. Rusting lumps dotting the countryside, returning to the earth, had been motorized vehicles that rolled on the once-smooth blacktop at unimaginable speeds, or so the stories went, told him as a child. Corroding remains of machines swallowed by time lay mangled and strewn—mountains of twisted and rusting steel. He had no idea what purpose they had served, none of them—just more things becoming lost to time. He picked up a heavily oxidized and pitted metal object that might have once been a hand tool. But what had it been used for? He tossed it aside and kept walking.

It became habit to look back and check on the girl. She was getting closer with each glance.

Intellect existed but systems of education and willingness to share know-how did not. Intellectually superior persons, able to think and reason, feared those who would manipulate them for greedy advantage. Jake did not view Satan as some wraithlike spirit. The devil stood for all to see as exploitation of man—an undercurrent in this world of disjointed societies where people with intelligence were sought as a perverse form of wealth. Jake wanted to make a difference, but how? What could he possibly do to change something as monumental and mutilated as this?

When governments crumbled so did urban life. People fled into the countryside. Some tried maintaining a semblance of society by forming 'corporations'. But the reality was stockades—walled forts housing people that stole and forced their will on 'independent consumers', those who chose to remain free of structured society.

Disease and desperation left entire cities vacant. Some crumbling metropolitan centers remained occupied. Like rats in a flood they bunched together devouring one another.

In the countryside, competition for basic resources made peaceful interaction on a broad scale implausible. From an era when commerce and doing business had become Godlike, the concept metamorphosed into something darker. 'Corporations' preyed on 'independent consumers'. Jake counted himself among the ICs.

All forms of long distance communication had gone away over a hundred years ago and transportation now depended mostly on how well a person's legs worked. The luckiest had horses but even those animals were often used as food and rare.

He fondly remembered having seen a working bicycle last year, a marvelous contraption. He'd never seen one or even heard of them before. He committed it to memory. It, too, would eventually return to the earth. In time it would become legend and dismissed as a bedtime story.

It was as if he played poker and knew the hands in advance, yet, had no chance of winning. Regression was an unstoppable wave. He feared it would not end until the entire human race reached a point after which only savages would remain without language and eating one another. It seemed as plain as the holes in his clothes and the grime streaking them. He lived within his thoughts, figuring it safer than conversation with strangers—people angling for advantage, sometimes ruthlessly.

He readjusted the knapsack to hang at his side instead of behind and renewed his gait. As he hastened his step, he glimpsed the girl breaking into a trot, gaining on him. So what if she is only a child, he thought. Should I trust her?

CHAPTER TWO
THE WORLD AS IT IS, PLUS ONE

Walking at a steady pace, Jake looked down at the girl now at his side. "You're spunky. I'll give you that."

The day was warm but comfortable. To look at the youngster's face, it could've been sweltering. It wasn't. She struggled to keep up. The end of the day neared. Her chin hung loose, bouncing with each step. Another mile just wasn't in her. Short legs chopped three steps to his one yet she doggedly matched his speed and had for two days—no complaints, nor words of any kind, nary a grunt. It wasn't only his pace she matched. Distrust of him and lingering wariness of her were close to even, too. Still, her desire to keep up was tenacious.

At the beginning of the day, when he'd woken under an open sky curled on a patch of tall grass having fallen under its own lush weight, he'd seen the child appear between parting eyelids—knees drawn up surrounded by skinny arms. She had stared unblinking as if she expected him to vanish if her eyes closed even once. He hadn't known how long she'd been sitting and watching but he figured a long while considering how she fidgeted.

The end of another day was now upon them. A place to spend the night approached the top of the daily priority list. The kid's stumbling behavior indicated a place to rest a short time might have to come first. Sneaking glances, Jake began to admire the youngster's resolve not to fall behind. He figured that he, too, might need a short breather. Another quarter mile came and went. The time had come to sit for a while, anywhere. Jake fared little better than the youngster—every joint ached.

He kept to an odd sense of schedule like a genetic appointment calendar was inside him. What once had been a mysterious urge, Jake eventually defined. Things done according to an agenda hadn't made much sense at first. During a rare moment of philosophical clarity, it occurred to him that schedule, even a vague one, equaled purpose and plan. It kept him motivated, a step ahead of hunger and, almost always, under shelter by dark when the weather turned bad. In truth, no timetable existed, no place to be, as long as he had a dry place to sleep and something to eat by day's end. Every day the same—forage, eat, sleep and then move on.

If only I could stay in one place and make a home, he thought. He puffed air into his cheeks then huffed it away as he looked down at the little girl. But, survival is key. That goes doubly now.

Rounding a bend in the path an overgrown cemetery came into view off to the side. No one made headstones so ornate anymore. It had to be a century old, likely older. Many had fallen and those still standing were mostly askew. One stood out as just right to sit on. He cleared tangled vines from its mildewed, gray and pitted top. A name was revealed: Carol Leann Flannery. He wondered what her story might have been. Beneath the name, the span of her life had been chiseled: 2016-2073. The epitaph read: "She made a difference".

He shuddered. Her age at death had not been much older than his present age. In all his rambling thoughts on the state of the world, mortality rarely crossed his mind. When it did, he ignored it. But lately, and with increasing frequency, it found a way into his head. Still, the length of his life stood in a dark shadow of those four words: "She made a difference". Goose flesh rippled his arm as if hit by a chilled wind. He'd made, and was making, no difference for better or worse on his small corner of the world he touched. Jake Henderson, he feared, would disappear from the earth without ever having made a mark. Dying unknown and unremarkable terrified him.

Nagging internal voices often tested him. But, this new one strummed an off-key note that knotted his heart and lumped his throat. If it weren't for the young girl at his side, he would've cried. He had to control the urge. The girl, he chose to call Annabelle, depended on him for survival. Emotional outbursts of any sort had to be contained.

Centering his aching butt, he moaned as he dropped exhausted onto the gravestone. The harsh realization that he'd someday pass without notice intensified his fatigue.

Annabelle stepped in close at eye level, a frail young shoulder inadvertently nudging him.

The warmth of human contact felt nice. He examined her profile. She can't be over ten. She remained speechless. Could she talk and refused to, or did she genuinely have no voice? The mind's eye visual echo of the child crying over the woman he assumed to be her mother had branded deep. It haunted him. He grappled with personal accountability to the young girl.

It was a pleasant surprise to discover that talking to someone and not just aloud to himself or lost in thought added clarity; a clear improvement over traveling alone. Earlier in the day he detected what he believed to be a smile. He glanced often, wanting to see it again. But then he thought, Why do I care?

He wriggled his butt until he hit a sweet spot of comfort atop the gravestone then swiped sweat from beneath shoulder length sandy blond hair that curled at its tips.

After a quiet moment, he again spoke. "Showing sympathy for a stranger can be dangerous. Did you know that? I've lived my life avoiding it." He glanced sideways at her standing near him and crinkled his nose. "It's safer. If you understand, it'd serve you to remember it. Trusting people will get you killed. Don't ever, ever forget that."

A flash of embarrassment reddened his cheeks. Even a speck of trust would've saved the youngster's mother. Conviction in the shared advice wavered. "Look, Little One, trust is almost as precious as food and water," he lifted an eyebrow, "but … not quite." The truth of it was suddenly questionable. It seemed less credible spoken aloud for some reason.

He examined her dirty face and tangled mop of hair that should've been straight. "Hungry?" He pulled a partially eaten turnip from his tattered knapsack and held it out to her. With doe eyes set sunken in a sallow face she stared at him. The distrustful gaze then shifted and locked onto the shriveled vegetable in his hand. As he moved the hand around, her eyes followed. Only then did he realize how hungry she was. "Go on. Take it."

Once in her grasp, Jake yanked his hand away or risk bitten fingers. Watching her eat, his heart ached. For the first time, he noticed how poor this child's condition was; ratty dusty blond hair, face streaked with filth, and snot dried and crusted on her upper lip.

Her pants had been crudely fashioned and stitched from several types of cloth, as was her shirt. Both were dirty and frayed, likely to disintegrate if laundered. The girl's mother may have been a fighting phenom but she was certainly no seamstress. Then again, maybe the child was simply outgrowing clothing faster than her mother could renew it. He considered embracing her and telling her that people were still around that cared, but couldn't muster the courage of such pretense. How could he? He had no faith there were—anywhere, and wondered if her generation would fix everything the past five could not.

He continued watching her, thinking, chewing the inside of his cheek, giving her time to eat the last of the food.

The wide trail ahead appeared as a ribbon through the woods that the flora had mostly reclaimed. The cemetery where they rested was situated about a hundred feet above the river paralleling the old roadbed. Trees grew in the middle of it, pushing up disintegrating asphalt-encrusted gravel. He imagined motorized vehicles whizzing by at great speeds.

A beetle crawled across the cracked leather of his boot. "You, my tiny friend, have been blessed with inability to worry." He looked sideways at Annabelle. "Yet, here I sit with something new to worry about."

Having always ruminated on the bleak future of the world, Annabelle's presence had moderated those views, now becoming less radical. It seemed to be happening exceptionally fast. Her presence might complicate things but it occurred to him she could also be an unexpected blessing.

He remembered a snippet of wisdom handed down from his father. "Knowledge, son, is what it will take to fix this broken world. To think, ponder consequences, and then act rationally with compassion is the key to humankind's survival. Always remember that what this world will become begins with you."

The advice sounded sage but aches and hunger had kept it hollow over the years. Nevertheless, it was all he had to pass on. Having no son, Annabelle had become his heir by default. She gnawed on that leathery turnip. Annabelle may be my last chance to make a difference—*my legacy.*

"I want you to know what I know. Okay?"

The girl paid him no mind, focusing on the shriveled vegetable in her hands; the strong smell of turnip filling the air.

She appeared inattentive but he thought it worth trying. "It's said that, once upon a time, harmony existed among diverse groups. But you and I know that could never happen." A wry grin widened, spreading his hairy cheeks. "I'll assume you agree."

Annabelle relaxed and sank to her knees next to the grave stone he sat on, eating, apparently oblivious to his commentary. The tone of voice must have comforted her.

"Small groups have formed that believe a genius, a savior, would emerge from among common people to save us from ourselves then guide us back to a peaceful, technologically functioning society. I know this because I've seen them. Last week I walked past a group standing before a rusting electrical transmission tower, wishing so hard for a return to a functional society that it sounded like a prayer complete with a worshipful gaze up it. Can you believe that?" He laughed. "They were actually worshipping a rusty ol' tower." he shrugged shoulders, "or, so it appeared."

His smile wilted away. He straightened and went silent. The opinion made less sense than it did while hovering in his tired thoughts. Maybe it wasn't preposterous. After all, what would life be if there was nothing to believe in and no hope for a better future? Was exhaustion to blame for questioning the long-held belief? Or, could this be another example of his cynicism abating due to Annabelle's presence?

He pushed a tangle of hair away from the girl's eyes, ensnaring his fingers—board straight except for the knots, darker in color near the roots. A smattering of freckles beneath the smudges across her nose hinted of the beautiful woman she'd eventually grow into.

She grunted and rolled her head away from his touch. Trust had not caught up to her level of need.

"My grandfather told me stories—stories his grandfather had told him—about how the world was put on a competitive course over two-hundred-fifty years ago, in the nineteen-fifties, throwing the industrial machine into overdrive. That's when Corporate America came to be. Something called the industrial complex flourished. Here, in what used to be the United States, growth seemed boundless. Complacency rose during the nineteen-sixties. A war that was not a war was waged in Indochina and split the nation ideologically." He scratched his chin then tossed out a hand flippantly. "I'm still not sure what 'war that was not a war' means ... or, where Indochina is." He looked away and thought on that for a moment. "Oh well, neither here nor there. We were no longer homogenous Americans, splintering into Afro-Americans, Asian Americans, Native Americans, Angry White Men Americans, Feminist Americans, Jewish Americans, Christian Americans, Muslim Americans and so on. We drifted apart. Misinformation became acceptable as the nineteen-seventies introduced high-level trickery to politics."

He snapped a twig between his fingers and flicked it. "By the nineteen-eighties, lying went mainstream to form public opinion. Grandpa called it lying. He said they, the politicians, called it 'spin'. I suppose it made an unpopular notion seem right and noble. I bet the public even laughed about it, like ... like it was some kind of joke! Can you believe that, Annabelle? No one cared." He attempted stroking her head again.

She snapped a startled look at him then ducked from under his palm and leaned away. Only a bite of that turnip in her hand remained.

"Well anyway, as the story goes, nearing the end of the twentieth century, people controlling corporations had grown obscenely wealthy and powerful—strong enough to manipulate whole governments that had become inconsequential and subordinate to them. Countries worldwide had become what Grandpa says were 'corpocracies'.

Affairs of government had become nothing but lesser divisions of big business in the twenty-first century, just another door down the hall of home offices sandwiched between the janitor's closet and the restrooms. Government's only function had become the printing of unsupported paper currency and making speeches on behalf of companies. Companies merged and grew until only one remained. America was one big company vacuuming money and resources into glutinous piles for self-preservation while the country hungered.

The hard stone of the grave marker now becoming uncomfortable, Jake squirmed, leaned over and rested elbows on his knees. He snickered under his breath then flipped his hands palms up and gave a lazy shrug. "That's right, governments were the puppets of business, plain and simple."

Jake sat up, just then realizing how low the sun had sunk in the western sky. About two good hours of daylight remained. He wondered about the summation of that legacy passed down to him. "'To think and ponder consequences'," he said slowly, exaggerating every syllable. "How can that be the key, Annabelle? The only consequence I worry about is starvation and the only consideration is how to prevent it."

As he spoke, Annabelle chewed the last bite of turnip, juice trickling down her chin—pulp decorating the corners of her mouth.

"Oh well ... are you ready to find a place to spend the night?" He didn't expect an answer but increasingly compelled to ask questions. *Someday, I hope to hear you speak.* He kept empathetic leanings to himself—selfishness deeply ingrained from having lived alone for ages. He was comforted by her presence. Someone to talk to was novel. He slapped his knees and rose. "Come on; let's see what's down the road."

Annabelle ... Annabelle. He rolled the name over in his mind as he walked. He liked the way it sounded. He'd considered calling her Waco, but only because he remembered it as the only distinguishable word remaining on a sign almost totally corroded away. He didn't know what the word meant or its origin. He just happened to see it near the outskirts of a decaying deserted town the day before he discovered her. But it had a hard masculine ring, whereas the name Annabelle had softness to it. It did make him wonder just how feminine this grimy little creature would eventually turn out to be. He settled on Annabelle, his mother's name, who died before he was two.

He recalled a time his father shared memories of her. What he remembered most about that day had nothing to do with the story of his mother, the tale of a woman he never knew. Resting in a crumbling movie theatre, the remnant of a stylized picture encased in glass caught his eye in an alcove protected from the passage of time. While his father told the story of the first Annabelle, his eyes fixed on the remains of that picture. It was the birth of opinions on the world he struggled to survive in.

After walking only a few yards, before leaving the cemetery behind, Jake stopped. Thoughts boomeranged to the present. He looked upon the headstone a final time that had provided a few precious moments' comfort. *Goodbye Carol Leann Flannery, whoever you are—were. I hope someday I make a difference, too.* "Come on, Little One. It'll be dark soon."

"You know," he said as they began walking, "Annabelle, as a youngster I saw a poster for something called a motion picture, a movie. I've heard stories they still exist somewhere far to the northeast of here but I've never actually seen one, someday maybe." He paused and looked at her. He hoped to see some animation, any kind of expression, but did not. "Anyhow, what was left of that picture depicted a world in shambles breaking into warring tribes. It was popular back then, or so I've heard, to believe humankind might be destroyed by an exchange of powerful bombs, leaving only a few to start over. I think those bombs were called *nucular* or *nuclea,* something like that."

He abruptly stopped walking. "You know what? It occurred to me that if those bombs really did exist, they're out there somewhere. They never exploded." He scratched his head and wrinkled his nose. "At least, I don't think so. Even so, I don't want to think about that. I sure don't need that worry heaped on top of all the rest." He walked on.

Annabelle stared straight ahead marching like a miniature soldier as though she traveled with purpose. If so, he wondered what that might be. If she feared he'd leave her behind again, that troubled him. But he bore the weight of fault on his conscience. He had, after all, walked away leaving the child in grievous pain over the blood-drenched body of her mother. It would have been a condemnation of death by neglect on someone as young and fragile.

"What was I saying? Oh yeah. No one realized back then that a collapse of order could be a slow decline that, once begun, couldn't be stopped. It followed such a logical path; family decay followed moral decay then greed that brought on corruption. Oversimplified?" He pushed out his lower lip. "I guess so, but that's what happened … minus embellishment of course. How can something so obvious not have been noticed? Now it's unstoppable, like my rotting teeth. If we—"

Annabelle stumbled hard to her knees after stepping into a shallow depression. She winced.

"Hey, be careful!" he barked, then squatted to lift her up.

She quickly returned to stoicism, as if she had something to prove.

Growing affection for the child frightened him. "Are you okay?" A trickle of blood appeared through a hole in the knee of her dirty pants tattered at the bottom. It was only a scratch. There were no doctors or medical facilities, only a few people with knowledge of healing herbs, but he wasn't one of them.

"Doggone it, girl! Watch where you're stepping!"

Annabelle recoiled. Tears filled her eyes.

"Wait. I didn't mean to snap at you." He stepped toward her.

She backed away.

He took another step.

She again moved to create a new buffer between them.

"Come on, don't do that. You scared me, that's all."

Fragile trust shattered. She didn't rejoin him at his side and again followed from the perceived safety of a few steps back.

He needed to stop worrying about the child. The only way to do that was think about something else. He ruminated over the history stories he had heard from his grandfather.

Greed had accelerated at unprecedented levels, becoming global in one generation nearly two hundred years ago. The world's wealth concentrated into fewer and fewer hands — the early stages of the New World Order. Countries no longer existed, only land and property holdings by individuals controlling all the world's economies. Once consolidated, growth stopped and that left the door open for economic incest. Desire for greater power and wealth turned ravenous; economic war raged. A sucker punch born of gluttony became the stone in the worldwide pool that rippled with destructive radiating waves — a tit-for-tat on a global scale, breaking the back of the world's economies.

Jake wanted Annabelle to know this history. But, he resigned to the notion she wouldn't comprehend and chose to save this part of the story for a later time. And then he wondered aloud, "Why do I care? I can't even guarantee it's true, for God's sake."

Only after it was already out there echoing back from the trees did he realize he wasn't alone and glanced to see fresh trepidation in Annabelle's eyes. "Not to worry, just talking to myself, Little One."

A perilously listing deserted farmhouse came into view as they topped a rise in the road. In another year it'll be collapsed, he figured. "Come on. Let's see if there's any fruit on those trees out back."

She trotted to catch up and clutched his leg. Two windows on the front of the house looking like big rectangular eyes and a severely tilting door between them left the appearance of a yawning monster.

"It'll be okay. That old house may give us shelter and protection for the night."

Before taking a step, she gathered two fists full of his pant legs and held him.

He peeled her filthy frightened little hands off, squatted, held her scrawny arms to her sides and looked into her eyes, realizing he could talk until sunset and still not convince her there was nothing to be afraid of. As their eyes remained locked, he smiled. He noticed the smile worked to offer more assurance than anything he said.

As he gazed into disheartened blue eyes, he wondered about the child's mother trusting that man she'd bested in hand-to-hand combat. Turning her back on a murderous stranger had been the ultimate faith — and stupid. What that man did should never have happened. Why did she so willingly give up the advantage? He hoped Annabelle knew and might share it someday.

He continued smiling at the youngster. Her expression did not change but her body language did. She stroked his long bushy beard with tiny fingers on each side of his face, as if petting a puppy.

Harboring so many fears of his own, how could he not sympathize with hers? Nowhere in the known world did there exist any organized law enforcement. Corporations protected shareholders and their possessions while independent consumers protected themselves. Existing laws were only those of nature and a few arbitrary ones set by greedy and powerful people meant for personal gain. All that remained was a personal sense of right or wrong, usually hinging on desperation. Jake remained ever mindful that, as ominous as the world had become, it could be worse.

He pulled her sweat-moistened hands from his face, rose and began walking toward the rear of the old farmhouse. "Stay here. I'll be right back … promise."

Approaching the remains of an orchard, he stayed within view of the girl but moved closer to the trees. Gangly and bore-infested, most of the trees were barely alive and hard to see within the overgrowth of Johnson grass that was taller than the trees in places.

He glanced back to Annabelle. She held her ground but fidgeted with each step farther he took.

Determination drove him closer to the trees to see if one of them possibly bore fruit. He counted thirteen trees scattered over an area once covering a half-acre or more. He felt kinship with the trees—proof that life would find a way. He searched every limb.

Jake shoved weeds and brush aside checking every green branch of each stunted tree, some close to the ground. His search came up fruitless.

On his way back to Annabelle, he stopped to check the last four trees. He looked her way and saw her wringing her hands but, when he returned his attention to the remaining trees, he beheld something beautiful: not one, but a cluster of four apples on the same branch of a sickly tree—red and ripe.

As if someone might challenge him, he ran and plucked them, claiming rights to dinner for two. He held the fruit in his cupped hands, staring, disbelieving such good fortune. For days all he'd eaten were leaves, a few berries and a couple of turnips. And now to have the crown jewels of dining, apples, seemed too good to be true. With a burst of enthusiasm, he trotted to Annabelle.

"Look, Little One! Look what I've found!" He held them high, two in each hand. She didn't appear enthusiastic. No matter. He knew they'd sleep well with nourishment.

Annabelle followed as he pushed aside weeds and vines that led to the concrete porch of the old farmhouse. He sat and waved her over as he shined an apple on a ripped sleeve then handed it to her.

An old man and woman abruptly appeared from around the corner of the house.

Startled, Jake snatched a rotted tree limb from the ground and leaped to his feet. As if it were a sword, he held it extended defensively.

The couple made no aggressive moves, no moves at all. Then the old lady wobbled. She went down. The man knelt beside her. Lines of hard living creased both their dirty faces. They were no threat, just hungry—lives and ability to survive spiraling down to a predetermined conclusion. Jake saw himself in the not too far future in their forlorn faces.

Even before he lowered the limb, Annabelle walked past him to where the woman lay and handed her one shiny apple. The old lady took it then clutched it in both trembling hands. She wept.

Jake couldn't very well hold on to his extra apple. Tentatively, he gave one to the old man.

Annabelle smiled—first at the couple then at him.

It occurred to Jake like a bolt from the blue, "Ponder consequences … act rationally." Then he said, "This is what my father was talking about." As soon as it cleared his lips another thought struck: That's what Annabelle's mother was trying to do. As the revelation jelled he began to slowly nod then faster while muttering, "If the world has a chance, it has to begin with Annabelle and me."

CHAPTER THREE
SOMETHING AMAZING
AND OTHER SURPRISING THINGS

With a sense of purpose now infused, Jakes' outlook, and along with it the overall situation, was improved. He pondered why things felt better, but not deeply—merely a fleeting mental notation. Deep seated superstition prevented it. Good fortune, no matter how small, was always welcomed, accepted and appreciated … but never questioned. Conditions didn't seem as dire as they did even a week ago. The only difference was the presence of Annabelle.

The worn knapsack he carried sagged with berries, carrots and spring turnips. Even though the climate was a temperate springtime, when these edibles should be most plentiful anyway, such abundance seemed odd. Has it always been this way? He had to assume the answer was yes. I should do more counting of blessings and less grumbling.

Following a path next to the Brazos River, Annabelle gamely kept pace. Jake heard a noise, pulled the child off the path into the bushes and began pushing her down.

She squirmed, protesting the rough treatment.

He put a finger to his lips and vigorously shook his head.

She must have noticed fearful wariness smeared across his face; she instantly stopped fighting and willingly sank to the ground, pulled her knees up and held them tight to her chest.

He leaned out and gingerly parted the brush in front of his face with a fingertip for an improved view.

Two elderly men, one white one black, walked the trail towards them. The black man walked in front while the white man held onto the black man's shirt from behind, both carrying fishing poles.

"Where in the depths of Hades are you taking me?" the white man barked.

"Huh? What'd ya say?" the black man countered.

"Where are you taking me, Andrew?" the white man said, still louder, "If you pulled the gall-darn wax wadding outa your ears, your hearing might come back. Ever thought of that?"

"Best shut up, John, before I leave you to walk in circles for a while, ya ol' blind toot."

Jake grinned and stood. "It's okay, Little One. They're just a couple of old guys looking for a place to fish."

Annabelle sprang up and peaked out from behind Jake's leg.

"Who's there?" the white man, John, said.

The black man, Andrew, glanced over his shoulder. "Are you back

---

there crackin' wise again?"

"Shut up Andrew, and see who's talkin' over there," John said, barely under a yell.

Jake stepped from behind clumped bushes. "Sorry. Didn't mean to startle y'all." He stroked Annabelle's hair. "The girl and I were heading north and had to make sure you weren't out to rob us."

"What'd he say, John?" Andrew said.

John stuck his mouth close to Andrew's ear. "He said he was afraid we were going to rob him." He guffawed. "Now, ain't that a hoot?" He laughed again, but then went serious. "Is it really just one man and a girl, Andrew?"

"Huh?"

Louder, "Is it just a man with a girl like he said?"

"Yeah … little girl, one man … that's right."

John extended his hand in a direction approximating Jake's position. "Glad to make your acquaintance."

Jake looked in the direction the old man held his hand. It was as if he pointed at something in the woods. Then it occurred to him; the guy was blind and waiting for him to step up and shake his hand. He hurried over and took the man's hand. "I'm sorry. I didn't realize right away that you were blind."

"The names John P. Blevins, blinder'n bat. This old black jackass is Andrew H. Conroy. He's almost stone deaf. We've sort of turned living into a symbiotic art form."

"Symbiotic art form?"

"I just mean living together works for us."

"My name is Jake Henderson and this is my friend, Annabelle."

Andrew perked his ears as if he'd just heard something. "Wait a dadburn minute! Did you call me a black jackass, you white drop o' pig snot?"

An uncomfortable pause ensued, then John and Andrew broke into boisterous laughter.

Jake's eyes darted between them. "I thought you boys were about to tangle."

"Tangle? Nah, if we didn't have each other we'd both die; I'd wander until I starved to death and ol' Andrew here would be lunch for a mountain lion before he heard it comin'."

"You must be talkin' nice 'cuz I can't hear it," Andrew said.

John put his mouth to Andrew's ear. "I was just tellin' the nice man that you'd probably be lion chow if I weren't around to hear it comin'."

"Don't go slingin' steamin' cow piles. I can see that man's no fool. He ain't gonna believe you'd survive any longer than me."

Jake's grin held steady. If they weren't talking in such a serious manner, he would've laughed aloud at John's and Andrew's antics. Annabelle reached for his knapsack.

Jake's smile vanished as he pushed her hand away, holding it shut. He gave her a stern headshake.

She looked up confused.

"We won't take any more of your time. It looks like you fellas have fish to catch and we need to be moving on."

"Nice to meet y'all," John said.

"Say what?" Andrew said.

"I told them it was nice to have met them."

"Oh, right. Yeah ... nice to meet y'all ... hope to see ya again."

Although the change in his thinking had been profound, it'd take time for actions to match emerging outlook. Forty-three years of a survivalist's mentality could not be overcome in a scant few weeks. They hadn't walked a hundred yards and he already had begun regretting such lack of compassion. He should've offered them some of the wild carrots foraged earlier.

Jake thought about Andrew and John, in awe of how happy they appeared, given the serious physical defects of both. After a time, he realized he looked at Annabelle as often as he did the trail ahead. She couldn't know that she was in the process of curing his blindness. His wasn't an inability to see the world around him, as was John's problem; he couldn't see the beauty and goodness still in it. He wondered how he'd managed travelling alone for so long.

Something in the youngster's changing expression was reminiscent of her mother. Where did the woman learn to fight like that? Although petite and young, the woman could've snapped that man's neck but chose not to. Why? To preserve the life of an intruder she didn't even know? Why take the chance? Her speed and strength went far beyond normal. The image of her flying through the air and getting a spinning scissor-lock on the man's head was as clear now as when he saw it unfold. She'd leaped high without a running start, like an antelope casually jumping over a fence. Yet, she was the one to die. The image had replayed in his head many times since witnessing it. "That was sure somethin' to see all right."

Annabelle stopped and looked up at him.

"Sorry, Little One." He patted her head. "I sometimes forget I'm not alone anymore."

Sidling close, she pressed her head into the softness above his waist. He squatted, placing hands on her shoulders and went eye to eye. Her gaze softened. He thought he saw desire to smile. "I wish I'd known your mother. She must've been extraordinary."

The twinkle in Annabelle's eyes spirited away.

21

She'd understood—the first time he definitely knew that beyond a doubt. "I'm sorry. I didn't mean to steal your good mood." He pushed hair away from her face. She made no move to prevent it.

Crunching of leaves and forest litter beneath towering oaks beyond where the girl stood captured his attention.

Then movement caught his eye.

He sprang to his feet as a rabbit appeared and then disappeared as quick. He spun in a circle looking on the ground. "If I had a sharp stick or a good throwing rock I might have fresh meat for us."

Annabelle turned and trotted a few steps in the direction the rabbit ran. She stopped, looked back and waved for him to follow.

"Where're you going?"

Her pleasant expression returned.

"What in the world ...?"

She ran a few more steps, twirling a fast hand for him to hurry. She then stopped at a thicket of dead and dying brush the rabbit ran under.

He caught up to her.

She picked up a rock about the size of her small fist and placed it in his hand closing his fingers over it.

"How can I hit something I can't see?"

She looked up at him as though he was the silliest man on earth, frowning and shaking her head. She trotted away.

He followed.

She stopped and extended a flat palm back at him, wanting him to stay. From a tattered pocket, she pulled a strip of leather no thicker than a shoelace and about as long as he was tall. A lasso-type loop had been fashioned at its end and a hefty pebble tied on the line above the loop.

"You don't seriously think ...?"

She cut a wide berth around the clump of bushes and with the agility of a monkey, swung her body up into a small tree, then out onto a low-hanging limb no larger than his arm, yet, she lay perfectly balanced and motionless upon the swaying branch, as if one with the wood, no more than five to six feet above the ground. She then tied the end of the leather string to her middle finger, coiled it and held it.

The child's incredible speed and dexterity set his mind to reeling with a fresh batch of questions but, now, they were about Annabelle not her mother. The flimsy branch continued swaying under her weight but didn't seem to affect balance at all. It was eerie and unnatural. It wasn't humanly possible to get in that position in less than two seconds with that kind of control over her body ... or so he believed.

She looked back at him, swinging her arm in a lobbing gesture.

He pointed to the rock that she'd placed in his hand. "You want me to toss it into the bush?"

She nodded.

"Is that what you want?" He waggled the stone.

She nodded again.

He pitched it up and caught it. "Okay. But I don't see how that's going to kill a rabbit." He took aim at the densest part of the bush near its center and threw it.

On cue, the rabbit scurried from beneath it, up the trail under Annabelle.

Within the span of an eye blink, she reared an arm and hurled the weighted end of the string into the path of the scared rabbit. The speed of the throw blurred her arm. It ran into the loop and she yanked it precisely, tightening on its neck.

Unbelievable—yet he'd witnessed it. If the evidence had not been struggling in that tightening noose suspended off the ground, he wouldn't have believed it. It was not his imagination. It had indeed happened. He whooped and applauded. "Holy jumpin' turtles, girl, how'd you do that? An adult can't move that fast. No one can."

Once again, the struggle between Annabelle's mother and a man he'd always remember by the name Hiram Baker caught up to him. He kept smiling but a quizzical expression shaded the joy.

***

The impaled rabbit roasted at the end of a stick. Jake jammed the end of the green wood skewer into the soft ground, placed a heavy rock upon it, balancing it halfway up on one of the stones circling the fire to suspend it over red coals and short flames. The fire crackled and sizzled from dripping juices causing lazy flames to come alive and dance. That and the rhythmic lap of the river upon the shore mellowed him. He sat back on his heels.

Annabelle copied the posture. She gazed into the flames that undulated with the light, cool, twilight breeze.

What're you thinking, Little One? What is it that holds your mind? He breathed in the fresh early evening air as his eyes followed the blinks of lightning bugs. His tired mind wandered. Time passed.

Finally, the last vestige of light squeezed off in the west. "What would you think about building a cabin right here and making a home?" He gestured with a quarter-turn swing of the arm. "Huh? What do you think?" He twisted the skewer stick, exposing a different side of the rabbit to the flames.

With each question, he hoped he'd eventually ask one she would attempt to answer, the one that might get her talking. He still didn't know if she had the capacity of speech. If the question interested her, she didn't show it. Her stare remained on the fire.

"A permanent residence sounds pretty nice to me right now." He flicked a twig into the fire and chuckled. "My tired feet must be doing my thinking for me."

Suddenly a rustling sound came from behind them. Jake leaped to his feet and whirled around. Annabelle clung to the bottom of his pant leg.

"Sir," a female voice came from the darkness, "We beg you not to be alarmed. We are unarmed and friendly. May we approach?"

Jake's eyes scanned the seeable trees and brush. "Who is 'we'?"

"Myself and my aging mother ... just the two of us. I swear it."

Annabelle released her hold on him.

He also relaxed somewhat, but kept his eyes in the direction of the anonymous voice. "Come into the light so I can see you."

Moving into the far limits of the orange firelight, he saw a woman, possibly mid-thirties, with skin not much lighter than the color of night and exotic features highlighted by large almond eyes, followed closely by another woman considerably older but of the same dark coloration with salt and pepper hair. The elderly woman appeared haggard, hair of tight curls escaping from a strip of cloth that should've held it back; wisps of it hung haphazardly to the sides of the old woman's face. Both wore men's canvas pants and thickly woven long-sleeve shirts. The younger woman carried two knapsacks, one on each hip, plus a backpack. The older lady carried a single knapsack. She coughed then muttered, "Excuse me."

The younger woman approached extending a sociable hand.

He glanced at it then back to her face, searching for signs of insincerity.

She held the hand suspended before him.

He made a quick perfunctory up and down examination of both women. His gaze settled on the younger one. She appeared tired. The knapsacks that rode slender hips and the backpack were loaded tight. Cooking utensils dangled from the backpack. He couldn't help but notice the leather straps of knapsacks crossing over her chest forced her breasts to stand out. His eyes hitched on that view—not a sight he was accustomed to. He swallowed.

There was a domesticated and soft look about both women— not at all trail hardened.

"Honestly, we mean no harm," she said. "We seek only to share your fire and, maybe, some of that meat. Rabbit is it?" She inadvertently licked her lips.

Although still unsmiling, Jake finally offered little more than the suggestion of a nod.

"Earlier we found lamb's quarter greens and wild onions in a meadow over that hill beyond the trees and ate a few." As she spoke, her eyes remained on the roasting rabbit. "But it has been so long since we've had meat, the lure of its aroma was hard to resist."

Jake remained skeptical. He began nodding, slowly at first. "Then you're welcome to join us," he said. Although the invitation was meant to be cordial, he couldn't hide the continuing distrust in his voice.

A smile came up on Annabelle's dirty face.

"Thank you, sir. We'll not forget your kindness." She guided her mother to soft grass beneath a tree and helped her sit.

The old lady leaned against the rough bark with a sighing moan, and then allowed her head to fall back against it—chin jutting, mouth agape. She coughed.

Annabelle hurried to Jake's knapsack near the fire, pulled out two short plump carrots then went to the river's edge and washed them. She gave one to each woman.

The younger woman bit off a chunk. "Umm, sweet. Thank you," she said, as she shoved it into her cheek. "You seem like a very special young lady. What's your name?"

"She can't talk," Jake blurted. "I call her Annabelle."

"Sorry. Is she your daughter?"

"No. Her mother was killed a couple of weeks ago and we just sort of ended up together." He tugged at his bushy beard and looked at Annabelle. "At least I think the woman was her mother. I can't be sure of that, but there're strong similarities, some extraordinary."

"My name is Glory Jackson and that's my mother, Myrna." The older woman smiled but kept her head back against the tree, eyes closed, stifling coughs. Glory took another bite of the carrot. Her hair was black as a crow's wing, long and thick with tight natural curls. She kept it loosely tied, splaying from beneath the strip of rag fanning across her upper back.

"Are you two from around here," Jake asked.

"We come from an area far to the south called the Hill Country."

"I've heard of it. Why so far from home?"

"Well," she said then sighed, "My husband built a cabin by a spring-fed pond and we, along with mother and father, lived quite well. We had a good association with a nearby corporation called Wellworth. We bartered cloth and staples. But then father died and Chauncy, my husband, left to hunt game one day and never returned. Months went by. Mother's health deteriorated." She sighed and then continued, tone gloomier, "Then Wellworth members began stealing from us by night. And with dwindling resources, barter became an unfair proposition that always tilted in their favor. Eventually they drained us of most everything of value."

Jake nodded. "It's not just them. All corporations look upon independent consumers as a quick source of stuff they don't want to gather or make. They see anyone not with shareholder affiliation as lesser human beings to be preyed upon."

"I never counted myself an IC since our association with Wellworth was so tight."

"Doesn't matter. If you're not in you're out, simple as that. Once your father died and your husband disappeared you were no longer of value."

"I don't suppose I'll ever understand how the world got into such a mess," Glory said.

"I'm pretty sure I do. If you like, I'll tell you the story." Jake glanced at Annabelle. "I have no children so I want to pass the information on to Annabelle. I've told her a little as we travelled but I'm not certain she understands."

"Sure," Glory said, "I'd appreciate even a smidgen of understanding on how we got to where we are."

"What I'm about to tell you has been passed down from father to child in my family since the end of the twentieth century."

Myrna cleared her throat, opened one eye and said, "You may not like what you hear, Glory."

"Maybe, but I'm sure I need to know it. I just never cared before we lost our home and livelihood. Please, go ahead Mister Henderson."

"It began with obscene amounts of wealth concentrated in very few hands. Over time, it worsened until the world woke up to corporations controlling entire governments. Right here in what used to be the United States, corporate America became the incorporation of America. Since government was forbidden to deal in commerce, the powers-that-be removed gold-backed currency, then state and federal governments incorporated. Supposedly working in the best interest of the population at large, government had become a company in the business of collecting taxes to accomplish little more than bribing the richest constituents for self-preservation. Lending sympathetic ears to public outcries was only for show. Action taken was always to the benefit of behemoth corporations and themselves. This was the birth of corpocracy. All people not holding management seats within these glutinous countries literally lived and breathed at the pleasure of them. Countries, at this point, ceased to exist. From their ashes rose corporations sucking money and materials at a rate which eventually collapsed the entire global economic system."

Glory, becoming uncomfortable with the story, said, "I can't believe we, as a people, allowed such blatant abuse of power like that."

Jake nodded. "I can see why you'd think that but, understand, we have the advantage of seeing it in retrospect. Remember, it began over two hundred years ago and happened so gradually no one noticed subtle changes until it was too late. You see, corporations went about strengthening the common bond that money and greed created." He chuckled. "The way they did that was by calling it patriotism. Anytime that began faltering, religious fear was used as a flashpoint to destabilize and then take over former countries. The control of wealth was the ultimate goal, and to set up corpocratic management systems in place of governing bodies.

"What happened to the huge corporations ... countries, or whatever they were called?"

"As the biggest swallowed the least, only a few global corporations remained. There was no more power, money or materials to be had; they began feeding off one another until even that wasn't enough. The end had begun. A squabble at the global level collapsed the entire world economy and began a decline that continues spiraling down today. Corporations, as we know them, are little more than stockades that send out raiding parties. No one has figured out how to reverse the decline. Machines, power systems, and all technology began a slow death and today are still continuing to disappear. Aside from food, clothing and shelter, the most important commodity today is the human mind. Intelligence is the new currency."

"You were right, Mother," Glory said, "It is troubling." She stirred the dirt between her legs with a fingertip. "We heard there was a mega corporation somewhere to the north called Stalwart that allows people into their fold without having to purchase shareholder status. We were told that we could work for room and board, sort of a sweat-equity system."

Jake shrugged. "If that's true, it might be a good thing. Don't know."

"I'm at a loss for what else I can do." She looked over to the older woman. "I have to try. Soon, I won't be able to care for mother without help."

The compassion Jake vowed to cultivate felt like it had a place in Glory's unfolding story. Should he invite the women to join them on their northward trek? It happened to be the same direction he and Annabelle traveled, although he had no desire to join a corporation and become locked into guidelines for living with questionable benefits to shareholders—not yet anyway. But it did remind him of aching feet, tired legs and painful shoulders that held up a sore neck balancing a heavy head. It had to be worse for them. "Are you certain you and your mother can make it? How far is it?"

"I don't know ... on both questions. We've been told that once we came to a river called the Brazos to follow it and we'd eventually find it."

Annabelle sat cross-legged near Glory but had begun glancing toward the older woman, Myrna. She rolled over to hands and knees, crawled next to her and sat. She, too, leaned against the tree. The elderly lady opened her eyes, looked at the child and smiled.

The sight sent a sentimental surge through Jake. "Look, Annabelle and I have no specific destination in mind. I've been searching for a permanent home site along this river." He gestured to his own body. "As you can see, I'm not that many years behind your mother and figure I'd better be thinking about the day my health forces me to give up moving from place to place all the time—"

"I did notice the smattering of gray in your beard and at your temples. Even the light coloration can't hide it."

He tugged at his beard.

"How old are you ... forty ... forty-five, perhaps?"

"Something like that. I'm not sure."

"That's not old, not old at all," she whispered.

Embarrassed by the sultriness in her voice, he cleared his throat. "Uh, back to the point, maybe my perfect home site is somewhere along the path you and your mother are taking. You're welcome to walk with us for a few days. Maybe Annabelle and I can find what we're looking for on the way to what you seek."

Glory's large dark eyes widened then settled as tears pooled in them. "You have no idea how wonderful it is to hear that."

***

Days passed. Conversation became light and forward-looking; various loosely conceived plans for the future were exchanged. Myrna tired easily; rest stops became frequent. The weather remained sunny and comfortable. Glory refused to be doted over. She turned away almost every attempt Jake made to help. Although attracted to him, she remained wary of this hairy-faced man's motives. Would he be looking for payback of kindnesses? If so, what would it be? She'd caught him looking at her in such a way as to be unsettling.

He seemed articulate and kind but his conversations vacillated between anger at the world to quiet humility. It was plain enough that he waged an internal battle of some type with rather abrupt mood swings. What troubled him so? Maybe a psychosis worked on him. Perhaps he could turn dangerous. She had to remain aloof for now. Still, her attraction to this enigmatic man strengthened—something about him touched her heart.

Each thoughtful look at Jake came with a vision of Chauncy. There remained no closure in her husband's disappearance. She didn't know what'd happened to him but the sun was setting on hope that he might still be alive.

28

Another week passed; still no sign of Stalwart. Myrna's illness slowed travel considerably. The trail next to the river now showed increasing signs of foot traffic. That seemed to be a good sign that they might be getting close. The path meandered but remained generally north.

Ducking under a low hanging limb, she held it back for her mother, then Annabelle, then Jake. As he walked by, she studied his profile then stepped in behind him. "I'm curious about something. But if you think it's none of my business that's okay."

"I can't say yes or no until I hear the question."

"Okay," she said, drawing out the word. "How long has it been since you've had a bath?"

Jake stopped and spun around. His mouth hung slack and that part of his cheeks visible above his beard reddened. "I … uh … well—"

"Say no more." She looked at a grinning Annabelle who watched their conversation. The little girl scratched various parts of her body; mostly her private area and her head beneath that long light brown hair—hair that was matted and knotted and just might be perfectly straight and blond if clean. It was easy to reason why the youngster might be Jake's daughter—hair near the same color and equally dirty. These two needed a scrubbing.

Jake scratched the ground with the toe of a deteriorating boot then squinted as if he needed to ask but didn't want a response, "Do I … uh … smell bad," he shrugged, "or something?"

"I'll just say as long as we're walking upwind I'd rather be in front of you. She crinkled her nose. "Sorry." She stepped around him to her mother and opened the small bag Myrna carried hanging from a long strap around her neck down to her side. Glory produced a rag with a lump in it and two small tools. "Since I've opened this conversation, I might as well keep it going; how long has it been since you've had a haircut or a shave?"

"Shave? Ya mean my face?"

"Of course; what did you think? I—never mind. Don't answer that."

"I've never shaved. But a couple of times a year I'll cut its length." From the waistband of his pants he produced a small handmade knife with a crude apple wood handle. "But I can't ever seem to get this darned thing sharp enough and it's painful—not something I look forward to."

She held up the tools. "Know what these are?"

"Hey, I haven't seen one of those since I was a kid. A razor, right?"

"Yep." She waved a tool in the other hand. "And these are scissors."

"I recognize them. An old man I met last year had a pair. He cut my hair in exchange for dried squirrel meat."

Glory unwrapped the rag and produced a white ball. "This is soap, strong enough to get your body squeaky clean and, maybe, kill a few bugs you can't see. I propose we set up camp early and devote a couple of hours to getting clean, all of us. What do you say?"

Glory assumed a positive response and didn't wait for an answer, immediately coaxing Jake to the river to sit at the edge of the short drop-off to the water.

He didn't resist and sat as directed. "What are you doing?"

"I plan on removing the hair from your face and most of that on your head." She stepped beside him down to the water and returned with cupped hands filled with water, splashing it on his beard. She then took the ball of soap and lathered his face.

Annabelle stood slightly behind Myrna on higher ground behind them. Clearly, the oldest and the youngest saw this as splendid entertainment.

Myrna cleared her throat and spoke as if Jake weren't there. "You know, dear, there might be a handsome man under that hair."

"That's what I want to find out."

"If there is, I do hope you'll remain ladylike."

"Hush, Momma." Glory removed one of her ankle-high boots and stropped the razor across the thick leather of its side. As she did, she told Jake, "Go stick your head in the river and get that mess on top wet, too, then come back and sit down."

When he returned and sat, she knelt and set aside the razor in favor of the scissors. She aimed them at a point on the side of his dripping face that might make a good place to shave away a beard but leave a sideburn.

He shied away, looked at the blade through crossed eyes and gulped. "Before you begin, I want to be sure I haven't said or done anything to upset you."

She smiled. "Not yet."

After the length had been severely shortened, she began with the razor. As she worked, dirty brown whiskers fell away in clumps like a sheep being sheared. Although it'd been a joke, Glory indeed saw a handsome man take shape beneath the razor. She felt like a sculptress, creating the perfect male face—lean with pronounced cheekbones. The skin beneath his jaw remained tight and muscle striations stood out down his neck—the nose thin and straight. As she finished, Glory stepped back to examine her work.

Annabelle moved in to replace her. With a beaming smile on that dirty little face, she stroked his slick cheeks with grimy hands.

Glory nodded. "Much better, but I'm not done yet." She retrieved the scissors and twice clicked the blades together. "Now for that mop on top."

Myrna coughed. "I'm sure glad we found you two."

Glory grabbed hair at the back of his head and sliced right into it, removing a fistful.

"Hey! How much are you cutting off?"

Myrna laughed then coughed, laughed some more then went into a coughing binge. She teetered backward, appearing faint. Glory sprang up but her mother waved her away as the elderly woman sat on the ground. "I'm fine, dear. This is the best medicine I've had in weeks."

Glory felt a sudden warmth of camaraderie and shuddered with its flush.

Successfully revealing the guy beneath, she studied her handiwork ... and then the gaze went beyond the cursory. Now she looked at this man with awe. The grime and hair had concealed handsomeness on a man who—added to the good looks—was apparently endowed with an extremely rare ... *caring* streak.

Comparing his white face to the dark coloration of her own skin, she wondered what their offspring might look like. I don't know about the color of its skin, but the baby would be beautiful. After another moment fantasizing, she finally shook off the crazy notion and returned precious barbering tools to her mother's bag. "Okay, Jake, it's our turn. You go over there somewhere and stand guard while the three of us make use of that soap and the river. You can take your bath later. Deal?"

"Deal."

***

Although the spring air was mild and comfortable, Jake had an urge to cover his head. It felt unnaturally cool. In all his adult life this was the first time his face had been clean shaven and the hair on his head cut high and away from his neck. He couldn't keep his hands off his face. It hadn't been so slick since pre-pubescence.

As he manually explored the new look, he watched three generations of women walk down the path, around a bush and beyond the trees to the riverbank a few yards from the campsite, just out of sight. A lecherous urge came over him. He wanted to follow them to see Glory naked in the river and began walking in that direction. A sly grin stretched his hairless mouth.

Even as he was giving in to the compulsion, a sudden image of Annabelle becoming forever scared of him if he should get caught brought him to a standstill. Feeling as though he'd already been found out, he kicked up a cloud of dust. "Dadgummit!" Trapped between desire and obligation wasn't at all comfortable. Reluctantly, he backed away and sulked. I'm in danger of becoming a good man and I'm not at all sure I like it!

"*Humph,*" He rolled his eyes and headed back up the hill. "Good man indeed."

CHAPTER FOUR
TIME TO DECIDE

Lying near the glowing embers of the dying fire, sleep came fast for the exhausted women — Glory spooned to her mother's back upon a blanket, Annabelle using Jake's belly as a pillow. A knapsack served as his.

Cradling his head on stacked palms, Jake lay awake listening to Glory's deep even breathing. He lolled his head to the side and looked at her studying facial features of this exotic woman. *What's your story, Glory Jackson?* Infatuation, still in infancy, glowed like one of those orange embers in the flameless fire illuminating her face. Dark streaking shadows that, under normal circumstances, should have created an unattractive appearance did not. A beautiful face overcame even this harsh visual effect. Turning back to the stars overhead, he mulled burgeoning interest in what she thought of him, more so than learning a deeper personal history. Or, could it be that he misread the smiles and whispered conversations that, alone, enchanted?

As he stared into a star-filled sky, it was pleasant to envision then explore her physical attributes. Glory's striking eyes set in smooth mocha skin, always twinkling; her small nose turned slightly at the tip — it was pixie-like. An easy smile came up. Full lips completed the inviting package. He closed his eyes for a better look at the object of fascination. The picture conjured and, playing out behind closed eyelids, at first took his heart rate into a higher range but, after a time, the image soothed him. Drowsiness began pulling him down. *No better way to end a day than an image of that face, those eyes ...*

He released troubles of the day and let them evaporate, drifting into a light sleep, listening to the song of a cicada in the distance and feeling the brush of velvety cool night air over freshly shaved cheeks.

He woke abruptly. He attempted establishing how long he'd been asleep. He could not — maybe minutes, maybe hours. His first thought: did I hear something? Or, did I dream it? Survival instinct stiffened his body and had control from the instant he woke. He didn't move, nary a twitch. He just listened. The air felt heavy with a presence that did not include traveling companions — of what or whom he could not determine.

Maybe an animal had wandered into the campsite that might be spooked into attacking. Mountain lions were known to roam the area along the river, in fact, common by all accounts. That would be the preferred situation. A big cat's wants and needs are predictable, not so with humans.

He shifted only his eyes side to side. The fire still contained a number of glowing coals. He couldn't have been asleep long. The moon was rising, washing out the abundant stars making it easier to see shapes.

A twig snapped to his left.

Brush rustled to the right.

Before another question could be posed, a wheeze and a dull crack sounded just beyond the end of his head—someone with a bad knee perhaps. *Crap!* We've been invaded.

Out of the dark came a bold voice, "We hate to disturb your sleep like this. But that's the price of doing business I'm afraid."

Startled from sleep, Myrna suddenly gasped. Her head popped up from the backpack pillow. She jostled Glory's shoulder, rousing her. The older lady knew what was happening but her daughter was groggy, heavy still with sleep. Myrna rolled over and shook Glory more vigorously. "Wake up," she said in an urgent whisper.

As Jake raised his upper torso, Annabelle was forced to roll off his belly. He gently pushed her upright. She rubbed sleepy eyes.

"What do you want? Why are you here?" he said, not yet facing the voice.

Wide awake in a flash and shocked by Jake's bold voice, Annabelle scooted nearer him.

"It's inventory time and, as business needs dictate, we have to replenish our stores."

Jake smoothed Annabelle's hair to keep the child calm as he rose to his feet. "What does that have to do with us?" Calmly as he could, he dusted his pants trying to display quiet defiance of what he already knew was coming.

Turning to face the intruder, Jake could see by the moonlight two others—a man and a woman—coming in to join him. Jake perceived the one who had spoken as their leader. Even in the dim light Jake saw they were armed with machete-like knives—the men clean-shaven with combed hair. They didn't appear to be run-of-the-mill thieves. The woman with them was young, or so she appeared. Without the revealing light of day she appeared pretty, too, with long light-colored hair, sandy brown or blonde perhaps. All three were well dressed and oddly courteous.

Annabelle stood and pressed against Jake's leg in full body contact, arms encircling his waist.

"It has everything to do with you and your party," the leader said. "You're in our network."

"Network? I don't remember signing up for any network."

"Are you a member of a corporation," the man asked.

"No."

"Then you are in our network. All independent consumers are."

34

"I am an independent consumer by choice," Jake said. "And, it's for the specific reason that I did not want to be bound by corporate rules and regulations."

"Sorry, but your personal desires don't matter. As an I.C. you must negotiate because it's commonly understood how important preservation of the corpocracy is. Without the orderly pragmatism a corpocratic society provides there'd be chaos. This is valuable information we provide to you at a nominal charge. Enough chitchat. We don't want to inconvenience you any longer than we must. We'll be on our way shortly and allow you good people to get back to sleep. Let's negotiate."

Although friendly of tone and demeanor, Jake remained on edge. "Well, I've been trying to be a better independent consumer and share when I can, so let me see what I might come up with." He peeled Annabelle's hands away from his waist and reached for the knapsack.

The man stabbed it with the point of his long knife, pinning it to the ground. "There's no need to dole it out." He pushed his hand past Jake's and snatched it away. "We'll take it and check it later. But thanks for the offer. You're very kind."

Jake took an aggressive step. The other man snapped his broad-bladed knife up to within inches of Jake's chest. As that standoff unfolded, the woman marched to Glory and Myrna. She yanked at the backpack.

Glory held it firmly.

The woman brought her knife up near Glory's nose while, at the same time, tugging on the backpack.

As the knife touched Glory's nose, her grasp loosened.

The woman forced it from behind crossed arms. The woman then backed away two paces and smiled. "Thank you so much for your business. You seem to be very nice people." She rejoined her two associates.

Jake didn't make another attempt. He watched them back away until darkness swallowed them whole. He slapped at the air in anger. "Damn it!" He paced in a tight circle, grumbling, kicking the ground.

Frustrated by impotence, he did the only thing he could; stir the remaining glowing embers to keep his hands busy, tossing on twigs and a stumpy log. After a few hard puffs on the dry kindling, it flamed up and lit the immediate area.

Glory was on hands and knees crawling back and forth and then behind the tree nearest them. A searching arm extended, feeling into the darkness, as if she were a blind beggar.

"What're ya doin'?" he said.

"Looking for the other three bags, you know, the ones with long straps Mother and I carried. The woman didn't take them but I don't see them. Where'd they go?"

From the darkness at the edge of the growing firelight, Annabelle reappeared clutching the three knapsacks. She dipped her chin humbly then slowly raised her head and grinned as she handed Glory the shoulder bags.

In clear amazement, Glory dropped to sit on the ground and leaned back against a tree, lips parted in surprise. "How did ... when did you get them?"

Still smiling, Annabelle sat beside Glory, nuzzling her head between Glory's arm and body then put an arm around Glory's waist. Glory stroked the girl's shoulder. "You're amazing. Those bags were at my side when those people came into camp. How ... when di—"

"There's something a little unusual about Annabelle," Jake said, thrusting a finger upright in emphasis. "I don't know what that *something* is, but to say she's *special* doesn't begin to describe her." He pulled Annabelle to her feet, away from Glory, and knelt before her. "But I'm proud to call her my friend."

After a lengthy admiring gaze into the child's eyes, he embraced her momentarily then pulled his face away. "She's family now." He sat back on his heels and noticed how the dark circles under the child's eyes had vanished and healthy color with rosy cheeks had returned. Now that her face had been cleaned, he saw the beautiful little girl that had been concealed behind the grime.

Annabelle wrapped her arms around his neck and patted his back as she laid her head upon his shoulder. She sighed.

But he heard more than that; a slight moan escaped. Jake again wondered about Annabelle's ability to speak. Could she? He still didn't know if it was a lifelong condition or, perhaps, silence forced upon her by the trauma of witnessing her mother murdered? If it was the latter, he thought it might return someday.

He eased her away and, while still looking at the child and stroking her hair, spoke to the older women. "Let's get our heads together and figure out if we can get by without the stuff they took."

The shared adventure of the robbery drew them closer together. Conversations became easier, more open, as days passed. They continued on the path northwest beside the Brazos River flowing the opposite direction. Talk became laced with inquiries of a more intimate nature and personal inquiries were no longer taboo, even becoming commonplace. Myrna's weakness kept the pace slow, rest stops frequent. Jake didn't mind, appreciating the opportunity to have more time with Glory. But, that was something he certainly had no intention of saying aloud. He enjoyed the company of both women a bit more every day.

Glory spoke of shared plans with husband, Chauncy. For one, she'd had dreams of creating and building a new corporate stockade, from concept to completion. The dream was alive and well, altered only slightly by his absence. She now dreamt of making it into what she believed Stalwart would be—a place ordinary people could live in peace and be welcome for a lifetime as long as everyone contributed to the greater good.

In turn, Jake told of a budding desire to create something—anything—so when the time came he could die knowing he'd left this world a little better off. He wanted to make a difference, no matter how miniscule, within the greater scheme. More importantly, that Annabelle would carry it on into the future, whatever it would eventually be.

They walked the trail, no one speaking for a time. Jake suddenly stopped, whirled around to face Glory and blurted, "I'm really afraid."

Myrna and Annabelle had to check their step or risk stumbling into him.

Shocked, Glory jerked her head back. "Afraid? You? I don't believe that at all."

Embarrassment reddened his face. "Well, yeah, sort of."

Annabelle stepped forward, leaned into Jake and pushed him closer to Glory. He yielded and took that step. He shot the child a quick half-grin. It wasn't the first time the youngster had made a not-so-subtle attempt to get the two of them together.

"I've seen many of your faces," Glory said, looking into Jake's eyes, "but I haven't seen fear, not once."

"It's not that kind of fear. Terror created by confronting wild animals or risking a long knife held to my chest by a robber is one kind. What I'm talking about is this gnawing in my gut that I won't know what to leave behind for Annabelle to remember me by."

He paced in a tight circle one time and ran fingers through his hair, frustrated by his inability to speak succinctly. "Look, I don't just mean leaving the world a better place. I want Annabelle to smile when she remembers me. I—I can't explain why, but ... *how* she remembers me is important. Does that make sense?"

"Jake, don't you recognize love?"

"Love?"

Annabelle again nudged him. Hard enough that he stumbled forward yet another step. This time annoyed, he glanced down. "Stop, Little One." When he looked up, his nose was within an inch of Glory's.

Her dark eyes twinkled.

His stomach fluttered.

She didn't give ground, just kept on looking pleasant, tilting her head slightly. Her already remarkable beauty was, suddenly, dazzlingly radiant.

He felt her warm breath on his face.

Eager to give reason to remain close, Jake rattled, "I, uh, guess that's what it is." Heat rose in his face.

He closed his eyes, swallowed hard and stepped back. He felt short of oxygen and drew a deep breath. He resumed stroking Annabelle's hair. "That's part of it, I guess, but there must be more, something larger than that alone. Maybe I'm afraid *no one* will remember me when I die. Is that possible?"

Even as the question left his mouth, he already regretted asking it. It was childish, self-centered and, most of all, unfair to expect an answer. "I'm sorry. I shouldn't be saying that kind of stuff. I don't know why this muck is spilling out of me. Forget I said anything."

"I certainly will *not* forget it. It's clear to me you've had no one to spill it out to." She made up the step he took back, bringing them together again. In softer voice she said, "I have little to offer, but I can, at least, offer you what you most fear you may never have." She placed hands on both his cheeks and drew his face within an inch of hers. "For all your kindness to Mother and me," she said, her voice soft and sweet, her dark amber eyes moist and penetrating, "you won't be forgotten, not by me." She kissed him on the corner of his mouth, then moved her head back enough to nod in her mother's and then Annabelle's direction.

His eyes followed.

"There're two others over there that won't either."

Jake didn't know how to respond, torn between years of practiced stoicism and the emotions bubbling within. It wouldn't take much more for tears to surface—and that he could not allow them to see.

Myrna placed a hand on Annabelle's shoulder and pulled her close. The youngster looked up and beamed at the older woman. No words were exchanged, just shared joy at both ends of the age spectrum accompanied by big smiles.

The ensuing hours walking the river trail were mostly void of chit chat. Jake had said much more than he really wanted to, so, he figured it was time to retreat into the perceived safety of his thoughts. With each step closer to Stalwart, desire to keep the four of them together became a hammer against a formidable wall of emotional stone that had taken a lifetime to mortar into place. Annabelle began the destruction but, now, Glory and Myrna were also blasting large chunks from it. What he planned to do about it upon arrival at Stalwart eluded him. He did realize it'd be the most difficult decision he'd ever have to make—to stay with them or move on. He inched closer to the raggedy edge.

The sun moved high overhead, not quite noon. The trail began angling away from the river ascending beyond the high water mark. Brush and trees on both sides of the trail ended. They now stood on a rise looking down a gentle grassy slope. Spring flowers dotted the landscape. Here, the river turned and meandered north-northeasterly. It'd served them well and guided them true.

On the flatter surface at the bottom of the slope stood, what appeared to be, a formidable stone stockade. Broad walls fifteen feet high enclosed a compound that included many stone buildings in neat rows covering twenty or more acres. People milled about within the enclosure and there were impeccably manicured gardens in a wide area outside. Water gurgled along an overhead wooden sluice from the river to the gardens—a peaceful and alluring view. He sighed. "Stalwart?"

"I think so," said Glory.

Annabelle wiggled between them. She grabbed his hand then Glory's. There was no elation; a somber cloud hovered over the child.

Glory shrugged without excitement. "It's impressive."

"Yeah. I guess it is."

Standing abreast, the four studied all that lay before them. Pain of the coming disconnection had begun squeezing his heart.

Shared quietness went beyond an examination of real estate. A monster followed them like a fifth member—the beast of separation anxiety eating away all the joy.

"Look," said Glory, "It's crazy that you and Annabelle should continue to wander. Your transient lifestyle is no life. Why don't you join us?"

And there it was: the question. He had no choice but confront it. The inability to decide began to pressurize. "I have a feeling no matter what I say, I'll wish I'd said something else."

"Mister Henderson," Myrna said, "I know you have misgivings about your lot in this world but you're a rarity—an honest man with good intentions. I'll miss you two terribly if you move on." She squeezed her daughter's arm. "I know Glory will." She coughed.

Glory's head bobbed sheepishly. "Yeah ... what she said."

Jake rubbed the nape of his neck. He looked everywhere but at Glory or her mother while he considered the offer. Finally he said, his voice low, a bit sad, "I'm sorry. I just can't handle the corporate lifestyle, too much like a prison." He looked down at Annabelle as he continued clutching her hand. "We've seen several good places along the river. Maybe better places will appear farther north." He kept looking elsewhere so sad faces wouldn't sway him. "For now, I think that I ... *we* should keep searching for the ideal home site." His eyes swept the ground.

Annabelle stepped back and pulled Jake and Glory's hands together forcing them to hold hands.

Jake squeezed Glory's hand then abruptly released it and turned to the youngster, dropping to a knee. He pulled Annabelle's shoulder to square with the child. "I like Glory and Myrna, too, but we have to follow through on our plan."

Annabelle shook her head.

"What are you trying to say? Do you want to stay with them while I keep looking upriver?"

Again, she shook her head.

"Then come on. This is hard for me. We need to go while I can." He came off his knee and began walking away, only to come to a shocked halt when he heard a shrill young voice split the air from behind—

"Stay!"

CHAPTER FIVE
SEPARATE JOURNEYS

As she and her mother walked the easy slope to the Stalwart compound, Glory looked back to shrinking figures walking the opposite direction. "What do you think? Should we have tried harder to convince Jake to join us?" They stopped about fifty feet out from the open gate. She turned and looked yet again at the pair growing smaller in the distance. "Annabelle sure wanted him to stay."

Glory's question hung in the mild spring air unanswered for a long pause before her mother said, "I believe, dear, that Annabelle wanted you and Jake to remain together. I don't think it mattered so much where."

Glory looked back through the open gate offering a view into the compound. Absently, she readjusted the shouldered knapsacks as she scanned the formidable structure top to bottom and end to end. A tall white stone wall was the backdrop to an expansive vegetable garden on both sides of the broad path they walked to get here. But the concept of Stalwart had lost its gloss. The absence of Jake and Annabelle left the experience hollow.

"Don't feel guilty about a decision Jake made. Questioning it will drive you crazy. He knows where we'll be. They'll be okay, as will we." Myrna smiled. "I sure hope Annabelle knows more words than 'stay'."

"Me, too. I think Jake is the right person to help her with that. I'll wager that within a year he won't be able to keep her quiet."

"A bet or a prophecy?"

"Little of both I guess."

A man approached from the end of a garden row with a hoe in his hand. "Welcome to Stalwart." His grin stretched wide. He wore a small wooden disc on his lapel. On it, an upturned crescent carved into its bottom with two vertical dashes above it.

"Thank you," Glory said, taken aback by his exuberance. "My mother and I are interested in gaining shareholder status, a permanent place within your walls. Is that possible?"

"As fate would have it an elderly gentleman and his wife passed away recently leaving sleeping quarters open that will accommodate two, I believe. But I don't have authority to offer it. Follow me. I'll introduce you to our chief executive officer and overseer, Mister F. Lee Tam."

Glory was compelled to remain where she stood a moment longer, watching Jake and Annabelle in the distance walking the trail until it turned downward nearer the river. As they disappeared into the woods over the knoll, she sighed. "Sure. We'd love to meet him," she said, but her eyes remained on the spot she last saw her friends. *I hope I see you two again. I love you both.* She held her breath for a heartbeat then exhaled sad air and turned toward a better life within the protective walls of Stalwart.

Myrna clutched her daughter's hand and tugged. "Come on. Let's go see what Stalwart is all about."

They followed the man through the open, massive oak double-door gate into the compound. He balanced the hoe on his right shoulder and walked with a cheerful bounce—itself a comforting sight. But there was something odd about his expression. The smile didn't look right, hinting contrivance—insincerity maybe. Had separation anxiety already begun tainting her opinion?

She scoped everything: the most obvious a stone obelisk standing almost as tall as the wall that enclosed the compound, roughly fifteen feet high she guessed, centered in the main courtyard between the gate and the nearest building which happened to be much larger than the others. That building was similar in style to the rest, mortared native stone topped by split cedar shingles. A knee-high stone retaining wall encircled the base of the monument filled with a kaleidoscopic array of blooming flowers, meticulously cared for as if it held reverential significance. Glory wondered what that might be. Symbols were carved into the obelisk; an upturned crescent with two vertical dashes above it like the wooden disk the man wore on his lapel.

As she walked past, her focus shifted to the building the man led them to. The monument would mean nothing without living quarters and shareholder status within Stalwart.

The man, hoe still over his shoulder, stopped at the door of the sprawling one-story and knocked. Glory turned a final time, taking in the view. Utter cleanliness seemed odd by the standards of today's world. It appealed to her. Not a weed or a stray branch beneath the oak and pecan trees dappling the grounds. Small yards of manicured grass fronted each of the stone cottages; all built to a particular style with split cedar shingled roofs, just like the building she stood before. Surprisingly few people milled about the compound. Where were all the others? Could they be in their cottages? Working?

The heavy door opened, startling Glory. She spun back and there stood a teenage girl smiling at them. But there was something unusual about her smile, too. Like the man escorting them, her eyes didn't match the mouth. Her youthful natural beauty was striking, but expressiveness and clothing certainly had nothing to do with the opinion. The girl had long, straight, unkempt dull brown hair clad in a collarless plain gray dress that hung like a sack to below her knees. Glory thought the uncombed hair unusual, considering the preciseness of everything else. Why was the girl's appearance in disarray? And, why was her hair only mussed at the back of her head? The girl's feet were bare—face pale. She seemed flushed and glowed with perspiration as if she'd been running. Whatever task she'd been busy with had clearly been strenuous. Glory guessed her age to be seventeen.

Their guide said to the girl, "We have guests who've inquired about gaining shareholder status. Is Mister Tam available?"

The girl didn't speak, just stepped aside and gestured them in.

As they walked through the door the opulence of what she saw took her breath. Glancing at her mother, Myrna's face mimicked her own. Small tapestry rugs lay over a smooth white flagstone floor. A chandelier hung from an exposed cedar log joist at the center of the room; all the joists had been stripped of bark and highly polished, otherwise left semi-rugged. Candles flickered from the chandelier and spread sparkling amber light through dangling crystal bobs. Beneath it, a round claw-foot table of considerable heft, intricately carved and glossy, were positioned in line with the front door. Beyond that, to the rear of the room, the wall was interrupted by a fireplace with a firebox that must have measured five-feet square. In front of the hearth, two leather wingback chairs faced one another. Artwork adorned the walls. Glory knew it'd been many decades since such extravagance had been more normal than not. Such finery in this part of the former United States, once known as Texas, began dying away over a century ago.

Gliding fingers over the burnished surface of the central table, she took note of a beautifully carved hardwood placard in the center of it: "Welcome to all who enter. —Fiam Lee Tam"

Glory hadn't noticed the young girl had left the room. Hearing the pad of feet, she turned toward a door left of the fireplace. A small man, distinctly Asian, entered. He stood no taller than she. He, like everyone else, had an unwavering smile. He wore a satiny red robe, legs and feet bare beneath it.

"Mister Tam," their guide said, "these ladies have inquired about staying on with us here at Stalwart."

"Thank you," Tam said, then casually gestured for the man to leave.

"Since I've brought replacements, I thought that—"

"That'll be all." The sharpness of the order belied his smile.

The man's smile wilted somewhat but snapped back as he nodded affirmation of the order. He stepped over the threshold heading out, but hesitantly so, as if he wanted to say something else. He retrieved his hoe from against the outside wall and closed the door behind him.

Tam's eyes remained focused on the closed door. "Please excuse him. He's a new member and having more trouble than most acclimating to the Stalwart culture. Complete unquestioning integration is important to serenity, most importantly to *family*. I'm afraid he still believes that if he does what he's told and smiles then that's enough. One has to internalize the concept, a total immersion into a lifestyle for a lifetime."

"I look forward to discovering what it is that I might be immersing in." She stepped forward and smiled. "I'm Glory Jackson and this is my mother, Myrna."

The elder Jackson moved to be at her daughter's side and bowed her head amiably.

"I honor your presence and am humbled you have chosen Stalwart." He took Glory's and Myrna's hands simultaneously kissing the backs of each. "How is it that you come to be here?"

"We traveled up from the Hill Country. A passerby heading south told us of your corporation. He passed on hearsay that your compound accepted new residents on a sweat equity basis for shareholder status and that we only needed to contribute to the greater good to earn living quarters and sustenance."

"Then you have heard correctly."

"Is there room for two more?"

"A cottage has just opened up. Your timing, purposely or not, is impeccable. An elderly couple has sadly passed on."

"At the same time?"

"It happens. One cannot survive without the other after many years together."

Glory thought it strange, but there was sense to be made of it. "I'm not sure how we might contribute, but mother has wonderful sewing and gardening skills whereas I'm strong and healthy and can work almost anywhere I might be needed. Plus, I'm a quick learner at most tasks. With your guidance, I'm confident we'll add value to your corporation."

Tam again bowed slightly. "Good answer." His smile broadened. "Consider yourselves welcome additions to *family* here at Stalwart."

Glory released a measured exhale feeling weeks of fretfulness drain away. She pulled her mother into a side embrace. "Thank you, Mister Tam."

"It is I who thank you for believing in Stalwart and the wisdom of devotion to *family*."

"If you don't mind me asking; why is it that everyone constantly smiles? Surely, everyone can't be that happy all the time, especially at the same time."

"You'll discover that to appear happy is to become happy." He moved to the window facing the main gate and gestured to the stone obelisk. "That is why the smile is a symbol of who we are. Pleasantness to all is a pre-requisite for residency."

"Oh, that's what the two vertical dashes over the upturned crescent signify, a smiling face."

"Exactly."

"That should be an easy rule to follow."

"Good, because that will be your first duty as residents, smiling at everyone you meet. Whether it be a shareholder or independent consumer, you'll proudly display the Stalwart smile at all times. Remember, a smile costs you nothing; it costs Stalwart nothing, but garners wealth. You'll come to know that. It will be your greeting to all you meet from this moment forward."

He clasped his hands together at his back. "I insist you and Myrna join me for dinner after you settle in to your new cottage. I'll expect you back when the sun sinks to the peak of the obelisk."

Since it hadn't been offered as a suggestion, Glory nodded. "Thank you. We'd love to." She offered her first obligatory smile and found it cathartic. Maybe this smile thing could have a lasting positive effect, she thought.

"Excellent. Now, my house girl, Lana, will show you to your new home."

Without having to summon her, the young girl appeared wearing sandals. She walked past Tam to the door without speaking and opened it. She stopped and looked at them while clutching the door latch handle waiting for them to respond.

Glory put a hand on her mother's lower back and gently urged her to walk. She adjusted her knapsacks then stepped lively toward the door. "See you in a short while," she said over her shoulder as the three exited and stepped into the brilliance of the late morning sun from under the porch overhang.

Lana led the way and stopped at the door to their new cottage.

"Thank you," Glory told her. "The name is Lana, right?"

"Yes."

"Pretty name."

Lana nodded.

It bothered Glory that the girl's eyes were sad, yet the mouth smiled. "Tell me, Lana, are you really as happy as you try to appear?"

The answer clearly hung in the girl's throat but, then, hesitantly, "Y—yes." Lana forced her smile wider and turned to walk away. She stopped. Head slumping, she stood momentarily then turned back. "I owe you a better explanation. The elderly couple living in this cottage before you was my grandparents, the last of my family. Fate brought us together after thieves killed my parents. I didn't know they were alive until they showed up at Stalwart's gates not long ago. They told me if it hadn't been for a man and a young girl offering them apples to renew their strength, they never would've made it, an—"

"Jake and Annabelle maybe?" a wide-eyed Glory blurted to her

45

mother.

"It certainly sounds like them."

"Anyhow," Lana continued, "my grandparents had only been here a few days when I was informed they'd passed away. It was too soon and too sudden. How could they have endured so much to get here and then die at the same time? It made no sense. I didn't understand then and I still don't. It'll take time to get over it." She didn't wait for a response and turned to walk away. She muttered, "They were so happy."

"I'm sorry for your loss," said Glory.

The girl kept walking and muttering. "I had been lost and alone before they came; now I am again."

Glory had questions but realized this was not the time. In raised voice she said, "Please accept our sympathy."

Lana kept walking.

"See you in a while."

Stepping inside the small cabin, Glory began a cursory inspection of the new lodgings as she shucked the knapsacks. The cottage consisted of three rooms: the front room with twin beds, a modest fireplace, bedside tables and two rocking chairs; a small kitchen with a wood burning stove and basin beneath an overhead can that held water—which Glory assumed was hauled up from the river. A table and two chairs graced the other wall. The third was a bathroom. It held a small metal bathtub in the center, toilet chair in the corner, and a table against the wall with a porcelain basin on it and a mirror above it. The cottage had been stocked with essentials. All the furniture was colorful, built with red and white cedar planks and posts stripped of bark.

The two women met back in the main room. "What do you think," Myrna asked.

"Perfect," said Glory.

"Then why the funny look?"

"Isn't it all a bit too perfect?"

"I'm not sure I understand."

"There's something not quite right, but it's just a feeling."

"Maybe it's the absence of Jake and Annabelle."

"It'd be great if that's all it is." She pulled the cloth binding tighter that held her long curly black hair in the back. "I suppose we've encountered too many people less than honest in the past few months. I must be turning into a cynic." She shrugged. "I guess it can't be too bad if Mister Tam is that concerned about family."

***

The farther from Stalwart Jake walked, the more he regretted leaving

Glory and her mother behind—worse yet, forcing Annabelle to decide between them.

Tears rolled down the girl's cheeks but she retained that unflappable look. Such stoicism was out of place on a child so young.

"I'm sorry it didn't work out like you wanted."

Annabelle rolled a shoulder high, tipping her head into it to sweep tears from her cheek, and kept walking.

"We'll see Glory and Myrna again. I promise." Although he put the vow out there, he wasn't sure it was in his power to honor. He simply wanted to divert her mind to a better place, as he did his own. "One good thing has come of it: you spoke a word. You know what that means? Somewhere inside you are many more; I want to hear them all."

He stroked her hair. A pain pricked his heart when all she offered in response was a weak smile, quickly returning to that bland face. He was left with no alternative; he had to let sadness play out and stop trying to soothe a wound that needed time to heal. *Glory would know what to do. If only I could glimpse the future and know for myself.*

Annabelle had become a constant source of apprehension, not knowing what might happen to her if he should be removed from the picture. What about Glory and Myrna—should he have forced Annabelle to stay with them? She would've been better cared for. Maybe he should have stayed at Stalwart, too? In a few short weeks his life had complicated. The general state of the world didn't matter so much anymore because his world now revolved around a ten-year-old girl.

As the trail straightened an elderly man, grizzled and slumped, shuffling along with a cane pole over his shoulder, came into view. Even at Jake and Annabelle's casual pace, they overtook the old guy in seconds, "Hey, old-timer, where ya headed?"

The man stopped and turned. He said nothing, just raked his remaining upper teeth over his lower lip and glanced in bursts at Jake then Annabelle then back. Finally, squinting up at Jake from beneath the frayed brim of a straw hat, he said, "If robbin' me is your plan then you picked a mighty poor mark, son."

Annabelle swiped at tears drying on her cheeks and began yanking on the knapsack over Jake's shoulder.

He laughed. "Slow down, Little One." He dropped the bag to the ground.

She flipped open the top and retrieved a small turnip. She trotted to the man and offered it with an excited smile.

"Tell me true; does that look like we're here to rob you?"

He looked to the vegetable as if disbelieving the child's good intention. After a moment of obvious contemplation, he cocked his head to one side. "Guess not." He took the turnip, winked, and nodded a thank-you. After rubbing the dirt from the purple and white vegetable on his threadbare jacket, he gnawed off a bite best he could with missing teeth. Juice dribbled from the corner of his mouth as he spoke. "I was headin' for that fallen willer tree up yonder. See it?" With the hand holding the turnip he pointed, extending an arthritically gnarled finger. "Right there, the one out over the water; crappy and bream tend to congregate under it. So, I thought I'd try to catch supper."

Root tendrils remained firmly planted in the muddy bank while green branches still grew at the other end of the willow tree shading the deeper water beneath it.

"What do you use for bait?"

"Crickets." He shook his head and sighed. "I'm gettin' so old and slow, though, that I'm havin' as much trouble catchin' the bait as I am the fish."

Annabelle trotted to a thin flat stone partially buried in the soil. She flipped it up and two crickets jumped in opposite directions. With amazing speed, she captured both insects in the air with a single sweep of one hand.

"Dadburn!" The old man pulled off his tattered straw hat and scratched his forehead. "Never saw anything quite like that. You're youngun there has a mighty fast hand."

Jake dropped hands on his hips. "Yeah, I know. Darnedest thing I ever saw."

Annabelle jogged back and pulled the cane pole from the old man's shoulder. He willingly gave it up. She unfurled the line of thin leather strips knotted together at intervals and skewered one of the crickets on the crudely fashioned crabapple thorn hook. She went to the fallen tree he'd pointed out and waved them over, appearing giddy by this respite from walking the trail.

"Tell ya what," the old man said, "whatever we catch let's split it in thirds. That way we all get fed."

Jake shook the old man's hand. "Ya got yourself a deal, Mister."

***

The dimpled and warped copper pan set on glowing coals of a dying fire. The last of the five fish they'd caught was in it, bubbling in the river water they'd used to steam-cook them. The fish was nestled in a mound of wild onion shoots and bulbs. The smell of it cooking was as satisfying as the taste.

"That last one's yours, old-timer."

"Nah. Y'all take it. If it weren't for your youngun there, I'd still be trying to catch something."

Jake peeled the flaked fish off the bone and gave an equal share to the old man anyway. As he did he wondered if the old guy might have wisdom to share. "Have you ever wished that you already knew what's up the road before you set out on a journey?"

Gumming small bites of fish, the old man took the question in stride. "Nope, if I knew beforehand, I might never go up the road or anywhere else." He popped the last bite in his mouth then wiped his hands on his pants and his mouth on his sleeve. "What's the matter, son, life gettin' ya down?"

"I guess it is." Jake patted Annabelle's hair. She sat close. "In the past few weeks I've gone from a wandering loner with no family or friends to having both, a worry I never thought I'd have."

"I see. Well, I've got no advice for you, other than to say I've been where you're going. As painful as it is to lose family and friends, it pales to never having had them when the end gets close." He stabbed the air with a stern finger. "That's not an opinion, friend, it's a fact. Memories are about the only comfort I get out of life anymore; wouldn't trade for any of 'em, no sir."

"You may not have intended it, but that sounded like pretty good advice." He flicked a twig into the glowing embers of the small fire, watched it flare, then heaved a sigh. "I yearn for direction, what I should do versus what I want to do. Those two things stay at odds in my head all the time."

"Well," the old guy tugged at his thin gray beard and sucked air past his gapped teeth, "the Oracle of Blister Knob might help. Don't know. Been by her place many times but never been to see her myself. I've heard she knows things."

"Knows things?"

"The future and such."

"Really? A woman you say?"

"Yep."

"Where's Blister Knob?"

He flipped a thumb over his shoulder. "Keep following the river north. You'll come to an area where the ground has been salted and left barren. Nothin' grows on it, nothin' at all. An equally bald hill rises up in the middle of it. That's Blister Knob. Dame Fortune lives in a partial dugout scooped out of its side. You'll see it. Not an easy place to walk by without noticin'."

At once Jake had a goal besides searching for a home site that he still wasn't sure he wanted yet. He fell back and laid his head on the knapsack. "Thanks, Old Timer. Maybe that's worth checking out." He moved his head around until he found a spot of comfort, then muttered, "The Oracle of Blister Knob ... weird title."

Annabelle scooted nearer to use his chest as a pillow; the sound of his beating heart must have been like a lullaby. She rubbed circles with her tiny hand on his chest and whispered, "Love you."

The new words intoxicated him. He lifted his head and looked into her sleepy face feeling her breath. Contentment settled over him like a warm blanket. "Good night, Little One."

Jake fell asleep with a smile.

The next morning, leaving the old man behind was troublesome. It occurred to Jake the man was so old they'd likely never see him again. He was an instant friend and a person of value. "You're welcome to join us," Jake told him.

"Can't do it, son. The legs aren't up to it anymore. But," he paused, "if the next time you pass by and find me … well, dead, I want you to take my fishin' pole, copper pan and this ol' knife o' mine." It's not much, but all I have to repay your kindness."

Jake didn't know how to respond. So, he simply smiled and touched a finger to his forehead in a friendly one-finger salute.

He took Annabelle's hand and began walking up the trail. The girl looked back as Jake pulled her along. He whispered from the corner of his mouth, "Come on, Little One. We've done all we can for him."

***

Glory woke to a mockingbird's varied song. For the first few moments, she relished a secure feeling. But then skepticism kicked in; a small voice echoed in her head. Guard your feelings. Be cautious. Take it slow.

She thought about dinner last evening. Mister Tam's charisma had her believing she would do anything to make him happy with her presence at Stalwart. On reflection, it seemed curious she'd think that. Exhaustion? Maybe. Fatigue coupled with appreciation for good food and a soft bed. That had to be the reason she bought into his charm so readily.

The feather pillow felt as though her head floated in a cloud. She didn't want to move. Now fully light outside, the sun had yet to breach the horizon.

Myrna stirred in the bed next to her.

"Did you sleep well, Mother?"

"Best in weeks." She stretched.

Glory heard a noise. The mockingbird stopped singing and took wing. "Is that clapping?"

Myrna rose up on an elbow and listened, turning her better ear. "I think it is."

Glory threw off the light blanket and rolled out of bed. She walked to the window and pulled back a curtain panel. People spilled from small cottages and filed by on the gravel walkway between small yards. Neighbors directly across the walkway came out of their cottage, began clapping in cadence like all the rest and joined the growing train of people. The leaders had already begun circling the tall stone obelisk between the front gate and Tam's house, all the while clapping in perfect rhythm and smiling. No one talked, made no sound of voice whatsoever. It was as if they were all in a trance.

She saw Tam's house-girl, Lana, coming.

The girl knocked on their door.

Glory took two lateral steps, opened the door and peeked around the edge of the jamb. "Good morning. What's all that about?"

"It's the morning affirmation."

"Affirmation? Of what?"

"Stalwart shareholders must jointly reaffirm allegiance to *family* every morning."

"Oh." Glory looked to her mother, shrugged and pushed out her lower lip. "Sounds worthwhile."

"Attendance is mandatory," Lana said.

Glory and her mother scurried about gathering clothes and quickly dressed.

Like all of them, Lana wore the obligatory smile but sad eyes spoke even louder. "Follow me."

The clapping became an irritating pulse; a ritual that would surely become tiresome fast. Everyone faced the obelisk, looking up to the carved smile. Now standing between her mother on the left and Lana on the right, a poetic chant began, augmenting the rhythmic smack of hands:

With the rise of each new sun
We re-avow that we are one.
It's easy to be and for all to see
That our reason to smile is family.

Lana chanted along.

Glory looked around the assemblage at curiously blank stares with heartless smiles.

Lana nudged her with an elbow. Her brow pulled down to a frown, although her mouth kept right on smiling. The chant began again as clapping continued setting the rhythm.

With the rise of each new sun...

Glory muttered, "We re-avow," she, in turn, elbowed her mother in the arm. Only then did the elder Jackson begin to harmonize, "that we are one. It's easy to be and for all to see that our reason to smile is family."

51

Glory shrugged at her mother and began clapping along with everyone else, getting into the melodic chant. It ended on the third repeat and the clapping turned random. Everyone left as methodically as they'd arrived. Still, no one spoke.

Glory saw it as a superficial exercise performed by people with artificial enthusiasm and pointless. It was clear enough that no one wanted to engage in the ritual but had no choice—likely the reason no one spoke—just something that had to be done to maintain an appearance of unity and happiness. She and her mother stood somewhat dumbfounded as everyone dispersed, leaving them standing with Lana next to the obelisk. "So, every morning we have this to look forward to?"

"You'll get used to it," Lana said, grim smile unchanging.

CHAPTER SIX
THE ORACLE OF BLISTER KNOB

Dodging a cluster of Chinaberry saplings in the trail along the river, Jake looked up to the high-water mark to a peculiar sight. A large patch of ground, void of all plant life, continued on from there to flatter ground higher up. A strange looking mound, not much more than a large pile of dirt, rose from its barren center. He realized now why the old guy they'd met on the river said it'd be hard to miss. The name Blister Knob fit perfectly; it appeared as a giant, whitish, festering sore on the ground.

The entire area surrounding the lump of a hill looked like a scar on the earth. Decades of erosion created an artistic series of gullies and sand drifts from the peak of the hill down to the river's edge below where he and Annabelle stood. A partial dugout structure, set in the center, protruded outward from it. The odd-looking building had been centered and dug into the side of the rise. Coupled with washouts and sand drifts, Jake could also imagine a Cyclops with a very unruly head of flowing hair—the vision an unsettling one.

"This must be the place." Somewhat spooked, he stared for several long seconds at the dugout. Finally, he shook off hesitance. "Come on, Little One; let's go see who this Oracle of Blister Knob is."

He took her hand. They climbed the gentle incline to the unusual, scanty dwelling. It looked like it had been partially covered over in a landslide. It was crudely constructed but neat and well maintained. The small gabled roof extended outward from the hill and was thatched over with a thick mat of cattail reeds—gathered from the shallows of the river, Jake surmised. There were no windows, only a front door of expertly fitted and bound cedar saplings. He wondered if he'd be capable of such fine joinery. A cluster of bluebonnets in full bloom grew from a hollowed-out stump next to a neat stone porch, superbly fitted together like puzzle pieces. Those plants with their delicate blossoms were the only vegetation for some distance in any direction, and obviously planted purposely.

The door flung open.

Startled, Jake stumbled back.

Once righted, Annabelle clung to his breeches leg and hid behind him, peering around at an old woman.

"If I be waitin' for a diddly dang knock, I'd still be waitin'."

"How'd you know we were out here? I didn't think we were making any noise."

"You weren't. I just be knowin'. That's all."

"Are you the one they call The Oracle of Blister Knob?"

"I be thinkin' you can call me Dame Fortune. It's a far sight better than Gladys Pitch."

"Bitch. Your last name is Bitch?"

She laughed with a hard sarcastic ring, ample waistline jiggling beneath a loose woven shawl. "Pitch, you blitherin' fool, *Pitch* with a diddly dang *P*." Her course word choice didn't fit her jovial manner.

"Sorry." He didn't know what to say next and then, again, took note of the bluebonnets next to the door. "Uh, nice blossoms. Did you plant them?"

"I be thankin' ya kindly, and no."

Annabelle remained in full body contact with Jake, arms reaching as far around his waist as possible, allowing only one eye to spy the woman from relative safety behind Jake.

Jake shifted his body position, withdrawing the shadow he'd cast over the woman; the sun struck her eyes—it was plain to see at a glance she was blind. They shone milky and glowed with reflected light when hit directly by the sun's rays. They set sunken in a face the color of midnight, scars crisscrossing both eyelids and cheeks. Long, tightly kinked, untamed hair hung in a wad, white as freshly fallen snow. Her sudden appearance at the door sharpened the wildly contrasting features.

"Don't just stand dere gawkin' at my beauty, come in."

"Aren't you nervous about inviting strangers into your home? You don't know us. We might have come to rob you blind and—"

"Think so, eh?" She guffawed, belly bouncing. She wore a floor-length full dress, somewhat ragged at the bottom. "Ya be too dang late for dat, I'd say." She dropped crooked black fingers upon ample hips.

"I'm sorry. That was a very poor word choice. I didn't mean to—"

"First impressions not be your strongpoint, eh?" The old lady cackled. "You be a diddly dang presumptuous fool. You know dat, man?"

"Uh … well—"

"I think your mouth be gapin' now. Close it." She stood aside and retrieved a long well-used cedar staff from its place leaning against the wall. "Get yaself on in here, come on now. Don't be wastin' my dang time."

"Thank you." Jake stepped tentatively inside. Annabelle walked in lockstep behind him. The old lady's home, scarcely wider than he was tall, extended farther back into the hill than he imagined it would. The furnishings weren't crude at all. Instead, all were well-crafted pieces. Two highly polished rocking chairs with small round tables at their sides faced one another and centered near the door. The entire house was one long narrow room transitioning from a living area to kitchen/dining and finally the sleeping area in the back, bed meticulously made over with a patchwork quilt. "Nice home."

She left the door open and walked toward them.

It then occurred to him there were no light sources—no candles, lamps or windows. Leaving the door open had been a courtesy because she didn't need the light.

"Dat be a fact; it *is* a nice home," she said with a broad grin, showing her gapped teeth.

"My name is Jake Henderson and this is Annabelle."

"I know who you be." With that long gnarled cedar staff held in one hand, she tapped one of the rocking chairs. "Sit. Let's visit." Probing fingers found the armrest of the other one. She dropped into it. "Dat feel good on my big ol' tired butt." The jovial look turned more thoughtful. "I be not disrespectful, but I don't give a diddly dang about what *you* look like. Da child, though, dat be different. She be of great interest to dis old woman. I be wantin' to see da girl's face. I been waitin' for days for you two to show up."

"See?"

"Not with dese dead eyes, you gall-durn fool, with my hands."

"Sorry." He had to force Annabelle's hands off his pant leg to sit in the rocker opposite the old woman but the youngster remained as close as possible. "I don't think she's quite ready to venture away from me."

"Not surprising, considering what be dat poor child's past." The old woman pursed her lips and shook her head. "No child should be forced to see such gore as she did when her mother's life be taken."

"So you do know things."

"From da time I be a child, I had a gift for seein' snippets of things to come and hearin' people's thoughts as if dey be tellin' dem for all to hear. My momma died when I be just da sprout of a youngun ... of some malady. Don't be knowin' what. Anyhow, it only be one dang month after my twentieth birthday; a wanderin' band of thieves slaughtered my father and older brother for a small bag of dried corn—killed for a gall-durn pound o' dried corn. Can ya be believin' dat, man? I be too young to be a problem. Don't matter none though. Dey branded my flippin' eyes with coals from da fireplace den just up and left like it was nothin', no big diddly dang deal." She snapped her fingers. "Just like dat, dey be gone. Ooh-wee dat be painful, but I be comin' to understand later dat it be a blessin'. Da day I lost my sight be da very day, man, I began seein' things clearly—things dat no other human could. And dat be da dang truth."

"Things? What kinds of things?"

"See dis staff?"

"Yeah. So?"

She ran a hand over its uneven surface. "If it be fashioned from an outer branch, I would only see da most recent events in dis tree's life. But it's a root, dat part of da tree responsible for its very existence. Just by knowing da staff, touchin' it, feelin' its form, I be seein' da entire life of dat tree from which it be taken, everythin' it ever experienced or ever will. I feel its pain from da time it lost half its girth to a gall-durn bolt of lightnin'. I know every squirrel dat be takin' refuge in its branches or ever will. I know every deer dat nibbles its berries or ever will. And, yes, I be tellin' ya true; I know da pain it will endure in da future and da span of its life, although it be healthy as we speak. Da root of a tree is its soul. To know anythin' fully, one must know its roots."

"What about us? Humans?"

"I use da tree as an example 'cuz it be quick. Humans be more complicated. But, like dis staff, I see humans I lay hands upon as if I touched dere souls directly. Dat be da root. I be sensin' things about both of you, but dere is somethin' ... somethin' about da child I feel compelled to be explorin' deeper, somethin' wonderful." She turned her attention to Annabelle. "Child, I mean you no harm." She smiled and sat silent for a moment. "I know dat you be a friend to all like me."

Annabelle loosened her grip on Jake's arm. She looked at the old lady then up at Jake. "Go on, Little One, she won't hurt you." He motioned her to go to the old woman. The girl took a step and stopped.

The old lady extended open hands and then held them out waiting for Annabelle to take them, all the while smiling warmly. "Please child, let me be seein' your face through my hands."

Annabelle looked back at Jake, eyes large and nervous, biting her lower lip.

He nodded in reassurance. "It'll be okay."

Annabelle covered the short distance in three wary and choppy steps to stand before the old lady.

Wrinkled black fingers touched the youngster's face and it was as if the old woman's breath had been taken from her. She gasped. "Oh my. You be blessed beyond flippin' words, child."

Jake didn't know what to think about the old woman's robust, almost abrasive, speech mannerisms, but coming from her, it seemed natural. Still, he appreciated that she didn't get too foul with it. Maybe she would have, if not for this impressionable youngster. There was a complexity to the odd woman, levels of deep compassion belying her caustic exterior. Somehow, he was certain of it.

Milky eyes darted side to side as if the old lady visually saw Annabelle's face and studied it. "I be knowin' of you people and hearin' da stories but you are da first I get to meet. I've heard dat your kind be dwindlin' in numbers, maybe gone by now. I not be knowin' for sure. But all dat doesn't matter. You, child, be da seed of things to come. Through you, the world will begin changin', followers will be risin' up around you. Give it time, child, give it time."

Jake slid to the edge of his rocker. "Your kind ... dwindling numbers? What are you talking about?"

"Quiet! Give me a few more dagnabit seconds, fool." Her lightly probing fingers swept over Annabelle's hair across the cheeks and then from the child's forehead down to her nose and on to the mouth and chin. She then took the child's hands. "You are not without weakness, but ya be havin' powers dat far exceed normal humans. Da depth of your heart be your strength but it will also be endangerin' you in time. Ya be spendin' a lifetime guardin' against carin' *too much*. In da years to come, you'll harness da power dat be your birthright, but dat tender heart must be controlled or you'll risk bein' swallowed by your own good nature ...," the old lady saddened in a long pause, then a morose sigh, "... like your mother. Bless her kind heart. She loved too gall-durn much. So do you, child."

Jake ran fingers through his hair, amazed by the old lady's knowledge, yet still confused. "I understand what you're saying, but why her? What is it about Annabelle that makes such things possible?"

For a time, the old lady mulled the question while holding Annabelle's hands, appearing as though she absorbed energy from the child. A near-rapturous look graced her black features. Shallow lines deepened. Her head swayed side to side slowly, rhythmically. It became obvious why the old woman said she could see things in blindness that she never could've seen as a sighted person, things he couldn't even imagine. The question became: how much of that information flowing into her head of Annabelle's life—past, present and future—would she share with him?

Finally, she kissed both the youngster's hands. "I be so dang privileged to know you." The old lady continued squeezing Annabelle's hands, kissing them repeatedly.

Now fully at ease, Annabelle threw her arms around the woman's neck and hugged her. The instant affection appeared strong and mutual. The old lady lightly pushed Annabelle back. The girl stepped to the side of Dame Fortune's chair and held tight to her wrinkled ebony arm. Annabelle's skittishness, so strong only moments ago, had vanished.

"Mister Henderson, Annabelle's existence be da result of genetic experimentation in da early part of da twenty-first century." Her voice filled with disgust. "Corporations grew dang glutinous and greedy beyond description. Dey raced to manufacture artificial DNA."

"DNA?"

She thumped the floor with her staff. "Quiet! Listen to Dame Fortune! It not be important dat you understand *what* it is, only how playin' God sent ripples to dis very day. You'll play a part in all dis. Survival of dis sweet young creature be up to you, man. You must know dese things."

Her voice rose with an edge. She tipped the staff in his direction. "Do you understand Dame Fortune?"

"Sorry." He shrugged. "I don't understand any of this."

"You be shuttin' your fool mouth and you will."

A flushed-faced and chagrinned Jake slid back in his chair and laced his fingers together in his lap.

"Dat's better. Da spin, at da time, be controlled characteristics for longer life, less disease and da 'limination of birth defects. Be soundin' noble. Don't it?"

Jake raised an open palm up. "I guess."

"Den you be flippin' gessin' wrong. Dat only be to make it sound legitimate to hide what da real reason be. Dey be manufacturin' humans capable of bringin' down competing corporations, whether by war or by outwittin' with superior intelligence. A worldwide race for control of manufactured genes to be clonin' into huge multiples of humans be underway. Eventually dey made it so. Fortunately, doze synthesized humans be so diddly dang focused on genetically coded tasks dey had no desire for da opposite sex. Oh man. Can you believe dat? Reproduction was practically non-existent. Da *preferred* candidates all be dead in less dan three generations. Dey had no interest in sex, so no heirs. So, as da world be spiralin' down and economies collapsin' all around, dey, along with da technology dat produced dem, be gone. Da first male and female, da Adam and Eve, where Annabelle comes from, be flawed, but only by da fool's standard. Dey still be successfully coded with great physical and mental prowess—speed, quickness, vision capable of picking out detail at great distances, amazing sharpness of da mind and other physical things dat be far superior to normal humans. But, deir idiot creators be forgettin' somethin' in deir rush, da most basic thing common to all humans, da need to be lovin' and desire to be loved. It came overly developed, too. Meanin' dey were worthless to da tasks set before dem because dey hesitated and, sometimes, flat out refused to harm another human. In fact dey be trustin' others way too much. Of all da synthetics, Annabelle's ancestors be da only ones to reproduce."

"I guess that explains her mother's odd acceptance of a dangerous man."

The old woman looked his way. "You not be as stupid as you act, ya know dat, man."

"I still don't see how I fit into all this, other than remain her friend and keep her fed?"

"Even with all doze abilities, she be just as human as you and I, subject to disease, distress, depression, fear, and so on. She be needin' an adult to guide her, to teach her dat everyone doesn't love as much as she be lovin'. Some'll seek to be harmin' or takin' from her. Mister

Henderson, dat child might lose everythin' and not lift a flippin' finger to stop it ... food, clothing, virginity ... even her life. You are da guidin' influence dat she be needin'. Don't you be forgettin' dat. You must be toughenin' her to da world as it is, not da way she wants it to be."

All Jake's ambiguous fears came into immediate, sharp focus.

CHAPTER SEVEN
DEVIL IN THE DETAILS

Glory passed on asking her mother to join her in a walk around the grounds of Stalwart, choosing to let the elder Jackson sleep. Her respiratory condition worsened during the arduous journey north to get here. It'd take several days for her mother to recuperate even marginally. Glory feared she never would return to the robust woman she'd known during her youth. Glory hovered over the sleeping woman appreciating the selfless lifetime of giving, a life well-lived. Her mind reeled off dozens of childhood memories up to the present. Now, as age took its toll, Glory could only love her.

She opened the cottage door and tiptoed outside carefully closing it behind her. Standing for a moment under the porch overhang, she thought on which way to begin an exploration of the compound. She might need to remain within easy reach if Tam wanted to begin orientation, but then disregarded it; he'd send Lana when the time came. No need to be antsy about getting that part of the Stalwart experience underway.

After a time, sauntering along the inside stockade wall, it became clear the entire community within this enclosed compound was nothing more than a continuation of what she already had come to know—every cottage the same size and identical in form with only a few scattered exceptions. Those buildings constructed to a different standard must also serve different purposes. As for the cottages, all had small grass covered front yards with rock walkways from the front door out to a common graveled path between cottages lining both sides. She strolled parallel to the front wall between the first and second row of cottages.

After morning affirmation at the obelisk, most residents vacated the compound; she assumed to put in a day's work beyond the walls. Only a few remained. She noticed two women shelling peas on one porch and a woman on another in a rocking chair knitting something. Similar sights were common. Interestingly, there was no banter, no conversations whatsoever within the walls. Of course, smiles were fixed like party masks but that seemed counter to some kind of pervasive mood she couldn't quite get a handle on. This gemstone called Stalwart lacked sparkle. It had no personality, no laughter, and certainly no sense of Tam's beloved word "family". She wondered if this, so-called, paradise might be farther from heaven than hoped.

Coming to the end wall, she turned right and stopped long enough to count sixteen rows of cottages. She considered the unnatural orderliness of the entire compound. Reservation became concern. The path she walked was straight—too straight. The compound was too clean. The cottages were flawless, evenly spaced and perfect—too perfect—like a fantasy. Glory suspected a nightmare lurked.

After traveling the full interior perimeter of the compound, she approached the open front gate, noticing the man who had guided them to Tam. She figured time had come to forge friendships. Developing alliances within the walls seemed like a good idea—an intuitive thing. She might as well begin with him. She picked up the pace to a purposeful gait to where he worked with a hoe cutting weeds in the large garden beyond the wall. He'd come to the end of a row of knee-high corn and stopped to mop perspiration from his brow with a long sleeved forearm before turning to work the next row.

"Excuse me," she called out.

He must not have heard and clearly didn't see her approach.

She tried again. "Excuse me, may I have a word?"

He'd been daydreaming or otherwise lost in thought. His head popped up, looking first in the wrong direction. Eyes eventually landing on Glory, he drew a smile that looked more like a smirk. "Need somethin', ma'am?"

"I just thought since you're the first one I met when mother and I arrived that I'd introduce myself." She extended a friendly hand. "I'm Glory Jackson."

He leaned on the hoe supporting his weight with both hands. "I know. I heard ya tell Tam." He didn't seem to care about shaking hands but reluctantly offered it when she refused to retract hers.

Glory stepped forward and grabbed his hand, shaking it solidly. "I don't think I caught your name."

"Hiram Baker."

"Shall I call you Hiram or Mister Baker?"

"Hiram'll do."

"Mister Tam said you're new here—how long?"

"Two weeks tomorrow."

"Like it?"

Baker fidgeted. Maintaining that required smile seemed laborious. His lip began to twitch. "I guess so."

"Is gardening your job?"

"For now." He wrung his hands on the hoe handle. "Tam told me I needed to improve my people skills before he'd let me become a supplier."

"A supplier? Is that what you want to do?"

"Better'n cuttin' weeds all day."

"Makes sense." She noticed his smile had become almost impossible to maintain, nothing more than a nervous tic. Smiling clearly didn't to come naturally for Hiram; on the other hand, angry frown lines between brows were deep and permanent.

Looking here to there as if expecting a reprimand, "I need to get back to work. Anything else you need to know?"

"No, I just wanted to get to know some people and you were here. Sorry if I bothered you."

Baker dropped his head and cut a weed. "I'd better stay after it. I'm supposed to finish this patch before dark. Don't want to make Tam mad." Before he turned entirely away, it was clear the already fading smile dropped as fast as his head. Then he added, muttering, "I damn sure don't want to keep cuttin' weeds the rest of my life."

As he walked away, Glory watched, confused by his aloofness. He didn't act like he wanted to be around people, or here, at all. "Well ... maybe we can get to know each other better another time."

"Sure." He didn't look up and continued working down a row of carrots.

Tam's right. Ol' Hiram's people skills need polishing. Giving up on igniting a conversation, Glory headed back through the gate.

Lana exited Tam's house.

"Hi," Glory said, waving from some distance.

Lana said nothing until they came together near the obelisk. "Mister Tam wants to see you."

"Sure." She followed the girl to Tam's house and on through the door.

"Wait here," Lana said, and then exited the room through the door to the back hall left of the fireplace.

Glory walked the room studying artwork adorning the walls, lingering over one in particular, the skyline of a city.

As a young child, she'd seen a city far to the south. Her mother called it San Antonio. She only got to see it from a distance. Like all smaller towns she'd seen and larger cities she'd heard stories about, that one crumbled in decay. She recalled the melancholy brought on by the sight of collapsing tall buildings and dreamt of its glory days. She'd begged her mother, then a young woman, to go for a closer look. Glory vividly remembered her mother's fearful response. "No, no. We can't go. Not now not ever. It's not safe."

But the painting on Tam's wall showed a viable city with tall buildings in pristine order. It fired the imagination. *I would've loved to live in a place like that.* Her fingers glided over its surface, outlining the tallest buildings.

"Beautiful, isn't it?"

Glory jerked her hand from the canvas and whirled around, embarrassed by having been caught with her hand on it. "Sorry, you startled me." She turned back to the painting. "Yes, it is magnificent." She sighed then glanced back. "Not so much the artwork but the picture, another time when the world made sense."

"That city, or the remnants I should say, is not far northeast of here. It was called Dallas. I've been told there are still people inhabiting parts of it but they're cannibals. Hapless people wandering into it pay with their lives and are eaten. Think about it; a carnivore with a taste for human flesh smart enough to outwit its prey. But that's not the most frightening consideration; I hear they are friendly and welcoming to strangers, seducing people into a level of comfort, similar to petting a goat before slitting its throat to calm the animal so the meat won't become charged with a gamy taste."

"I wasn't aware of their welcoming attitude, just that they were man-eaters. Surely there's a city out there somewhere that has maintained a semblance of sanity."

"I'll share that hope with you." He took a moment to consider her words further. "You seem quite intelligent and well informed."

"I love visiting with people and listening to stories and, when we had a stable residence in the Hill Country, I read a lot ... whenever I could find material that is." She glanced back at the painting. "Why did city people become that way?"

"Starvation. It started after the economy collapsed. To stave off death, people began consuming those who starved first. Then it became a craving and the only source of nourishment within a world they were too frightened to break away from. It happened to be the only food aside from the occasional unfortunate animal that wandered into town. Inner city inhabitants have still not learned that the future is in the countryside because all their forbearers had known was an urban existence and didn't know where food came from. They waited for more. None came. Markets ceased to exist. Even before the worldwide decline began, street gangs roamed inner cities. That was the beginning. In time it turned into more than turf wars, it became hunting expeditions for food. They couldn't see beyond the city limit signs. Now they're simply bands of terribly misguided people. Cannibalism as a steady diet drives people insane. That makes them extra dangerous yet appearing quite normal."

He waved off the conversation. "That's enough about that." He put a hand on the back of a chair and gestured to it. "Let's turn the conversation to pleasant topics. Please, have a seat. I'll have Lana make raspberry tea."

"May I make a request?"

"Ask."

"After Lana makes the tea, would you mind if she joins us?"

Tam's smile never wavered but he hesitated. "I suppose that would be acceptable." He nodded to the girl. She left the room.

"So tell me, Mister Tam, how does a supplier operate?"

"A supplier for Stalwart seeks out goods and services and returns them for use and distribution within the corporation."

"I must say I'm a bit confused because in my travels I seldom encountered peddlers with wares for barter. All Mother and I encountered during the trip were thieves." She then gestured with outstretched arms. "This entire corporation is well stocked. It all came from somewhere."

"Indeed. Our suppliers seek out people that are in need of the Word about the corpocracy and its benefits to humankind and that the future of our world hinges on the rebirth and growth of corporations like Stalwart. In return, food and tools are taken as payment for such valuable information."

Glory's mind reeled back to that night she, her mother, Jake and Annabelle were roused from sound sleep and robbed. They, too, spoke of the corpocracy and how it was the way and the future. "I think I'm beginning to understand."

Lana returned carrying a wooden tray of three steaming cups. She held it out to Glory and then to Tam. The girl placed the tray on a small table, took the last mug and sat in a ladder-back chair across from Glory. She alternated quick glances from Tam to the floor and back, clearly uncomfortable.

"Our method of garnering supplies is a fair arrangement." Tam took a sip. "Wouldn't you agree, Miss Jackson?"

Lana's simple straight-line dress rode above her knees. The nervous action of sliding her sandaled feet back and forth over the tapestry rug pushed the dress higher up her thighs. She likely worried about Tam's opinion of her sitting as an equal.

Glory saw dark splotches on the inside of the girl's thighs just above the knees. *Bruises? My God!* She was forced to turn away to address Tam's question. "I'd say yes, it could be fair if those independent consumers felt obliged by the information." She sipped tea.

"Our suppliers are instructed to assume that. After all, it is valuable and worth the price."

As she took a sip, Glory sneaked another glimpse at the girl's legs.

Lana finally noticed the curious look and pulled her knees together, smoothing the dress down over them.

Glory suspected what bruises meant in such an intimate area. A nervous flutter tickled her stomach. "Mister Tam, if you don't mind me asking, do suppliers resort to the use of weapons ... large knives for example?"

"Despicable hooligans wander the countryside these days. Should our suppliers happen upon people not willing to negotiate, then yes, weapons might become necessary. Suppliers have the corpocratic right to defend themselves." His smile broadened in a lazy way. "And sometimes persuasive measures are called for during intense negotiating sessions." Tam dabbed his lips with a small linen napkin. "You see, we must never forget that the future of humanity lies within each corporation and the corporation cannot exist without the input of the independent consumer. We all choose our lot in life. Sometimes people need to be reminded of that choice, a place they have willingly chosen for themselves. There are consequences to all life's decisions?" He set the teacup on a side table, rose, and sauntered toward the fireplace with his hands clasped together at his back. "Does that make sense to you now?"

Convinced that she and her mother's presence at Stalwart was a blunder, the stomach flutter now tightened as a knot. Still, she couldn't help but see Tam as sincere. The man believed in the righteousness of Stalwart's mission. His hypnotic charm calmed her although she vehemently disagreed with his philosophy. To her way of thinking, his antiquated reasoning was the same perverse sense of right and wrong that spun the world out of control two centuries ago.

Glory remained composed. She needed time to figure a way out without raising suspicion. A man bent on extreme order would not allow people of Stalwart to think he'd failed in the conversion of an independent consumer. She hadn't seen or heard anything to indicate this way of existence was life threatening, but why test it? "The philosophy of Stalwart is impressive," she said. "And, it obviously works judging by what I've seen."

Tam faced her, hands still at his back. He seemed pleased. "Your ability to reason and discern order from the midst of chaos impresses me, Glory. I hope you don't mind if I call you Glory?"

"Not at all."

"Please call me *Fawm*."

She glanced again at his name printed on the placard atop the table spelled F-i-a-m. "I would've guessed the pronunciation to be *Fee-um* or *Fee-ome*."

"It's an old family name. I'm actually Fiam Lee the fourth."

Glory mentally toyed with the name. In a flash of realization, the morning affirmation rang loudly in her mind:

With the rise of each new sun
We re-avow that we are one.
It's easy to be and for all to see
That our reason to smile is family.

The word isn't *family*. It's Fiam Lee, she thought. Difficulty in remaining neutral began to rise at an alarming rate. "Thank you, Fiam. I appreciate your gentle manner," she said, her tone faltering but she struggled to remain demure.

"Would you care to join me again for dinner?"

This time she hesitated but reasoned that it wouldn't be wise to rebuff the invitation. "That's very kind of you. Mother and I will—"

"Just you, Glory. Once Lana has set our table, I'll have her deliver the same meal to your mother in your cottage when she fetches you."

"Uh ... all right, that'd be lovely."

As if the conversation had become boring, Tam dismissively waved her toward the front door. "I'll see you back when the setting sun hits the tip of the obelisk. Lana, see Glory to the door."

"Yes, Mister Tam," she said bowing slightly.

Tam left the room.

Lana held the door open. As Glory walked by, the girl whispered, "He favors you. I haven't seen such tolerance toward any of the other shareholders."

Glory leaned in to the teenager and spoke directly into the girl's ear, "I want to know how you got those bruises on your legs?"

"We all must pay our way in Stalwart." Her lip quivered as her eyes fell away from Glory. "I don't just cook and clean for Mister Tam."

The squeak of a loose floor joint of the little dugout home provided a slow monotonous rhythm as Dame Fortune rocked in her chair. She extended the cedar staff and nimbly swung it until it struck Jake's leg. He faced her from another chair. "No need for you and da girl to be runnin' off to God-knows-where, ya hear. I be privileged to offer adjacent site for a permanent home. What ya say? I know ya be lookin'."

"Uh ..." It was the last thing he expected to hear from a person who lived far away from people and seemed to relish isolation. *Maybe it's a joke and she's looking for another reason to curse at me.*

"I don't be needin' no damn reason to be cussin' ya, boy. I be doin' it anytime I see fit."

"How'd you know what I was ...? Never mind." Void of human habitation for several miles in all directions, he'd assumed the distance from others was purpose driven, but, maybe not. "You caught me by surprise with that question. I don't think I'm prepared to answer it."

"You be such a gall-durn fool. You know dat, man? Can't ya see I not be trustin' you to teach Annabelle in ways vital to her development."

Jake was nettled. "What's that supposed to mean, that I'm not good enough for her?"

Annabelle took a step away from him. She hadn't heard him snap in anger like that.

Dame Fortune tilted the staff in his direction. "You be keepin' a rein on dat temper." She rose and walked to a nearby shelf and removed a large jar filled with smooth colorful river rocks, most pea-size. "Open da door all da way. Let's be gettin' more light in here for da child. Now, Mister Jake Henderson, I be showin' ya sumthin' dang good dat you not even be realizin'," She touched the side of her nose and nodded, "but Dame Fortune do." She set the large barrel-shaped transparent jar on the table. "Child, how many of dese smooth little pebbles do Dame Fortune keep in da jar?"

Annabelle's smile broadened when she realized a game was afoot, seeing the request as if it were a toy for her amusement. Stepping to the table, she studied the jar for only a second then held it between her hands, as if calculating diameter. Holding one hand on the side of it, she rotated it with the other. Finally, with that same hand still against the outside of the jar, she slid it from top to bottom slowly.

At that point, she looked at Jake and grinned as she removed the lid and dumped all the pebbles on the tabletop, sweeping a hand over the surface of the rocks until they lay flat and individually. Annabelle then slid one stone away from the others. Near it she pulled three more into a separate grouping. Next she formed a seven stone pile. Then she slid another single stone into the line and placed it near the seven to form a straight line of four groups of pebbles.

Jake frowned. "What does that mean?"

"You think I be seein' it, man? What has the child done?"

"She spread them flat then created a straight line of four piles with a few of them. I don't understand what she's done."

The old lady slapped the side of her face and muttered, "Heavenly Mother, Gimme strength." Her tone became aggressive. "The number of stones in each pile, man. Gimme da number, ya dang fool."

"Sorry. It's hard to figure what you know and what you don't sometimes."

"I be givin' ya dat one. Still, I need da number."

"One in the first, three in the second then seven and another one by itself."

The old lady laughed so hard she had to grab her staff with both hands so her huge pendulous bosom didn't sway her off her feet. "It be plain enough to an old blind woman dat da child be tellin' us da stones total one-thousand-three-hundred-seventy-one.

"Oh. Now I feel stupid."

"It be good dat you be havin' da sense to say it before Dame Fortune have to tell you."

"But ... how? I mean she didn—"

"Ya see now what I been tellin' ya? She must stay close to Dame Fortune. You know nothin'; I know every diddly dang thing." She laughed again then swung her staff, this time clipping his shin.

"Ow!"

"Maybe you be awake enough now to listen to dis old blind woman. I be too smart for you to keep up with, eh?"

Jake massaged his stinging shinbone. He saw wisdom in the old lady's words. He sat quietly—a little amused, a little frustrated and a little disgusted with having been so slow to understand something so simple. "So, you want Annabelle but you'll settle for both of us if you have to. Is that about it?"

She laughed loud. "See? Sometimes you show you not so stupid after all." With the aid of the staff, the old woman shuffled from the table where Annabelle stood to an open shelf. From it, she pulled worn blankets and threw them at Jake's feet. "Here. You and da girl sleep on da floor until you finish your week's work for me. Then I decide whether to let you stay to build a cabin of your own. I be thinkin' yes right now, but things have a way of changin'. But, you be knowin' dat. Don'tcha, Mister Jake Henderson?"

He now understood he didn't need to respond directly. She'd know he was about to agree. But he smiled and nodded anyway for Annabelle's benefit. Then he winked at the girl. "Week's work, huh?"

"Let me be makin' it clear; I think you not so stupid ... at dis very minute. Don't be changin' my mind on dat. Ya hear? I charge a week's work on my home and gathering me some food to store away in return for valuable insight." Her voice lowered. "Surely you not think dis house look good from my own doin'. If dat be true den I take it back. You be stupid *and* a damn fool. I be blind and old! What you be thinkin', man? I can't find food, fix roofs or build furniture. I be seein' da future and such, not da rabbit or da wild hog." She smacked her lips. "And I surely be lovin' da taste of both, especially with a hefty steamin' pile o' turnip greens." The old lady threw her head back and moaned. "Oh my. Now dat's a delicious thought." She appeared as though the act of *thinking* about it could become orgasmic.

"Sorry, I wasn't thinking. It does make sense. I just hadn't thought about it. I sure like your food choices though—sounds great."

"Thinkin' not be your strongpoint, eh?"

All Jake's annoyance with the old lady vanished. She was not only gifted, but had a sense of humor he harbored a growing appreciation of— regardless how abrasive she made it sound. "Okay then, in return for that wonderful information and the hospitality of offering your home, I'll do what you desire for one week. Then we'll discuss where we go from there. Is that satisfactory?"

"Good!" She stamped the staff on the floor like a judge's gavel. "You back to not bein' stupid. I be thinkin' I might like you." She turned her head toward Annabelle as if she could see the child.

The girl moved back to Jake's chair and knelt at his side. The youngster held a satisfied expression as though she knew all along that things would work out. Maybe she did. Maybe her gifts included such things, too. As his eyes moved from Annabelle to Dame Fortune, Jake felt an acute twinge of inadequacy.

"Girl, you an' me have a lot to be talkin' 'bout; might take years, ya know. Yessiree, I sure be darn glad to be knowin' ya."

That brief moment of inferiority was overridden when he realized a great weight had been lifted from his shoulders. He now had someone to share responsibility of Annabelle with. He clapped his hands. "The first thing I'll do is put a window in this place."

The old lady's head snapped back. "Why? I can't see. No use for light or a view of da river. Are ya slippin' back to stupid so soon?"

"Not at all, but you live in it and apparently are not aware this place smells dank, like a root cellar. I'm surprised your blankets aren't mildewed."

"Humph!" She rubbed her cheek with an open palm. "Hot dang ... you know what? You close to becomin' a smart feller."

"What else would you like done?"

***

"Here she comes, Mother, find out what she knows about this place." Glory continued looking through a narrow space between curtain panels watching Lana approach their door. "Something's terribly wrong around here. I don't know what it is but I'm determined to find out. Lana may know and, for whatever reason, is not sharing it with us. If so, I want to know why she's afraid to talk."

Myrna pushed off from the armrest and rose from the rocker, her age showing in the stiff ascent. "Don't worry about me. Just go have dinner and try not to rouse Tam's suspicion." Myrna opened the door. Lana appeared holding a covered tray. "Hello, dear, come in."

Glory approached Lana. She clearly wanted to quiz the girl about the bruises on her legs, but didn't, possibly thinking there wasn't enough time to get into it right now. She squeezed Lana's arm, offered a sympathetic smile, and then walked out the door.

Myrna remained quiet until Glory closed the door behind her. "Thank you so much, Lana." She uncovered the tray in the girl's hands. "Oh my, look at all this food." On the plate was a whole sweet potato, a piece of well-done red meat, radishes and lettuce leaves. She took it from the girl and placed it on a small table beside her rocking chair.

Lana turned to leave.

Myrna snagged her hand. "Wait. Keep me company while I eat?"

"I—I shouldn't."

"Please."

Lana's eyes flicked side to side. "Maybe just for a minute or two." She looked toward the door, as if expecting someone to storm through it and punish her for even thinking about it. "I have to get back soon, though. Mister Tam gets angry if I don't answer on the first call."

Myrna pulled the other rocker around so Lana would face her. "Please dear, sit. And for heaven's sake, relax." While waiting for the girl to make up her mind she sat and pulled the tray of food into her lap.

Lana fidgeted. "I really shouldn't be staying at all." Hesitantly, she lowered her body into the shiny cedar rocking chair, sitting on the edge of it appearing as though she might bolt.

Myrna ignored the apprehension. "If Glory and I are to live here, I'd like to get to know you. Tell me about your grandparents."

The mention of her grandparents brought a rare, sincere smile to her pretty face, not the manufactured Stalwart version. It didn't last. She nervously slid sandaled feet back and forth over the wooden plank floor, rubbing both armrests of the rocker with flattened palms. "They were beautiful people. Old and weak perhaps, but they worked hard at becoming accepted here. We soon became a family again." Her face went dour. "I don't think Mister Tam liked me spending so much time with them." She picked at a peeling thumb cuticle. A spot of blood developed.

Myrna poked at the sweet potato with a fork. "What changed, dear?" Casually, she lifted a forkful to her mouth, treating Lana as she would a skittish fawn. She made no sudden moves. She offered only passing eye contact to further emphasize the lightness with which she engaged in conversation.

"I—I'm not sure. I remember Grandmother quizzing me about Mister Tam." She dropped her voice to a whisper. "I don't think she trusted him."

"Should she have?"

Lana looked down at her wiggling toes. With rapid fingers, she hooked straight hair behind her ears. She shook her head and diverted her eyes to the front door. "I don't think so." Her head wilted forward and she sat unspeaking for a moment before looking up again. A watery film covered her eyes. "I think Mister Tam became aware of Grandmother's suspicion." Her lip quivered. She cried.

Myrna dropped her fork, rose in a hurry and leaned over Lana, embracing her. "It's okay, dear."

"No it's not. I think, because of me, Mister Tam had them killed." She cried harder, wrapping her arms around Myrna, clutching at the older woman's shirt. Her body shook.

"Do you know this for sure?"

"No, but they were alive one day and gone the next." She pulled her face back and looked into Myrna's eyes. "If they'd been sent away for being too old to contribute, they would've contacted me. Since then I've noticed how older people at Stalwart seem to disappear. I—I worry about you."

Myrna wondered about sharing too much with Lana. She was still a virtual stranger after all. The girl seemed sincere but she might pass information to Tam just for temporary favor. Finally, she determined that a later opportunity to talk with Lana privately might not present itself. She took a chance. "Lana, would you rather be somewhere other than Stalwart?"

"I can't survive on the outside alone. I'd starve or be killed in a few days."

"You wouldn't have to be alone. You could stay with Glory and me."

Lana swept away streaming tears with a shaky hand. "You mean it?"

"Sure I do. There's no need for you to live this way. Glory told me about the bruises and how you likely got them."

She exploded in sobs.

"What's the matter, dear? What's wrong?"

"I think I'm pregnant. I'm scared what Mister Tam will do when he finds out."

***

Glory knocked but didn't wait for an answer; she went on into Tam's house. Running fingers over her curly black hair, she then tightened the cloth strip forming the gather of tightly kinked locks at the neck then smoothed down her shirt in front. She wanted to impress Tam, but didn't know exactly why. Food was on the table. It was set in Tam's preferred style, formal. Steam curled from a platter of meat and a separate bowl of sweet potatoes.

Tam entered the room gesturing to the table. "There's no reason to wait."

He pulled Glory's chair back.

She sat.

"A dinner should be eaten while it's hot." He leaned over from behind, placing his face so close that it almost touched hers. "It's the only civilized way to dine," he whispered. Wouldn't you agree?" His breath smelled of mint.

"I guess so." She smiled up at him over her shoulder as he assisted her chair nearer the table. "Thank you, Mister … I'm sorry, Fiam."

"Yes, please, let's keep it casual," his eyebrow went up seductively, "Glory." He sat and lifted a folded napkin, snapped it open and placed it in his lap. "I do love your name. It conjures images of bright colors, brilliant light and all things good."

Although seeking reasons to, she didn't trust the man. She wanted to glean something—anything, no matter how remote, to believe that her suspicions would turn out groundless. Because she saw that, in all he did for her, he trusted her implicitly, clearly smitten. She had to resist his charismatic charm, remain skeptical, and maintain an objective distance to learn what he did and was capable of doing. Even if successful, how to use that knowledge remained unclear. Still, the compulsion to learn the secrets of Stalwart was strong. The only way was to play the grateful role and hope to produce the wherewithal to resist his wiles. She was a woman, after all, and had already assumed Tam believed in what he did. She just didn't want to be sucked in if suspicion of morally reprehensible methods proved true. His delicate Asian features and manner exuded sexual magnetism that attracted her. She wanted him, not his ideals. She couldn't stop fantasizing that the man and his beliefs might be separated long enough to enjoy his company without loyalty to satisfy a physical itch.

It dawned on her she needed a mental safe room to retreat to in case the urge became overwhelming. Jake Henderson was that refuge.

After a short time thinking about Jake, she began to smile. Tam clearly assumed she smiled at him. It was obvious by his inflection as her face went dreamy. But the smile was for the first time she saw Jake's smooth face and the affectionate rush that coursed through her body at the time. It comforted her.

For the first time, Glory allowed the belief that gratitude toward Jake and her infatuation with him might be more than a passing fancy. As she listened to Tam talk of Stalwart things, her mind danced in another pasture. She sat with chin cradled in hand. But the look had become an empty façade. *Where are you, Jake Henderson? What are you doing? Have you found a home site? Oh, how I wish you were here.*

CHAPTER NINE
THINGS TO REMEMBER

Jake tossed the wooden mallet to the ground. With a sweep of the arm, he removed streaming perspiration from his forehead then stepped away to examine the handiwork, a modest framed-in window next to the front door of Dame Fortune's dugout home. Having no glass, he'd fashioned shutters that could be left open during nice weather. He snatched up the borrowed tools and, with a prideful grin, opened and closed one side on cleverly crafted wooden hinges.

He walked down the gentle slope of the featureless lump of a hill to the river's edge and fell to his knees. After splashing water on his face, he ran cool wet hands over his lean bare upper torso and then splashed a little more on his face noticing his beard had just about covered again—a thick curly blond. He wondered if he should try to sharpen his little knife and attempt to shave it.

It reminded him of Glory; almost everything did. She held a special place in his thoughts, taking up more of that space as time went on. Although imaginings varied, Glory's dark smooth skin and striking eyes framed by thick curly hair spilling down over her back had become a cherished image. He stared at his reflection in the shallows of the Brazos River, enjoying the parade of recollections.

After a time, he saw a face appear next to his in the rippling water. Annabelle hovered near holding three rabbits. He fell back onto his elbows and laughed. "Well done, Little One!"

"Thank you."

Jake bolted upright. "Hey, you're talking more now. That's wonderful."

She dropped the carcasses, fell to her knees and threw her arms around his neck.

Her weight forced him back onto his elbows. He laughed again.

"Love you," she whispered.

"You're really something. You know that?" Then he remembered Dame Fortune's warning about her weakness—she loved and cared too much. He pulled her hands from his neck and sat up. "Annabelle, you need to stop believing that everyone loves you or the world around them as much as you do."

Rising to her knees, she scooted away from him and appeared as though she'd been slapped. Her lip began to quiver.

"Wait a minute. I didn't mean that I don't care for you. I do, very much."

Although only words, every one could've been separate daggers thrust one at a time into the child's heart. The damage was done. Tears spilled from her eyes. She rose, shoulders slumped and she sobbed. She turned away leaving the rabbits where they lay.

She walked up the rise toward Dame Fortune's dugout, shoulders bobbing as she wept.

"Come on, Little One, you don't understand what I was trying to say."

With no hint of having heard him, she kept walking.

The old woman opened the door of her house and stepped outside. "So," she called out in a loud voice beyond the youngster to Jake, "You be stickin' your foot deep inside your mouth again, eh?"

Jake came to his feet and rubbed away the damp earth that stuck to his elbows. "I guess I did. Please talk to her."

"Hah! Now you see what Dame Fortune be tryin' to tell ya all along. Annabelle be too young to be talked to like an adult. She needs soothin' words. Not dat crap dat be fallin' out of your mouth, man. What is it you not be understandin' 'bout gentleness, fool?" Then she mumbled, "Ooh-wee, dat man sure be high maintenance." She waved the staff, sweeping it across her body. "Come on, girl, it's time you and dis old blind woman had our first little sit-down chat."

Annabelle glanced back but kept walking up the slope to Dame Fortune.

What am I to say? And how am I supposed to say it? He turned away so neither the old lady nor Annabelle could see him. He clutched hair on both sides of his head and hissed to the sky, "Damn it!"

It was becoming clearer that staying close to that wild woman had been the right choice after all. Her craziness had to be more act than substance. Dame Fortune, he realized, was brilliant and had the knack. He didn't. The old woman offered guidance that he could not.

Annabelle stopped before the old woman.

Disappointment subsided, seeing them together like that. He picked up the axe and drawknife he'd lain nearby and walked toward the woods to gather and groom more building materials from the scrub oak down the river.

***

Annabelle stood in front of the old lady.

Dame Fortune groped with an outstretched hand until she touched the girl's head then stroked it.

Annabelle leaned on one of the old woman's thick legs and held Dame Fortune, her arms not making it half way around the rotund waistline. Within that sense of security, Annabelle let it all out and cried.

The old lady channeled the sadness and felt its intensity. "You still not be trustin' him to keep you around. Do ya, child?" She rubbed soothing swirls on the girl's back and felt Annabelle's head against her above the waist. "Sweet Baby, if you could see what Dame Fortune do, you'd know dat not be true at all, not anymore. Dat foolish, foolish man be lovin' you so much that he's hurtin' 'cause he made you sad and didn't mean to be doin' it. You have touched dat man as deeply as anyone in his whole life, maybe more."

She pushed Annabelle away. "I need to get off dese fat old legs, child." With the aid of her staff, she shuffled to her rocker, sat, and then waved Annabelle over. Dame Fortune took the child's hands into her own and held them together in her lap. "Girl, da first thing ya need to be knowin' is dat no matter how dat fool behaves, he worries so much 'bout you dat his stomach gets sick. He be too stupid to say it out loud, dat's all. Ya know what dat means?"

Annabelle rubbed her eyes with balled fists and shook her head.

She couldn't see the response but that didn't matter. "Dat means he loves ya, baby. He just be so silly dat he may not realize it." She chuckled. "But he do, very much." She then laughed. "He be scared outa his mind dat you might find someone else to go to and leave *him* behind."

She pressed Annabelle's hands tighter then abandoned them in favor of the child's face, palms on each side. "Now, I want you to be givin' this old blind woman a thrill by smilin' big. Whatcha say, child? Wouldja be doin' dat for Dame Fortune? Whatcha say?" The girl's cheeks pulled back as the old woman danced fingertips over deepening dimples. "Dat be more like it."

How much do I be tellin' dis child about her future? Divulging too much could alter a person's future because they ceased working toward an outcome she'd already seen. Overconfidence instilled a belief that no matter how they behaved or what they did, the end result would be as she foretold. Expectant complacency could change the future. She remained ever mindful of that and kept it at the forefront while discussing such things. It was vital to present the girl with something to reach for but never say too much. She couldn't tell Annabelle that she'd already divined the path the rest of her life would take.

Again, she clutched Annabelle's hands between hers. "Child, humanity be leanin' on ya heavy when ya be growin' into a young woman. People will be searchin' ya out for help in fixin' lives and beatin' back enemies. You'll come to bear da burden and da scars of mankind's freedom. Everyone be trustin' Annabelle as a deliverer from doze dat control, manipulate and kill for greedy advantage. All da things dat make you who you are, physical speed, quickness of hands and mind will be a small part of who ya be growin' into. Da very day you become a woman, physical strength will start developin' fast. Charisma be drawin' people to you like flies to honey. By your fifteenth birthday, you'll be stronger dan any three grown men. Things will happen 'round dat time, child, marking you as a savior in da minds and hearts of doze knowin' ya. But listen to what I be tellin' ya now, child, it'll also make you a target by dark forces. Do you be understandin' dese words, child?"

Annabelle frowned. "N-No."

"Can ya remember what I be tellin' ya?"

She nodded. "Yes."

"Den dat's good enough for now. 'Cause it'll come clear to you as time be goin' on."

She patted Annabelle's shoulders, feeling the threadbare fabric and holes in her top. She ran hands over the full length of Annabelle's clothes, fingering irregularities in the tattered fabric. "Ya know, Dame Fortune usually charge plenty for good information but dis be a special time for dis old blind woman. So, I be doin' things differently. Dis time I sew you up some wonderful clothes. Whatcha say 'bout dat?"

Annabelle fell across the old woman's knees into her lap and wrapped her in a hug.

"Ol' Dame Fortune knows better dan to say dis but … I guess I be tellin' ya anyhow." She cupped her mouth in mock show of secrecy. "Because us girls be needin' a hush-hush or two, ya know. Mister Jake Henderson knows a woman and thinks 'bout her all da time. She be changin' his life real soon. Oh yeah, he'll fight it. But she be too powerful." She chuckled. "She be a woman, too, after all." She pushed Annabelle back and waved a cautionary finger in front of her face. "But you must be swearin' dat dis be kept our secret. Do ya promise Dame Fortune?"

"Y-yes." Annabelle said nothing else for a moment, then said, "I … love … you."

Dame Fortune laughed. "You don't need to be tellin' me dat. 'Cause I know you love every-damn-body." She pounded the floor with the staff as laughter hit a higher note.

CHAPTER TEN
CAUSE FOR CONCERN

Glory flung opened the cottage door. Curtains fluttered over a nearby window. Scarcely altering stride, she ran inside and closed it behind her.

On age-weakened hands, her mother pushed out of the chair and stood. "What's the matter?"

Glory didn't answer, just hurriedly slid laterally down the wall to stand next to the window. With a single finger, she parted the curtain panels and glanced out looking to a space between cottages across the way. She searched the area.

The sun had set. Coming darkness and deepening shadows made a thorough examination difficult. Streaking rays of pink, orange and blood-orange painted the western horizon.

"What are you doing, dear? Is something wrong?"

"That Hiram Baker guy is beginning to spook me. He stalked me with his eyes from the time I left Tam's place until I walked through this front door."

"He's a strange one. But let's worry about him later. I have news."

Glory continued spying on Baker through the window. "So do I."

"You first; what'd you learn?" Myrna returned to her rocker.

"I barely listened to Tam most of the time. I didn't want to be seduced," she glanced back, "by all the promises, mind you. So, I retreated in my head to thoughts of Jake, and," She let the curtain fall back into place then faced her mother, "Annabelle, too, of course."

"Of course."

"Anyhow, he finally said something that brought the daydreams to a dead stop and honed my focus razor-sharp." Glory went to the other rocking chair, pulled it close and sat.

Myrna twirled a curious hand. "Don't keep me in suspense."

"He wants me to take Lana's place as his live-in housekeeper. And, well, I think you know what that means?"

"Surely you didn't agree to that."

"No. I asked if I had a choice and if I might consider the offer for a while. He told me everyone at Stalwart has choices and that a thoughtfully considered "yes" would be the better one. After that, he dismissed me as if it were business meeting."

Glory rose and paced. There was no alternative if she wanted to stay at Stalwart. Tam's response was nothing more than a twisted sense of political correctness. "I can't help but wonder; If I tell him no, would I be *forced* into servitude?" She spun to face her mother. "Worse yet, would I have sentenced myself to death and not even know it?"

"I don't know but you can't willingly agree to it. I won't allow it!" Myrna's hands shook. "But I don't want you endangering your life either." Her voice became strained. "Oh God, what'll we do?"

"Calm down." Glory knelt before her, scooping up the elder Jackson's hand. "Being *in service* to him is certainly not my first choice as a means of livelihood." She paused and thought, then grimaced. "One minute I'd be polishing the furniture and the next minute I might be polishing ... well, I'm sure I'd be doing despicable things. Do you really think I want to do that?"

Myrna covered her ears. "Please stop. Don't say anymore. I don't want to think about it."

"Then don't. What'd you learn from Lana?"

"Something disturbing." She pulled her hand from Glory's grasp and dropped it into her lap. "Lana thinks she's pregnant with Tam's baby."

Glory's eyes fell to the floor. "Oh no," she said, voice trailing.

"She's scared for her life."

"Rightfully so; more is sanitized at Stalwart than the grounds. Tam's utopian corporate society has to be maintained somehow. Problems within these walls, this insane asylum, aren't solved, they're eliminated. Masterful decision-making has nothing to do with it. I'm absolutely convinced." She pressed her lips into a thin line. "I'd bet there's a graveyard somewhere filled with executive decisions."

"I wish there was something we could do for the girl."

"There is."

Accusingly, Myrna lowered her voice. "What are you talking about?"

"Let's just say Tam's proposition has now been 'thoughtfully considered'." Glory sprang to her feet and began walking toward the door.

"Please, hon, don't do something you'll regret."

"Sorry, Mother. If I don't do this, Lana may disappear from Stalwart. Tam would have her killed to maintain appearances. I've got to do this." She opened the door then stopped. She clutched the door handle looking into the mild spring evening. Nature's color display in the western sky had disappeared, replaced by a rising moon. The heady sweet aroma of jasmine, witch hazel and rosemary filled her nostrils while lightning bugs flashed and, for a fleeting second, she wished she could sit in a rocker and enjoy this beauty. But the serenity of it was a façade, like everything else around Stalwart, a Satanic temptation that lured the unsuspecting with superficially beautiful promises concealing treachery. Nothing was as it seemed. There was nothing beautiful about what she had suddenly become compelled to do, either.

"Don't go, Glory. Please."

"I don't have a choice," she said without looking back on her way out. "Otherwise, I'm no better than Tam." She pulled the door closed and headed to the main house. As her eyes adjusted to decreased light, she noticed movement across the way and down one cottage. *Baker, what're you up to, weirdo?* She shuddered but forced uneasiness aside to focus on a more important issue.

Standing before the door of the main house she hesitated to knock. She needed a moment to give courage a chance to equal to intent—once she rapped on the door there'd be no turning back. A guttural groan died in her throat. She snorted away fears through flared nostrils and solidly knocked twice. The plan was on.

Lana opened it and offered the obligatory smile. Still, it was obvious the girl was shocked to see Glory again so soon. "Yes?"

Glory offered a sincere smile. "I need to talk to Mister Tam." She leaned near and whispered, "No matter what you hear from me, or Tam, go with it. I'll explain later."

She reluctantly nodded; a show of trust unto itself. Glory appreciated it and felt calmer for it. The girl disappeared through the door into the back hall.

Glory visually swept the room with nervous eyes, wringing hands while she waited. All the things that awed her in the beginning now left her cold, realizing the probable price of such garishness. Contempt drilled deep as she gazed at the gaudy display—furnishings, the chandelier, tapestry rugs, artwork—everything: all assembled from the pieces of other people's lives that none gave up willingly.

Tam appeared through the door left of the fireplace, walking in front of Lana. "May I assume you've thought over my offer?"

She stopped the nervous hand gesturing and began the formidable task of appearing at ease. "You may. I think it'd be to our mutual benefit that I accept your generous offer." Maintaining a mask of calm became difficult, much more so than anticipated. Disgust filled her at the mere thought of engaging in this type of prostitution.

When Tam looked away, she flicked eyes to Lana. The girl wouldn't understand the motivation, scared witless that she'd be turned out to make her own way. *Pregnant and alone might not be survivable—in Stalwart or beyond the walls. I can't turn back now,* she thought.

As Tam's eyes came back around, Glory met his gaze. "I'll be your housekeeper and ... in your service." She offered Tam a Stalwart smile.

"Excellent." In disgustingly casual manner he turned to Lana and said, "Thank you Lana, but I no longer need your services. You must find other living arrangements. Close the door behind you, please." He waved her toward the door and turned his back on her—literally and figuratively.

Oh, how I'd love to slap that smug look off his face right now. I can't help the girl at this moment. It has to be this way, for now.

Lana crumbled. She attempted keeping the smile but the corners of her mouth and chin quivered. Tears coated her eyes. She hesitated, uncertain what to do or where to go. She shuffled through the door and pulled it closed.

Glory heard her sob. She twitched, wanting to chase the girl down and explain it, but could not. Not yet.

"Now," Tam said, "Lana was about to take the garbage cart to the far corner of the compound where a small door in the wall opens to the outside. A large wagon is located just the other side. Unload the contents of your cart onto it. That will be your first job." He took two steps away then turned back. He eyed Glory with a lustful glint. "When you return, bathe. Afterwards, I'll show you what else is expected of you." With an almost feminine flutter of fingers, Tam dismissed her. "That'll be all for now."

Glory obediently dipped her chin and left the house to take care of the assigned chore. Stepping into the night, it felt as though she'd been holding her breath. She stood for a moment drawing in deep the night air and then walked to the rear of the house. She located the small two-wheel cart loaded with odorous food waste buzzing with insects. She pushed it onto a path for the trek to the back side of the compound. The mindless task offered a chance to think about what her next move should be.

The decision was not whether to get away from Stalwart but how to get it done safely. Tam would send people to kill them if she bolted. Egomaniacal as Tam was, he wouldn't allow gossip of failure to spread. Regardless of cost in human life, arrogance would dictate a course of action preventing suspicion over his reputed benevolence and wisdom. The world needed to know the truth, but that should come later. The safety of her mother and Lana must be assured first.

Glory located the small unobtrusive double-door gate; a passageway intended for the sole purpose of ridding waste without having to take it through the front gate. It was lower and wider than a normal door, held closed by a corroding black wrought iron slide bolt at its center. Other than the main gate, it was the only exit through the walls. Walking around the cart, she fumbled with the rust-coated door bolt, trying to slide it free.

A large calloused hand came around and covered her mouth.

She attempted to scream but couldn't get a sound past the hand.

Grabbing the middle finger over her mouth, she pulled it back.

The knuckle cracked.

There was a groan. The breath stunk.

She peeled the hand away from her mouth.

The brief advantage disappeared. A tight fist connected to the side of her head.

Pain exploded from her cheekbone as she whirled a one-eighty face down into the dirt.

Dazed and desperate, she pushed up to hands and knees. No thoughts, just instinct to run, to get away.

A booted foot landed hard to her stomach lifting her up as all the air left her lungs in a violent wheeze. Paralyzed, she rolled onto her back, wrapping her midsection with both arms. She wanted to cry out but had no wind to make a sound.

A shadowy male figure dropped and straddled her, ripping her shirt open. He then pinned her spread arms to the ground.

Glory regained a measure of clarity and saw Hiram Baker forcing his mouth toward her chest.

She wrenched a hand from his grasp and slugged him on the temple.

His head went with it. Slobber strung from his open mouth.

With a rabid growl, he slapped her across the cheek then backhanded her across the other; he kept on as he ranted. "I'll teach you a lesson you'll never forget, damn you! I was next up for promotion! Just because you're a woman, I get shoved to the rear of line! It's always a woman standing in my way!"

The slapping stopped. She felt hands at her waist, yanking at the belt buckle, attempting to unfasten it.

Each time she pushed at his groping fingers, he slapped her.

Her flailing arms grew weak. It was as if the appendages belonged to someone else. Pain in her battered face lessened as it numbed. The slaps no longer stung. The ordeal turned dreamlike. She drifted in and out of consciousness.

Then the mauling stopped.

He fell off her.

Glory opened one eye, the other blood-engorged and swelling shut. The full moon beamed in from the right and cast a harsh shadow on Lana's face. No more smiles—the girl glowed hatred as she stood over Baker holding a flat paving stone in both hands.

Baker moaned then squirmed.

Lana growled and hit him in the head a second time.

His body collapsed, then went limp.

Lana didn't move, holding her ground, the stone high overhead ready to bring it down again if necessary. Once certain he'd remain out, she tossed the stone aside and dropped to her knees, working Glory's pants back up over her waist and pulling her shirt closed. She lifted Glory's upper torso, cradling her head in her lap. "He can't hurt you anymore."

Glory slurred through swelling lips, "I know about your pregnancy.

You have to live with Mother. That's the reason I replaced you. If Tam believes he won't be seen as the father, he may ignore you. If you started to show while living with him, he'd have you killed." Forming words became difficult. "I wanted to tell you but I couldn't. I'm sorry. I just wanted you safe and out of there." The words gurgled through bloody drool oozing from the corner of her mouth.

Lana's eyes grew larger as Glory's intentions became clear—that she was indeed a friend. "I'm so sorry for getting you into this. It's—"

"Don't … say … anything. We have to help … one another … to … survive." Her head lolled to the side. She looked at Baker.

Lana glanced to him as well. "You must tell Mister Tam what happened. You'll have to explain your injuries anyhow. Tam will have Baker held, then executed, a very public execution for damaging his property, you." She spat on Baker. "It's what the pig deserves. If he should get away, Stalwart suppliers will hunt him down and kill him for an unforgivable crime against an associate. If he runs, his ability to survive would barely be a bump above zero."

Lana gently stroked Glory's injured cheeks. "Mister Tam and I finally have something we agree on, destroying garbage like Baker."

***

Jake woke on his back and looked to see Annabelle sleeping, her head lying cozy on his stomach. The child's warm breath felt velvety on his face, coming in slow even puffs. He smiled and petted her head, studying delicate features of the child.

Even though Dame Fortune had given them pillows, the girl preferred his torso to goose down. The soft thump-thump, thump-thump of his heart was the only lullaby she needed.

From the pallet on the floor, where he and Annabelle lay, he finally looked beyond her angelic face to see small points of daylight escaping through cracks in the closed shutters of the window he'd finished building the day before. A cacophony of singing birds filled the air outside—the varied songs comforting. Fortunately, the gurgling snore of the old lady from the rear of the house didn't drown out the more cheerful sounds.

The day started as planned: up before Dame Fortune so he might work for a while on a personal project. The old lady's whims could wait until forced upon him by rapier wit once she woke.

He removed Annabelle's head and laid it on the pillow then went outside to greet the day. From beside the door, he retrieved a piece of sun-cured Bois d'arc wood and a strip of strong leather he'd shaved from a hide draped over the footboard of Dame Fortune's bed. The wood was

86

strong as oak yet more flexible. He sat on the edge of the stump next to the door, bluebonnets growing from its rotted center. Taking the drawknife, he clenched the perfectly straight, knot-free, two-inch diameter branch between his feet and shaved it, shaping it into a flatter piece, tapered at both ends with a round hand-grip at its center. It took over an hour to get the look of the wood the way he wanted.

Grabbing it by the ends he bent it. Flexible strength proved phenomenal. "Yes," he mumbled. He notched both ends of the strip of wood then slipped the knotted end of the leather string into one. He then pulled the wood into the more familiar bow shape slipping the other end of the leather through the gap at the opposite end. He continued pulling until the string had drawn tight and the bow arched sufficient to tie off. He beamed with satisfaction as he twanged it.

He heard a throat cleared and looked up at Dame Fortune standing in the doorway, arms crossed beneath those pendulous sagging breasts. A crocheted shawl around her neck draped over her elbows.

"What you be wastin' Dame Fortune's hard earned time on, man?"

"I saw a wild hog by the river yesterday. If you'd like some tasty pork, I have to build a bow and make some arrows. You don't think Annabelle is going to snare it like a rabbit, do you?" He had another reason for wanting that pig, to strip sinew from the animal to back the bow with and fashion a finer but stronger string—modifications that should increase the bow's power and longevity. He didn't explain that part but had a notion she already knew.

"Clever man. You be actin' like a smart feller again." She waved a finger at him. "But don't you be wastin' too much time. Don't forget, I know what you be thinkin, but dat's okay, for now. Dat roof o' mine needs thatchin' or da storm dat be comin' tonight will drive da rain right on through to wet us good. And, ooh-wee, dis old woman sure don't like to be cold and wet."

"Storm?"

"Don't ya be askin' stupid questions. Just hustle your butt down to da river and gather more of dem cattail reeds."

Jake grinned. "Yes ma'am. I'll get right on it."

"See dat ya do. If you be good and fast 'bout it, Dame Fortune might just give you somethin' to eat. Whatcha say?"

Annabelle ran around Dame Fortune to the outside and caught up to Jake. He'd already begun walking toward the river. She hugged him around the waist then rubbed her eyes and yawned.

"Tell you what, Little One, go to that grove of cedar saplings," he pointed to an area about fifty yards down river, "and find me some really straight limbs this long," he held his hands about three feet apart then held up his thumb, "and about this big around. Ten should do it. Okay?"

Annabelle smiled big and nodded enthusiastically, looking thrilled to be trusted.

Later, roof re-thatched, Jake took the limbs Annabelle had gathered, peeled the fibrous bark then shaved off irregularities to fashion arrow shafts, frequently sighting down their length, gauging trueness.

Clouds gathered. The sun oozed lower, eventually swallowed whole behind a bank of clouds before it had reached the plane of the western horizon. Approaching darkness accelerated. Lightning flashes appeared in the distance then seemed to take no time at all to come close enough to hear rumbling thunder. Jake abandoned arrow-making and moved inside the dugout closing the shutters and securing the door. Wind strengthened and blew in gusts.

"You were right. It does look like a storm coming."

The old lady snorted and stamped her staff on the floor. "Whatsa matter with you, man? You not be believin' an old woman just because she be blind? When I tell ya a storm be comin', listen to me, fool."

"I, uh, didn't mean to sound doubtful, just making conversation."

"Dat better be all." She grinned. "Now dat you been set straight let's heat up some of dat rabbit and have supper. Whatcha say?" She stoked the small clay oven in the corner and had it flaming in seconds. She placed a pot with rabbit meat and broth in it over the flame. "Maybe after supper, we tell stories to pass da time until da storm moves on."

Jake looked up as a gust of wind hit the dugout, rustling the reed thatching on the roof. Course sand peppered the front of the small abode. "I do hope those reeds are woven in tight enough to hold."

"Well, if you be believin' an old blind woman den I tell you dat you have nothin' to worry 'bout."

"Oh, I believe you all right."

The old lady's face went grim. "Din you be hearin' dis and be believin' it, too. Listen well. Another storm be comin', one dat be havin' nothing to do with da weather. Tomorrow, finish your bow, make your arrows and kill da hog. Dis be more important dan you know. Dame Fortune be needin' you more dan you be needin' her … very, very soon."

***

Baker regained consciousness, sprawled just inside the compound wall at the back corner of Stalwart near the garbage portal. The Jackson woman was gone. A sharp pain rifled through his skull; his face tightened, head canting and eye fluttering. He wondered who'd hit him and if his skull might be cracked. It couldn't have been Tam's people. He would've been killed on the spot. Then the danger of his situation caught up as lucidity returned. Stumbling to his feet, he fought the slide bolt on the passageway door, pulling it open. Unable to stand erect, he stumbled into the night beyond the wall.

After several awkward minutes, meandering without direction or plan, equilibrium and a measure of alertness returned. Still, his head throbbed. He made it to the path by the river and hesitated long enough to question: South or north? He looked both ways.

His first encounter with Stalwart suppliers had been south of the stockade and he remembered they tended to scour that area in greater numbers. He began walking north, intending to be miles away by dawn. Tuning his ears to every strange sound in the dark woods, he stopped frequently until noises could be identified or not repeated. Lightning flashes added to an obsession that eyes followed his every move. Some of the suppliers worked in darkness to their advantage. He had to assume word of what he'd done had spread.

The pain in his head settled. As it did, anger increased. As usual, Baker believed himself the victim. *It's always a woman that steps in and ruins things for me!*

The first betrayal had followed him into adulthood. As a boy he'd been turned out to make a life on his own. He pleaded with his father to stay in the home he grew up in. The elder Baker was sympathetic to his plea. But his mother, whom he saw as a selfish hoarder, instigated action to send him away. Even now, he could not accept how his own mother could do such a thing to an only child. But, she did. On his thirteenth birthday, Hiram Baker was exiled from his family and from a father he'd trusted until that day.

His heart had turned to stone as he fought hunger, disease and dangers that a boy, barely a teen, shouldn't have to deal with. The mantra guiding his existence then continued on: Take what's needed. Kill if necessary. Trust no woman ever.

Stinging hail became mixed with the rain. Baker could no longer ignore the storm. Lightning flashed across the nearby woods. Covering his head with both arms he glanced about for shelter from pelting ice, pausing long enough to assess how far he'd walked. Coming to no conclusion how safe it might be, he acquiesced to the will of nature. Pea-size ice stung his face. If he couldn't run any farther, maybe no one else could either. He scurried beneath a large flat rock cut under by flowing water at the river's edge and sat in the mud barely above the water line.

After a time, exhaustion overtook him. He fell onto his side then rolled into a tight sodden ball. While fingertips probed throbbing bloody knots on his head, a final thought knifed through his aching head: Women ... I wish I could kill them all. He clutched a clay disk at the end of a leather thong around his neck beneath his shirt. An inscription scratched into it read: Love Always –Glory.

***

Myrna stepped to within inches of Glory. "If Tam expects you back right away, the longer you stay may put you in danger of retribution and, no doubt, perverted."

"Your mother's right," Lana said. The teen stood in the corner of the room of the small cottage hugging herself, rubbing away a chill born of tense fear.

Carefully dabbing swollen and bloody bruises on Glory's battered face, the older woman looked at Lana. "Thank you, child, for saving my Glory."

Lana nodded, accompanied by a flash smile.

Glory sat, eyes closed, listening to her mother speak, offering only an occasional flinch when the dampened cloth touched a nerve.

"Oh honey, I—" She coughed then cleared her throat. "I can't bear seeing you like this, carrying such a burden. The sacrifice you're making is too great." Concern stained the elder Jackson's dark features.

Glory opened the undamaged eye and looked at her mother. "You're right. I can't go through with this." Her puffy lips began to quiver. "I thought I could handle it but, God help me, *I'm too weak*." She dropped to her knees in front of her mother. Myrna stroked her downturned head. Glory continued, "I'm so afraid my cowardice will be committing you to an early grave," she said between sobs. "This was our last best hope for a place to live." Reverting to a childlike state, Glory began to rattle. "I tried to take the reins of the family when Chauncy disappeared. I really did. I wanted to be brave. I worked hard at it—"

"Hush!" Myrna pushed Glory back and lifted her face. "Stop talking." She cleared away clumps of curly black hair from her daughter's face that had abandoned the cloth tie. The older woman backed into the rocker behind her and sat. She then leaned forward and kissed each injury on the younger Jackson's face. Glory remained crumpled on the floor between her mother's parted legs. "You really don't see how courageous you are. Do you, dear?"

Lana hurried over to stand beside the two women. "You're very brave, Miss Jackson. You've saved my baby and probably my life. I see that now. No matter what you do from here on, I'll always see you as my personal savior from a life I never wanted and a death that might have been."

Glory stopped wailing but every breath came in fits from a spastic diaphragm. "Oh mother, I—"

Myrna placed a light hand over Glory's mouth. "I don't want you to say anymore until I've had a chance to speak. It's my turn to make a plan. Now, here's what we'll do: first, go to Tam and tell him what happened and who did it. Second, beg off participation in whatever sordid plan he might have for the night, citing your injuries. His anger will be directed toward Baker for a while. Then come back here. While it's raining, we'll rest. When the storm passes we'll make our way to the trail next to the river and head north. Let's go find Jake and Annabelle."

Glory regained composure. "I hope you're up to it." She sniffed. "It sounds like an excellent idea." She looked to Lana. "Let Tam sleep with his precious shareholder status."

Lana nodded. "Yes, excellent idea."

"I've had about all I can stomach of Stalwart's twisted vision of paradise." With renewed purpose, Glory rose and walked away from her mother and Lana. "With a little luck, I'll be back shortly. I have to endorse a man's death warrant and say what I must to preserve my honor as a woman."

As she walked through the darkened compound, clear visions of Jake Henderson provided motivation to get away from the spotless, yet filthy world of Stalwart.

CHAPTER ELEVEN
A LIFE'S COURSE CORRECTION

Jake had scrounged black buzzard feathers near the water's edge and was now busily fletching arrow shafts. He sat on the hollow stump next to the dugout door watching the work of his hands while also keeping an eye on debris floating down the swollen river from last night's storm. Logs and limbs washed into the water in great numbers. He'd finished several arrows. The task now had become repetitive and monotonous. Thoughts dwelled on Dame Fortune's vague warning that her safety would soon be threatened. That, alone, caused his hands to work a little faster than he would have otherwise.

He tried getting more information but she rebuffed him. Wouldn't or couldn't, he did not know but believed her refusal was purpose driven. Where detail stopped, assumption took over. He guessed she saw herself injured and thought if she shared too much then the scale of likely occurrences might tip in favor of death. If he were to have faith in Dame Fortune then he must develop a comfort level with ignorance. He didn't want to get her killed. Still, his own survival instinct drove him to wonder: Is it possible I'll die saving her? Although the notion crossed his mind, he dismissed it—refusing to believe that Dame Fortune would selfishly withhold information.

He held up a completed arrow sporting a triad of feathered rows just below the nock then sighted down its length and spun it between fingers. *Perfect.*

Sharp killing points of stone or metal were the next order of business. But, he chose to simply sharpen the points for now. Dame Fortune's warning instilled a sense of dwindling time. He'd add points later. He figured he could get close enough to a wild hog to get a clean heart or lung shot without the long distance stability of a weighted tip.

Annabelle had taken to staying close to the old lady. He was okay with that, a pleasant diversion of accountability. He hadn't yet come to terms with bearing full responsibility for the youngster. Somewhere along the way simple concern for the child had turned into love, complicating things immeasurably. Mysteriously, he was okay with that, too. Want it or not, he realized he was becoming a parent. To so much as think it was unsettling. He was a loner by habit. Annabelle was changing that, by means of her presence.

He admired the old lady's way of drawing the youngster into conversation; something he hadn't been able to do. Although he heard them chatting amiably inside the house, specifics of the conversation were difficult to understand from where he sat. He heard his name mentioned then whispers laced with laughter. Regardless what they said, it was like warm water on a chilled body. It soothed him hearing his name mentioned in a lighthearted way. Death held no greater dread than being forgotten.

Dame Fortune kept her promise of new clothes for Annabelle. The old lady labored on ankle length pants and a shirt. Jake glanced to see her working on the clothes. The material came from remnants of a rotting canvas tarpaulin, but enough good pieces remained to make a sturdy suit of clothes for an active youngster. The sightless woman felt the contours of Annabelle's body, cut material with a sharp knife, then threaded the mesquite thorn needle with salvaged thread from the same material and began stitching. As a special favor, the old woman promised a rabbit skin vest once the hides had been cured and tanned.

"Hey, Annabelle, want to shoot my new bow?" he said over his shoulder into the house.

The child beamed with enthusiasm.

"Go on, girl," Dame Fortune said. "Get out dere and enjoy some o' dis day. I know you'd rather be doin' dat, dan watchin' an old woman sew."

Annabelle ruffled the cloth in the old woman's lap to lean over and hug her.

"Go on, girl. You be slowin' me down here."

As Annabelle skipped through the front door, Jake held out the bow. "Ever see one of these?"

The girl nodded eagerly and took it from him. She plucked the string. "Know how to use it?"

Again, she nodded, sliding a hand the length of its spine, still admiring the form.

Jake handed her an arrow. "See that big leaf on the side of that knoll?" He pointed to a barren spot not far from the dugout where a cottonwood leaf had settled after the storm.

She nocked the arrow and pulled to test the bow's strength, then drew it half way, pointed it at the leaf and let it fly. It hit high and slightly right. Grunting disapproval, Annabelle frowned, confused that the arrow didn't find its mark. Apparently she'd never missed a target before and was surprised when she did.

"Remember, Little One, the arrows have no weighted tips. They'll rise in flight." He flew a hand in front of her face to emphasize the point.

This time Annabelle didn't smile. Her eyes drew down, determined. Holding the bow in her left hand, she double-checked the nock point on the string, watched the breeze push leaves on nearby trees then drew the arrow fully, fingertips settling at the corner of her mouth, as she sighted down the shaft's length. This time the shot was dead on, whizzing at lightning speed and skewering the leaf to the dirt behind it.

Scratching his head. "Well, I needn't wonder anymore if I can hit that hog because I'm not going to try. You can do it. Come on. Let's go see if the storm chased that big ol' porker away or if it's still hangin' around down by the river. If we're lucky, we'll have meat but I'll also have sinew I can back that bow with and make a better string. Then it'll last for years. And it'll be yours."

CHAPTER TWELVE
A KILLER WILL DO WHAT A KILLER DOES

Baker crouched behind a cluster of birch saplings watching two Stalwart suppliers down the hill on the trail next to the Brazos River. They walked south. The pair of machete-wielding men had obviously worked overnight, laden with cloth bags presumably stuffed with stolen goods to be laid at the feet of Fiam Lee Tam. Clean shaven and well dressed, the men were typical suppliers. Baker ground his teeth, angered by anything or anyone connected to Stalwart.

His stomach growled. He hadn't had food since that bowl of beans day before yesterday—the day he made the fateful decision to beat and rape the Jackson woman. He was still angry that he'd failed on the latter. Hot butter beans now seemed infinitely more important than Glory Jackson. Something to eat hit the top of his priority list, fast becoming an obsession. Void of remorse, he still planned on killing her if their paths crossed again. A couple of lumps on the back of his head were a sore reminder why. But that could wait. His mouth watered, staring at the bags the men carried, conjuring visions of tasty delights hidden away.

As he observed every nuance and move by the two, he reasoned the men had been notified and would kill him on sight. It made sense. It also made sense to kill them before they had the chance and take as much bounty as he could carry.

Remaining a safe distance behind trees and brush up the hill above the path, Baker stalked them for over an hour, diligent to remain unseen. As the two came upon a rock shelf, extending out over the river's edge, he heard distant conversation. They stopped to rest.

Baker sneaked closer, staying under cover, preparing to take advantage of any opportunity. He bent low and walked down the slope hiding behind the remnant of a building that only had one triangular corner of stacked stones still standing, draped in vines. He sank to his knees then eased back onto his heels realizing he'd managed to get within earshot.

One of the men shed his backpack, knapsacks, and even the scabbard for the long knife he wore belted to his hip. "I'm going to take care of nature's business behind that stone wall," Baker heard him say.

"Don't take long," the other said. "I want to get back to the compound before dark. I don't want to sleep on the trail another night."

Baker dropped back down behind the right-angle heap of stones. It was the only thing between him and where the man intended to be.

The guy hurriedly unlaced his pants, pushed them down and squatted against the shoulder-high remains of the crumbling wall Baker hunkered behind.

When Baker heard the man moan, then sigh, he figured there'd be no better time to act than now. He cautiously rose just high enough to peek over the collapsed wall. He saw the top of the man's head. He then looked to see the other one down by the river place his baggage and knife in a small pile, then take the short but steep descent to the river's edge — probably to wash his face, get a drink, or both. The two were now separated and unarmed. Glancing about, he spotted and picked up a heavy stone with both hands. Rising to stand erect, he looked down over the rock partition.

The top of the guy's head was just below him. Too easy, he thought, slamming the rock down on the man's skull.

By the thudding crack, Baker confidently assumed he'd be no trouble. The guy fell over and didn't move — not a twitch.

The blow made more noise than he'd planned. He glanced to the other man almost to the water's edge. He saw the guy stop and scan the vicinity of the rock wall. "Hey, are you all right up there?"

Baker crouched. "*Damn*," he hissed through clenched teeth. He cupped his mouth and, in a loud voice said, "Yeah." He hoped the other one didn't recognize the difference in voices.

"I thought the wall might've collapsed on you," the guy shouted, "You sure don't want to get caught with your pants down that way." He laughed.

Rising to look over the stones again, he saw the man continuing what he'd begun, going down on his knees at the river's edge.

The window of opportunity had just been flung open. He came around the stone wall, took the dead man's long knife and then broke into a full sprint down to the river. By the time the man raised his face from the water Baker arrived and snatched up the other unsheathed knife. He now had possession of both weapons.

Hearing the commotion, the man leaped to his feet, looked up at Baker and reached for his hip before realizing he'd left his knife behind. Trapped between a fallen tree on his left and the protruding stone shelf on his right, he wanted to run but there was nowhere to go except back up to where he'd come from.

Baker grinned. He had the advantage and knew it.

The man could only do one of two things, face Baker unarmed while climbing up a steep slippery slope or swim the swollen river. It was really no choice at all. He spun and dove into the water.

Baker didn't want him getting away to tell the story or come after him later. He came down the steep embankment so fast he slid on his butt the six feet to the bottom.

The man's arms reeled in a desperate attempt to swim fast enough to avoid Baker's murder attempt but had swum less than a body length when Baker came to stand at water's edge.

Holding the end of the broad blade between clenched palms over his head, he hurled it spinning toward the man.

It found a mark in the man's back. Not a killing stick, but debilitating. The guy choked on river water and began thrashing about, batting the water's surface with outstretched arms trying to stay afloat. After several unsuccessful attempts, he sank beneath the surface. A circle of blood spread in the water.

Untrusting, Baker watched. Eventually the man surfaced face down. "And, that's that. You and your pal will be no trouble now," he muttered then sneered at having pulled it off.

Returning to the cargo, he strapped on the scabbard and shoved the one remaining long knife into it. He rummaged through the bags, picking out food and other items. As he did, he thought it best to avoid close proximity to the river for a while but decided to stay near enough to follow its course.

In a perverse sense of male camaraderie as he shouldered two of the knapsacks and adjusted them for comfort, he looked at the crumpled, lifeless heap of a man with his pants around his ankles up near the stone wall, then back to the body, tangled in floating debris, just then drifting out of sight down the river. "A different way would've been better, but I just didn't have a choice. Sorry, boys. I really am." Again, he believed himself the victim.

Feeling the stubble of a beard on his face, he wished it'd grow faster, needing his appearance to change. He walked; still unable to think of a better direction than north. He had no plan, other than get as far away from Stalwart as possible.

***

Jake smeared bright white swine sinew lengthwise on the back of his prized project, the bow. Afterwards, taking great pains, he wrapped the fibrous pork byproduct four times around the handgrip at the center of it, then reduced it to a double layer beyond that and, finally, down to a single layer to just below the string notch. He then began repeating the process on the other end.

"Dat pig gonna go good with dem lamb's quarter and dandelion greens young AnnieB done brought back from over yonder."

Jake's hands, slathered in slimy tendon strips, suddenly stopped working and looked over his shoulder at Dame Fortune. "AnnieB?"

The old lady came to stand next to where he sat on the stump. She centered the staff between here hefty legs and, steadying her girth, sat on the stump next to him. "Scoot your butt over. Dis fat ol' woman wants to sit and feel da sun on her face for awhile, might as well be 'side you."

Jake moved as far as he could without vacating the stump entirely and resumed working on the bow.

The old woman sighed.

"Something on your mind," Jake asked.

"No more dan usual."

"Where did the name AnnieB come from?"

"Da girl's birth name be Constance Elizabeth Spencer but she be lovin' you so flippin' much, she didn't want to change it back from the name you gave her. 'Sides, da birth name be draggin' her down to even think about it now, ya know. Her momma's pet name for her had been Con-Con, too sad for the child to be rememberin'."

"Really?"

"Yep." She shielded her mouth then whispered, "But she tell me dat Annabelle sound like some diddly dang flower and felt she be more substantial than a rose petal, or some such."

"I hope she didn't say it like that."

The old lady cackled. "Dat be my style, not hers. But da message be da same."

Jake shrugged as he continued wrapping the bow with the slick but tough material. "Okay, AnnieB it is … I guess. I'll have to get used to it." He stopped working for a moment and thought about it. "But, ya know, Constance Elizabeth is a beautiful name. I wonder why it makes her so sad and why she didn't want to go back to it?"

"Dat girl be some smart little thing, more dan you realize. She loved her mother so much dat even da name, Constance Elizabeth, would be a reminder of dat dark day." Her head took a mournful bend. "Poor child, to be seein' somethin' as tragic as dat; just ain't right, ya know."

"That's for sure."

"No youngun should ever have to be carryin' dat load."

He stared into the distance remembering the gruesome sight and his regrettable role.

"So she be decidin' to remember only da love of her mother and look to da future with you as AnnieB."

"You're talking about Annabelle, right?"

"Now don't be gettin' stupid on me. I done tell ya she don't want to sound like a gall-durn flower petal."

"Okay. Geez. AnnieB then." He glanced sideways with a grin as he shook his head.

"Why you be workin' so hard on dat bow? Isn't it good enough yet? It done killed a hog."

"Simple. I want it to last the rest of my life then I want to pass it on to

100

Annabelle, I mean AnnieB. It's not just a weapon or a tool for hunting. It's something to remember me by when I'm gone."

"Hot-dang, man, you too worried 'bout bein' forgotten. You know dat, man?"

"Maybe."

"No maybe 'bout it, fool. Just do da right thing den people will be rememberin' ya. Simple, eh? Dat's a Dame Fortune guarantee." She slapped his knee. "You do be knowin' right from wrong, don'tcha, man?"

"Now you're making me mad."

She howled with laughter and pounded the ground with the cedar staff. "Dat be a flippin' good answer."

Elbows resting on his knees, Jake worked on the bow. The old lady offered no conversation or new insults, just sat for a time. He glanced and saw her blind eyes staring into space as if she were looking at something and certain that she was—equally certain it had nothing to do with the world he saw. "What do you see?" he said.

"Jake Henderson, you may not be realizin' it yet, but our lives have become intertwined and now be inseparable. I hope you come to be knowin' dat soon and not be fightin' it."

She turned to face him as if sighted and wanting to make eye contact. She became serious. "You be askin' me what I see? Clear as day, I be seein' dat no matter what our futures bring, I see me and I see you and I see AnnieB standing between us for many years. You might be thinkin' of yourself as her anchor. If you do, dan you be da *big* fool, ya know. She be *your* anchor and she be mine. You think she be cute, cuddly and special, and she be dat for sure. But I see further and so much more, a world in need of savin' dat be knockin' at her door for a lifetime. Dat's what I see."

She walked her hands up the staff to rise to her feet. "Yessiree, dat's what I see," she muttered then snickered, but not in a happy way, and turned to go back inside. As she walked she said, "Dat youngun may not think of herself as a flower, but she be blossomin' jes the same; and you, Jake Henderson, will be seein' a little sample of dat real soon."

She walked away muttering and Jake tried to hear every word, listening as she moved off. She shuffled inside the dugout and disappeared behind the closing door. He stared at it and thought on those somber words laced with hope. Hackles came up on the back of his neck. He saw no reason to question her but wished to know more.

Time pressure to complete the bow now became paramount. Soon, he had to finish it. He couldn't say why, but felt it was only a matter of days, maybe hours, before it might be of lifesaving significance. Why would a sense of time running out consume him like that? Did Dame Fortune's talents extend to that kind of influence? She was a magnificent enigma.

Striding to a spot on Blister Knob above the dugout that caught maximum daily sunshine, he laid the bow under Sol's direct rays to cure the freshly applied wet sinew. Once cured, the bow would be almost indestructible. He tilted his head and looked upon it because, to him, it represented more than the sum of its craftsmanship.

He saw Annabelle playing near the water down the hill at the river's edge, behaving as any child would. *For God's sake, she's just a little girl. How could that old woman place the weight of the world's shortcomings upon such tender shoulders?*

As he watched the youngster, a flame flickered that singed his heart. He loved her and hoped he could muster the gumption, someday, to tell her so. Dame Fortune's warning tied the young girl and that bow together, yet he couldn't answer the simple question: why?

***

Myrna's coughing accelerated. Cool damp predawn air didn't help. Lana walked close at her side aiding her—the assist almost constant now. A few yards up the trail, Glory led them north. "I'm sorry for the fast pace, mother, but we have to put safe distance between us and Stalwart."

"Don't worry," she coughed, "about me. Just keep leading the way." She fluttered fingertips in a gesture of encouragement, urging Glory to keep walking.

Glory looked at Lana. "How about you—are you okay?"

"I'm fine." She rubbed the bump on her belly. "And the baby seems okay, too. I know it's not a girl's dream to become pregnant this way, but I'm excited. I hope I'll be able to care for an infant."

Myrna lifted Lana's hand and patted it. "Glory and I will be at your side the whole time." She adjusted the knapsack strap on her shoulder, coughed, and added, "I'm confident we'll find Jake and Annabelle soon. When we do, we'll have the makings of a wonderful self-sustaining collective."

Glory stopped and looked thoughtfully at her mother. "Yeah, almost like ... well, almost like family." She again walked, now somewhat lighter; the spring in her step returned.

Two more days passed. It was a warm late spring afternoon. Glory became more at ease with slowing the pace and allowing longer rest periods. Regardless, Myrna's condition continued deteriorating. She'd begun expelling phlegm with spots of blood. Exhaustion on top of the respiratory condition combined to speed the downturn. Glory became scared. She had to find Jake soon. Three women without talent for wilderness travel didn't bode well for longevity—one sick, one pregnant, and another never trained or desirous of guiding anyone anywhere. Food had dwindled but Glory thought it dangerous to take time to forage.

On this day, they'd walked about two hours. "Let's take a breather," she announced then looked at her mother and added, "I mean that quite literally for you."

Myrna wheezed and cleared her throat. "I'm glad to see your sense of humor is intact."

Glory offered a grin but it quickly drooped. She scanned the woods above the trail as she removed knapsacks that rode her hips from straps around her neck. "Am I the only one that feels we're being watched?" She turned a complete circle, looking. "I suppose I'm just paranoid?"

Lana dropped the small cloth bag she carried, backed up to a tree, and slid to the ground to sit, the simple gray dress riding high above her knees. She brushed pebbles and dirt from her sandals. "Working for Tam, I always felt as though eyes were on me. I do have that feeling but I'm not sure it means much. It became part of me a long time ago."

"Dear, I think you're sense of responsibility to us is driving you to imagine things," Myrna said, as she guided her bottom onto a fallen log with both hands.

Glory massaged sore shoulders. "I hope you're right, but I—"

The crunch of forest litter sounded off near a large cottonwood tree high above the trail.

"Hear that?" she rattled with wide eyes.

Myrna and Lana nodded.

"I knew it wasn't just my imagination."

Glory looked about for a weapon, then threw open the flap of a knapsack and retrieved her straight razor.

She heard it again. But this time it was continuous.

She glimpsed a human form disappearing over the rise just behind the tree.

"Who's there?" she yelled.

No answer.

"Did either of you see who it was?"

Even as she asked the question, Myrna and Lana were gathering things to get back on the trail and on the move. Glory snatched up knapsacks. Her voice quavered. "Come on. Let's get out of here."

In a fast walk, they continued northward. As the next hour rolled by, grisly images of attack and slaughter whirled through Glory's mind. There'd be little she could do to prevent disaster if it came to that. She choked back a whine. The trail angled left away from the river and, as they walked around a cluster of Chinaberry saplings, a strange looking spot of ground appeared, an obvious break in the woods void of vegetation with a small structure that looked to have been partially covered over by earth, sliding down from the top of a whitish bald hill that rose up behind it.

Lana continued as a crutch for Myrna. The elder Jackson couldn't maintain the grueling pace unaided. Lana threw the woman's arm over her shoulder and held tight to that hand with both of hers.

Glory still held the folded straight razor.

Again, the crunch of dry foliage sounded off—this time below them, near the river, next to a huge tree that tilted at a severe angle out over the water.

She flipped open the razor and shouted, "I'm warning you! Stay away from us!"

From behind the tree, Jake's head popped up. "Glory?"

The razor slid from her trembling hand. She began to shake. "Jake!" she shouted then ran crying down the hill.

Jake climbed over the mostly exposed mass of gnarled roots at the base of the tree. His feet had barely touched the ground on the other side when Glory slammed into him, knocking him off balance. He stutter-stepped sideways. She hugged so tight it forced air wheezing from him. "What're you doing here? What's the matter?"

Holding her face firmly against his chest, "Somebody's been following us. Oh Jake, I was so scared." She sobbed.

"What about Stalwart?"

"I'll explain later. I'm just relieved to find you." She looked back up the rise to her mother and Lana. She released her hold on him then took his hand. "Come on. I have someone I want you to meet." She swept escaping tears from her cheeks.

"Good to see you again, Mister Henderson," Myrna called out as Glory and Jake approached.

"You, too, Myrna." He looked at the girl. "Who's your friend?"

Lana extended a hand and blurted, "Hi, I'm Lana, Lana McAdams." Her mouth stretched as wide as a Stalwart smile but with a difference; the eyes glistened with joy.

Myrna and Glory looked at one another and said at the same time, "McAdams?"

"We never knew that," Glory said.

Lana shrugged. "It didn't seem important before; now it does. I guess it's all part of reclaiming my life." She looked up to the dugout structure. "Is that your home, Mister Henderson?"

"No. But there's someone up there I sure want all three of you to meet. Has anyone ever heard of the Oracle of Blister Knob?"

Lana said, "As a matter of fact I have. Tam told stories about a strange woman that lived alone in the woods, a fortune-teller I think."

"That's the one. She lives here. She's up there now with AnnieB. Come on. I want to introduce you to her. You're in for a special treat."

"AnnieB? Are you referring to Annabelle," Glory asked.

"Oh, yeah. You tell me all about Stalwart and I'll explain that to you."

Glory squared her shoulders to Jake and pulled him around to face her. Her eyes went dreamy. "God, you can't know, even in your wildest imaginings, how good it is to see you again." She kissed him lightly on his hairy cheek and jerked him into another tight hug pressing her cheek into his chest.

He blushed then pushed a matted swirl of black hair resembling an errant dreadlock away from her bruised and swollen left eye, plucking a dried leaf from it. "It looks as though life has been rough on you lately. Maybe a bath and washing your hair will make you feel better." A wry grin came up; he then screwed up his nose as if smelling something foul.

Glory slapped his chest. "I guess I deserve that." She zipped a flattened palm over his sandy-colored beard that'd grown long enough to curl. "And you could use a shave."

Myrna took the lead. "Let's walk up to the house. I'm curious to meet the new woman in Jake's life."

Jake chuckled. "Get ready for a shock."

CHAPTER THIRTEEN
LABOR PAINS TO A NEW LIFE

Dame Fortune muttered to herself, "It be a fine day and a warm feelin' to finally have da circle complete."

Jake stood several paces ahead of the old woman, watching AnnieB accompany Myrna, Glory and Lana to the river to bathe. He picked up the ax planning to resume work, but paused upon hearing Dame Fortune's softly spoken appreciation. "What circle?"

She sighed. "Dat Myrna lady and Glory be a long time comin', but dey finally here. You be findin' no better people in all of dis world. Be kind to dem Jake. Be very kind."

He frowned and then said hesitatingly, "I will." Clearly not understanding her mood or the tender refrain, Jake began turning to walk away.

"Don't be goin' just yet." She reached out. "Take my hand."

"I really need to get to work. I—"

"Just be takin' my hand, fool!" She felt his palm slide across hers.

"Why? What's so all-fired important about holding hands?"

"I be needin' to know your energy and you be needin' to know mine."

"Huh?"

She patted his hand and released it. "Okay, now go 'bout your bidness and cut dem logs for dat retainin' wall by my house, got no time for stupid questions."

Dame Fortune knew she was acting unusual. She also understood Jake was confused. But there was no other way. The vision of what was to come must take precedence. She sensed all his unasked questions. But he wouldn't delve any deeper into what she saw in that future vision. She was comfortable he'd come to understand how knowing too much could adversely alter what she'd seen. In that way, the trust between them tightened.

Finally, he said, "Okay."

She heard him turn and walk toward the door of the dugout home.

"I'll go down river to that cedar grove and get busy on it right now."

"No! You be goin' to da grove nearest da house. You got dat, man?"

"But those are flimsy saplings. None are substantial enough to stop the erosion of Blister Knob on both sides of your house. They'd get pushed right over to the ground with the next big rain."

"Please, jes be doin' what Dame Fortune say," she whispered with uncharacteristic sensitivity. "Go on now."

She followed him as far as the flagstone stoop outside and listened.

She must be certain he walked in the direction she asked of him. As the sound of his footsteps faded, she stepped back inside and closed the door behind her. The pieces of the dangerous vision had begun coming together swiftly, confirmed by Glory's emotion-filled telling of having been stalked along the river less than a mile down-river.

She assessed the situation. Jake was gone and AnnieB likely sat on the river bank chatting with Glory and Myrna as they bathed, while she stood alone, just as she'd envisioned. It had to be this way. She'd be injured but alive, not ideal but better than dead. She'd taken a chance on two minor initiatives that might tip advantage to her: urging AnnieB to take the bow and some arrows to practice with while down at the river and keeping Jake closer than he might have been otherwise.

The door swung open.

Even expecting it, her heart stuttered. "You not be welcome in my home but I be expectin' ya, so let's be gettin' dis bit of nastiness over with, Mister Baker."

She felt his anger. Visions of a man haunted by a lifetime of rage drenched in hues of red swirled in an ever-tightening montage that, to Dame Fortune, appeared as a tornado coming from a dark cloud to catastrophically touch the ground in this very time and space.

The stench from his mouth indicated how close he came to stand. "You be seein' for yourself that I jes be an old blind woman, unable to defend myself."

"I know. That's why I waited for the others to leave," he said in his normal deep raspy voice.

She felt his probing eyes.

"So, what they say about the Oracle of Blister Knob is true; you know things before they happen, the future. Tell me old woman, do you know why I'm here and what I want?"

"I know what you be sayin' you be wantin'. You want food and trade goods, but deep inside your black heart I see da truth of it. I surely wish you be unlockin' dat part of your heart. Your momma be a bad woman. But every woman not be like her, don't ya know, man."

"Shut up, hag! Don't be talking about my family. I don't care what you think you know. You know nothing. Ya hear me, nothing!"

"Ya need to be hearin' it, man, 'cause nobody has ever told ya. It be the source of your torment, can't ya see. I already know you won't let me live. So, I might as well be givin' ya da truth. Ya see, man, ya want so bad to kill your momma dat ya see her face in every woman you cross."

"Shut up!"

Dame Fortune straightened and conjured a fast image of Jake. *It's time, Jake Henderson. Come to me. Come to me now. Run, man, run!*

She then brought her attention back to Hiram Baker. "Ya die a little more each time ya be endin' a woman's life, yet ya be driven to keep killin'. I feel so flippin' sorry for ya, man."

"Shut up! Shut up! Shut up!"

She heard a whoosh and quickly held her staff out in time to catch the hard blade of a large knife chopping deep into the wood.

She heard the rhythmic thud of rapid footfalls becoming louder and shouted, "Hurry Jake!"

She felt the blade land hard against her upper arm. The densely knitted shawl she wore absorbed some impact of the slicing blow, but the sting told her it still penetrated deep into her flesh. She grabbed for the wound and felt blood streaming from a gash as long as her fingers and as wide as two of them.

Then she heard Jake shout, "It's you!" Jake's voice dropped to an intense growl. "You'll not get away with it this time, you … you sonofabitch!"

"He be dat for sure. His momma be a bad woman."

Punctuated by clanging metal upon metal, Jake engaged Baker — broad knife against ax head. The room was small and the ceiling low, a disadvantage for Jake's unwieldy ax.

She stood unmoving for a time, uncertain where the fight would take the two men.

The old lady heard the struggle take them to the table at the rear of the front living area. She made her way in the opposite direction to the door and yelled, "AnnieB, get your behind up here! Da time has come for you to be shinin', girl!"

***

Jake gripped his ax in one hand and the wrist of Baker's knife-wielding hand in the other, but glanced when Dame Fortune shrieked like a banshee shouting for AnnieB.

Baker swung him into the old lady's back, knocking her stumbling outside.

He saw her bloody fingers clutching her arm. A glance was all he had time for. His was a struggle with a psychopathic killer that would only end when one of them was dead. And, he was learning quickly he had no strength advantage over Baker. His adversary yanked free, spun, and lunged at him, both of them grappling and rolling; they rumbled out the door and split apart, both vying for fighting stance and advantage.

Before Jake had regained his full balance outside the dugout, Baker was advancing. He snarled and pressed for more advantage. With a foul curse bursting from his stank-of-a-mouth, he leaped forward, swinging his weapon, missed, but seized Jake by the collar, readying for another strike.

Jake had to put distance between him and that machete-like knife. Summoning a burst of strength, he shoved Baker away, then clutched the ax at both ends holding it out defensively.

Baker yielded, stepping backwards but swung the knife in a right-to-left looping arc as he did.

Jake blocked it with the ax handle, but then made a mistake by sliding his hand near the ax head down the handle to join the other so he could swing it full bore. In that fraction of a second his body was unprotected.

Baker reversed his swing.

Jake jumped back.

The blade contacted his abdomen, slicing long and deep above his navel.

He stumbled backward holding the gash, uncertain whether viscera would fall out or not. He tripped and fell with a thud on the hardpan, grassless ground still holding tight to the wound.

Baker came to hover over him.

In those eyes, Jake saw the glazed look of a remorseless killer.

Jake had nothing left. He lifted his free arm to cover his eyes.

A screech split the air.

He looked. *AnnieB!*

"Jake!" AnnieB was incensed and on a mission, running as though the wind carried her, tiny feet barely touching the ground as she blurred up the hill from the river.

Hair sodden, Glory tried, but in no way kept pace with the girl. She carried a single arrow and the bow, yelling for AnnieB to take the weapon.

The girl had no time to slow down.

Baker lifted the knife high over his head for a killing chop to the center of Jake's skull.

Moving at unearthly speed, AnnieB ran up Baker's back to stand upright on his shoulders. She leaped high and came down with the points of her knees smashing into the trapezium muscles.

Temporarily paralyzed, he went down.

As he was falling she flipped backwards, landing upright on her feet.

Regaining a measure of composure, Baker bounded back to his feet and abandoned his attack on Jake.

He faced the girl with a white-knuckled grip on the long knife.

That's when Jake saw something glowering in AnnieB's eyes. She recognizes Baker as the man who killed her mother, he thought.

Sprinting up the hill, Glory caught up. "Take the bow!" Still running, she held it and the arrow out for AnnieB.

AnnieB ran toward Glory away from Baker.

Baker followed.

She snatched the bow and arrow from Glory's grasp.

Baker came close. He took a swipe with the knife but the youngster simply rolled her upper body with the direction of the swing as she leaned back then took off running again.

Blinded by anger because he couldn't best a child, he ignored Glory.

AnnieB ran up the steep hill next to the dugout, then on to that portion of the roof extending outward from it.

Baker sneered.

Jake realized in that moment that Baker believed he had a defenseless child trapped on the roof and needed to simply climb up the small hill, join her on the roof and kill her.

Jake watched but lay helpless. "Annabelle, you're trapped! Get down from there!"

With no sign of fear on the child's face, she strung the arrow and slid it to the ideal nock point then said to Baker, "My mother's name was Lilly Katherine Spencer."

In the time it took Jake's heart to beat once, AnnieB raised the bow, drew and let the arrow fly. It plunged deep into the left side of Hiram Baker's chest.

He gasped, dropped the knife and fell, rolling to the bottom, coming to a lifeless rest next to the hollow stump filled with blooming bluebonnets. Slung to the side of his head was a bright orange clay disk on a leather string that he wore around his neck beneath his shirt. On it was scribed Glory's name.

Jake's discomfort paled in comparison to what a ten-year-old girl had just done.

Glory ran to his side and dropped to her knees. "Oh God, Jake!" she said, her voice strained to a whining hiss. She pulled his bloody hand away from his belly.

For the first time, he felt he could look down at his wound and assess the extent of damage. He observed the laceration had penetrated deep into the dermis but had not cut into the intestines. Somewhat relieved, he smiled weakly at Glory. "You once told me that your mother was a good seamstress. I think Dame Fortune and I will have the opportunity to see just how good she really is."

Glory sat back on her heels, covered her face and shed tears of relief.

Jake looked around her to the girl. "Look at Annabelle."

Glory dropped her hands into her lap and turned to see.

The youngster cradled Baker's head, crying, filled with remorse for having taken his life.

A curious look came over Glory.

"What is it? What're you looking at?"

Glory rose and walked to Baker's body. She ran a hand over the grieving child's head but her eyes and interest were on that disk around Baker's neck. Upon close examination, she straightened. "I gave this to Chauncy the last time I saw him. I'll never know exactly what happened, but it's clear he didn't survive." Softly, she began to weep again. It was the closure she needed.

Lana was working her way up the hill from the river, taking it slow, aiding Myrna.

But his concern remained with the girl. She mourned for a man that only knew evil as a way of life. "Annabelle, please child, come here," he said as gently as he could through his own pain.

Glory guided her to Jake's side.

"You had no choice, Little One. Baker would've killed all of us and then kept on killing if you hadn't stopped him."

The little girl fell to her knees and hugged his neck. She whispered in his ear, "You called me Annabelle."

Speaking directly into the little girl's ear he whispered, "Is that okay? I really don't like the name AnnieB."

"How about Annie?" she said, pressing her cheek into his.

"I think I can love Annie." He tightened the embrace, kissed her cheek and whispered, "The name and the girl."

Dame Fortune, still standing away, finally spoke. "Hot-damn, people, y'all be makin' dis fat ol' woman burst into happy tears."

CHAPTER FOURTEEN
A NEW LIFE BRINGS NEW ADVENTURES

2213 A. D.
Five Years Later

Annie crouched in her favorite hunting blind near the river—uncomfortable because the canvas pants Dame had made for her rode up into the crotch—this after patches had been added twice to extend width and length.

The wind shifted. The air began to cool. Dry leaves swirled at her feet, another sign of changing seasons. She sought to build stores of dried or smoked meat for the cold months ahead.

At daybreak, she woke to warbling turkey gobbles providing a great idea on how to spend this day. A fat hen or a big tom would make an excellent feast to celebrate season's end and her birthday. Add plump fall turnips from Glory's garden and maybe mashed pumpkin sweetened with the juice of boiled cane pulp and they'd have another genuine reason to be thankful.

She didn't know what the true date of her birth was. But the day Myrna had passed away, Annie honored the elder Jackson by adopting her birthday as her own, November fifth, celebrating it for the first time in 2209, thirteen weeks after the funeral.

Finally, she noticed movement.

She crouched lower behind the tangled thicket. She watched a specific place down the slope. From the shadow of a shedding willow tree stepped a turkey hen with a beard so plush it almost touched the ground. "Yes," she breathed and began to rise. From behind that same tree strutted a larger tom turkey and two smaller hens.

She again shrank into hiding, wanting both but unsure if she could get off two shots quick enough. A slight miscalculation might cost her a clean kill on even one. Never the one to back away from a challenge, she pulled another arrow from the quiver strapped to her back and placed it between her teeth.

Again she rose. As her head cleared the top of the low thicket, the tom's head popped up.

She'd been noticed.

All four birds turned and began walking away.

No longer attempting caution, she sprang tall, drew and released the first arrow.

Before the point of that arrow found its target on the hen she had the other arrow nocked and drawn.

The tom took wing and lifted off.

Leading it slightly, she released the arrow.

By the time the hen had fallen over with an arrow through its middle, the flying male bird tumbled to the ground, stopping inches from the other in a puff of dust.

"Yes! That's how it's done!"

Trotting around the thicket she danced down the slope to the birds.

Just as she lifted one up by the legs, a deep guttural growl came from dense undergrowth beyond the cluster of willows.

A mountain lion leaped out and hunkered into attack pose, claws bared, letting out a thunderous growl. It began slinking laterally in a stalking maneuver.

Annie held her ground. "Hey, big fella, were you hunting these turkeys, too? Sure sorry about that. You're just a little slow on the kill, buddy." She squatted and sat on her heels. "Ya hungry?"

The cat snarled baring its teeth.

"Oh hush. That's not nice." She laid her bow on the ground and draped her arms over her knees. "Hmm. Now that you've shown up, I have quite the dilemma on my hands. It would appear you agree with me. Let me think about this. I could give you the tom but it's big enough to feed six people and you're just one hungry cat."

The lion snarled again and stepped forward threateningly.

Annie dropped her chin and grinned. "I told you to be nice." She glanced at the two birds. "Now, where was I? Oh yeah. Or, I can give you the hen. Granted, it's a little smaller but much more tender, I bet. What do you think?"

The mountain lion seemed bent on taking one or the other, but it also appeared the cat had developed a confused sort of respect. It continued snarling, baring its teeth, and carrying on, but tensed muscles in its shoulders relaxed, as if it no longer saw her as a threat. It paced to and fro not ten feet away—well within attack distance. But the animal came no closer, as if it were in a cage and couldn't.

"I'll tell you, old friend, you have really sharp looking teeth, so why don't I give you that big ol' tough-as-boot-leather tom and I'll take the tender succulent hen. All of us humans can't handle tough meat as well as you. That's a talent we don't share. How about that? Sound fair?"

The cat growled but didn't change the pattern of its side-to-side pace.

"Ah, you must agree. Okay then, the tom it is." She laid the dead bird in front of her, pulled the arrow from it and said, "Well? What're ya waitin' for? Dinner is served."

Leary, the big cat hunkered down and eased forward, extending its neck and head toward the bird but never taking its eyes off Annie. It snatched the turkey by the neck then trotted away, disappearing into the woods.

Annie sprang to her feet. "I knew there was a reason I needed both those turkeys." She dusted her hands, shouldered the bow and picked up her prize.

Walking north into a cool breeze, she relished the feel against her face and arms. Harsh sunlight flickered through the trees in an ultra-clear sky as she strolled along. After such a hot muggy summer, she welcomed the dry cool of autumn, enjoying kicking through and crunching the layer of leaves along the path. Turning her head upward, she also took pleasure in the tickle of leaves still coming down and kissing her face.

Taking the curve in the trail, Blister Knob came into view beyond the chinaberry trees that had grown to an imposing size since she'd first come to this place. She stopped for a moment to admire the progress, starting with the spacious and comfortable cabin Jake designed and they all pitched in to build. It stood within a stone's throw of Dame Fortune's dugout home, whom they'd begun calling simply Dame a few years back.

As she climbed the hill, approaching the cabin, she saw Jake sitting on a crude bench, drawknife in hand, building a cedar rocking horse for Eva Louise, Lana's child. "Looking good, Jake," she called out.

"Thanks, but it's more difficult than I'd counted on," he said before looking up. He glanced, then again. "Hey, speaking of good looking, that's quite a turkey you've got there."

She held it high. "You think Glory and Lana can do something with this?"

"If those girls put their minds to it, they could make rocks taste good."

"I think so, too." She looked around. "Where's Glory?"

"Spending a few minutes with her mother," he said then sighed.

"She spends a whole lot of time at that grave. I wish there was something I could do to take her mind off it."

"Believe me, Little One, you do every day. She loves you very much."

Four-year-old Eva came running out the cabin door when she heard the talk. "Annie," she shouted and ran down the hill. According to what the child's mother, Lana, had told her, the girl's delicate Asian features came from Eva's father, Fiam Lee Tam. Eva was a beautiful child who would grow into a gorgeous woman someday. Glistening straight black hair and Asian eyes set in delicate features highlighted an innocent face.

Annie dropped the bird and snatched the girl up, spinning her around. "Whatcha been doin' all morning, Punkin?"

Eva wrapped her arms around Annie's neck. "Waitin' for you."

Lana appeared in the doorway wiping her hands with a rag. "By the looks of that turkey it would seem I have work to do." She tossed the cloth aside. "Come on Eva, let Annie have a few minutes to herself. She's probably tired."

Annie put the child down and whispered in her ear, "We'll play later." She winked at the youngster.

Eva beamed and ran to join her mother.

"I'm going to check on Dame," Annie announced after handing the turkey to Lana.

In no rush, she sauntered to Dame's dugout home. As she was about to knock, she heard the old lady making noise, moving about inside. "Comin'. Keep ya breeches on."

Speaking up, "No hurry, Dame, just haven't seen you today, thought I'd drop by."

The door opened. The old lady, clearly winded, blocked Annie's entrance. "And I be so flippin' glad ya did."

Annie stepped sideways and peeked around the old woman's substantial girth. "Dame," she said, drawing out her name, "why are you acting so secretive?"

"Hush up and don't be askin' foolish questions, child. You know da Dame be tellin' ya when da time is right."

Annie noticed a ragged quilt covering something in a heap at the foot of the bed in the rear of the little house. "Okay. No more questions."

With the aid of her staff, Dame shuffled around and dropped into her rocking chair. She huffed as if it were a major expenditure of energy. "Come on in. Been a busy mornin', child. Busy, I tell ya, yes indeed."

"Besides busy, how've you been?"

Dame sat silent, then finally said, "Been seein' things this mornin'."

"Future things?"

"Uh-huh, bothersome, too."

"Why?"

"It be things that'll put you on a course to fulfill your destiny."

"I've heard you mention this many times but never in detail. Are you talking about dangerous things, wonderful things, or just," She shrugged, "things?"

"All three. But ya know well enough, child, I can't share details or I be riskin' changin' what I see." The old lady leaned forward in her chair, tapped the side of her nose with a finger then waggled it at Annie. "But I be tellin' ya dis much, and it be truthful enough; new people be comin' into your life soon. Your heart will dictate what you do after dat, not Dame or what she sees. Okay?"

"You can be so mysterious."

"Gotta be, child. It be da nature o' what I do."

Annie kissed the old black woman on the cheek and then patted down Dame's snow white hair into a better balanced arrangement on top of her head "I know. I love you just like you are." She straightened. "You haven't forgotten it's my birthday have you?"

The old lady threw her head back. "Ooh! Dat stings! I can't believe you'd think I be forgettin' somethin' so diddly dang important. I be a blazin' fool if I forgot, child. I be blind but my memory be gooder'n gold. Dame always remembers what be important. I have a big surprise for ya." She pointed a finger at Annie. "But ya gotta wait."

Annie's eyes sparkled. "Surprise?"

"You betcha."

Annie smiled so big the corners of her mouth disappeared into her cheeks then suddenly went curious. "You know what? I have no idea what *your* age is. How old are you?"

"Don't know ... don't be givin' a blitherin' damn either."

"I guess that means you don't know when your birthday is, huh?"

"Dat be true enough." The old lady swung the tip of her staff and tapped Annie's foot with it. "But I be sharin' a tidbit o' wisdom with ya, child; if you be bent on tracking dat gall-durn number, you be an old woman too soon. Listen to dis ol' fat woman, Annie, don't concern yourself with da number of years dat be passin'. Track good deeds, goals achieved and all da friends ya be makin' along da way. Dat's da main number and what be most important. Keep up with dat, why don'tcha?"

"Hot-damn, you're flippin' smart."

"Don't be usin' dat foul language around Dame!"

"Why? You say it all the time."

"You may look all growed up but you still be a child, just a youngun. I be older." The old lady turned her nose up, feigning superiority. "I earned da right."

"According to your tidbit of wisdom, age means nothing. You and I might as well be the same age."

Dame's face went bland for a moment then she drew a smile. "You not only pretty, you flippin' smart, too." She jiggled all over with laughter.

***

Annie looked around the table, thankful her eclectic family could be together this way. As her eyes settled on the amusing sight of the picked-clean turkey carcass, loving warmth soaked her so fast she shuddered.

She watched as Jake teased Eva. Glory sat close to him with an affectionate hand on his arm, laughing along with his good-natured joking. Eva giggled while Lana and Dame discussed better ways to cook a turkey using available herbs. There was nothing extraordinary about any of it. And that's exactly what made it so special. At this table was Annie's wish for the world.

She looked at Dame. *It can be this way everywhere someday. I'm sure of it.*

Dame smiled. "It be a wonderful celebration and I agree. One day it be dis way everywhere. What you soon begin, Little One, be spreadin' like a prairie fire. Dis be a Dame Fortune guarantee, girl."

Everyone stopped chattering and stared at the old woman. "What in the world are you talking about," Jake asked.

"Just sharin' my thoughts with Annie, since she be kind enough to share her's wit' me."

"But I didn—"

"Oh yes you did. You be wantin' me to know your mind."

"Why do I even question you?"

"Yeah. Why?" The old lady slapped the tabletop. "Now it be time for Annie's birthday gift."

Annie clapped like a little girl and let a breathy squeal escape. Eva leaped up and ran to Annie's side, wanting to share in the surprise. Annie scooted her chair back from the table, dropped her hands into her lap and sat prim. "I'm ready."

Dame reached down beside her chair, lifted up a hefty cloth bag with a grunt and offered it to her.

Annie's eyes widened at the size of it as she took it into her hands. Eva jumped up and down. "Open it. Open it."

Reaching into the bag, she pulled out a pair of knee-high pig-hide boots with delicately pointed toes. "Oh my …" She reached in again, this time withdrawing lightweight buckskin breeches adorned with colorful wooden beads near the waistline. She looked again in the bag and pulled out a new furry rabbit skin vest. The one she had, she'd outgrown with the last growth spurt and hadn't worn it in nearly two years. Finally, she removed an off-white linen shirt with long loose sleeves. She held that the longest and studied every inch. "I've never had anything so fine." She held it to her cheek, languishing in the texture of the cloth.

"Mother wanted you to have it," said Glory. "She told me the day she died. I was just waiting for you to grow into it and, of course, the right time. Your fifteenth birthday seemed appropriate."

"Thank you." She turned to Dame Fortune and held up the array of leather goods. "These must have taken weeks to make."

The old lady shrugged. "Eh, what else do I be havin' to do?"

Annie leaped up. "I have to wear all this right now." She disappeared into the bedroom and reappeared moments later. "What does everyone think?" she said, twirling full circle. She wore the buckskin breeches tucked into the top of the tall boots and the gauzy shirt tucked into the pants laced up the front. Over that she wore the rabbit-skin vest, left open, and went so far as to tie her long, straight, silken sandy-colored hair back with a strip of red cloth to set off the ensemble. The hastily fashioned red bow created a long ponytail and offered a softer, more feminine look.

Jake's jaw hung slack. He stammered, "You're, uh … it's … y-you're beautiful!" Then he added smugly, "But I always knew the cute child you were had to someday turn into a ravishing woman."

Her eyebrow went up. "Sure you did."

"You look great," Glory said.

Lana quickly added, "Absolutely enchanting."

Everyone jumped with a start when something crashed into the cabin door, silencing them.

Jake leaped to his feet and snatched up the ax from beside the door. Holding an open palm toward the rest he said, "Everyone stay back."

Annie rose and stepped to the side of the floor-to-ceiling pantry cupboard retrieving her bow and quiver without taking her eyes from the door.

Jake flattened against the wall next to the door then gingerly pushed the wooden locking rod from its hold.

Weight bearing against the door pushed it open fast.

Jake raised the ax over his head.

Annie strung an arrow and had it drawn.

As the door slammed the wall behind it, a young man fell inside, dazed and mumbling.

Jake leaned the ax against the wall and knelt, rolling the man onto his back. It appeared he was little more than a boy, seventeen—eighteen perhaps. His hands were covered in crusted blood and his face appeared to have been clubbed—knots and bruises dotted it. Blood had dried in a zigzag streak from his temple. His nose may have been broken, judging by the deep varying shades of purple radiating laterally from the swollen bridge and the clotted blood on his lip below both nostrils.

"Do da boy be wearin' a robe like a monk?"

Jake looked at Dame, his eyebrows pulling down. "Yeah." He shook his head. The things you know …"

"Never mind dat. Take care of da boy."

Glory raced to the small kitchen and poured water from clay pots, wetting several rags. She ran back and dropped down on the cedar plank floor on the side opposite Jake. She cleaned blood from the young man's face then began mopping his brow with a clean cool wet cloth.

"Let's get him onto my bed," Annie said, stepping in to replace Glory.

Jake wiggled his arms beneath the boy's limp body. "Give me a hand, Annie." Together, they carried him to the bedroom.

Annie sat on the bed next to him and put an ear to his chest.

Jake probed arms and legs for fractures.

"His heart sounds strong and steady," said Annie.

Jake straightened and planted hands on his hips. "I don't know where he came from or how far he walked to get here, but I'm surprised he made it. He's been badly beaten."

Annie's eyes moistened. "Why would someone do this?" Her lip quaked. She looked up at Jake. "Why do people have to be so cruel?" Stranger or not, Annie could no more control how she felt about the brutality than the movement of the planets, and didn't try.

Glory came to Annie's side, lifted her up, and embraced her. She whispered in her ear, "It'll be okay. He's young and strong. He'll get better soon."

Annie pulled away. "No it's not okay! What happened to him happens all the time in this crazy world." Her voice went up an octave. "People are afraid of one another. There is no trust among people. I don't care who he is, what he did or where he came from, no one deserves to be beaten like that." She sobbed. "Whoever did this didn't care if he lived or died. And for what? A turnip? A piece of shiny junk? Or, God help us all, maybe they *just* felt like beating someone to death!" She rested her face on Glory's shoulder and wept.

Annie heard the tap, tap, tap of Dame's staff. She lifted her head, sniffed and saw the old woman heading for the front door.

"Come on, Annie girl, you be sleepin' with me tonight. Let da boy rest. Tomorrow be da time to find out his story."

Annie sat on the bed next to the boy — the early autumn sun already high in the sky. He slept. She pulled a cool damp cloth across his face in feathery sweeps to soothe the badly battered face. With the other hand, she toyed with four short braids in his sparse beard dangling from his chin. She thought it an odd style choice on an, otherwise, handsome face.

He began emerging from slumber. Eyes parted slowly. The light of non-recognition suddenly popped them into saucers. He tried to bolt but Annie held him down. "Welcome to Blister Knob. Are you in pain?"

Resting on his elbows, eyes darting about, threatened by unfamiliar surroundings, he remained tensed and ready.

She didn't attempt to say anything further, but kept him from sitting upright with a hand in the center of his chest. He made a weak attempt to come on up anyhow but couldn't force his way past her palm.

After a few anxious seconds, his eyes relaxed. Fear left his face. He calmed and stretched his neck to the side. "I hurt all over," he said in a hissing rasp, and then eased back down, head sinking into the pillow. "Who are you?"

"I'm Annie." She flicked her chin toward the bedroom door. "Jake is the man of the house. He's off cutting cedar trees to build … something. He's always building things. Lana and her daughter Eva Louise are in the front room. Eva's four, she's watching her mother carve a wooden plate and Glory, Jake's life partner, is foraging for edible roots to put up for winter. And, finally, Dame Fortune lives in a dugout next to us, just over there." She flipped out a northerly pointing thumb.

"Dame Fortune?" He touched his nose and grimaced. "Is that a title or a name?"

"Both. She's a dear friend, a psychic, a seer and deeply intuitive. She's known as the Oracle of Blister Knob."

"I've heard of her."

"Most people have. She's earned a well-deserved reputation. It's phenomenal what that woman can see, considering she's blind."

"Blind?"

"Yep … blinder'n a bat but, take my word for it, she can see a whole lot more than you and I. I bet she knows what I'm tellin' you right now, and she's not within earshot, I promise."

"Are y'all a family or a small corporation?"

"Well, aside from Eva and Lana, the rest of us aren't blood related; of course I'm sure you could tell that by the variety skin colors, when you see all of us, but we're a family for sure. You'll not find one stronger anywhere, guaranteed. Glory has spoken of wanting to start a corporation that actually does what that Stalwart place apparently pretends to do, allow shareholder status to anyone willing to contribute to the greater good, but no stealing or playing shenanigans with people's lives like Stalwart does."

"Stalwart," he said, drenched in disgust.

"Know of them?"

"I don't just *know of them*. See this nose and all these cuts and bruises? I know 'em very well, intimately even."

"They did this to you?"

"Yes. Our Order has been determined to be a threat to the corpocracy and has endured lesser attacks before by smaller corporations ... but never like the violent raid day before yesterday. Wait a second. What day is this?"

"Thursday, almost noon."

"It happened Sunday night." He rubbed disbelief from his face. "That means I wandered the rest of that night, all day Tuesday and Wednesday, too, before happening upon your place. I only have a vague memory of standing by your front door."

"That's because you fainted before you knocked. When Jake opened the door you fell inside, totally unconscious."

"It'd seem the Order and everyone in it has become targets to be discredited, disbanded, maimed, killed ... whatever. None of the corporations want us to succeed because it lessens their precious control over independent consumers."

"What 'Order' do you speak of?"

He touched his nose again and winced. "I suppose I need to back up and introduce myself. My name is Ethan Turlock. I'm an ordained member of the Order of Theocratic Minds."

Jake entered the bedroom mopping sweat from his forehead. "That wouldn't happen to be the same group I saw worshipping a rusting electrical transmission tower and few years back, would it?"

"Don't know for sure, although I'm inclined to say yes. If it were original members of Theocratic Minds, they weren't worshiping, just wishing."

Jake smiled. "They were certainly doing some powerful wishing."

Theocratic Minds is not a religious order, not really. In this godless world how could it be? But, we do adhere to rules and try to set an example on how to behave in the world. Theocratic Minds has developed a plan to bring together the smartest people we can find to re-establish technology and sanity. We insist everyone joining take a vow to harm no one. Whatever we develop and build won't be used for individual gain or as weapons. We're hoping The Order can help re-establish plain old common sense on how people should treat one another. Unfortunately, corporations, Stalwart especially, see us as competition. Regardless what we say, they believe we want control like they do. We allow our example to guide us. If corporations want to call it control ... well, okay. We can't control how they think. But, as for the Order, we'll never profit from hungry people scratching out a living from the earth. We are determined to stop that kind of desperation. We just want everyone to have choices, real choices."

Glory entered the bedroom. "I've been in that trap. Hunger and lack of hope are powerful motivators."

Ethan again came up on his elbows. "Exactly. Our Order doesn't insist on shareholder status or any kind of inclusion; we freely give of what our machines can offer to anyone in need."

"What kind of machines," Annie asked, "and if I may also ask, for someone as young as you, you speak like an intellectual far beyond your years. How is that?"

"Living around brilliant thinkers day in and day out, it's only natural I pick up some of the speech style but, as for me, I just have a gift for designing and building machinery. It comes naturally; thinking deep and philosophically does not."

"Oh." Annie nodded, satisfied with his explanation. "Go on, about the machines?"

"Sure. Well, as for the machines, there are many kinds. We've put our heads together to create steam and methane engines that power looms for cloth, mills for grinding grains, drilling systems for finding water deep inside the earth, and pumps to lift it out to irrigate long-deserted farms. But those are just examples. We've built them to be difficult and too complicated to operate by one person, purposely cumbersome. If stolen, they're useless by design. And, since ordained members cannot be coerced, Stalwart is on a campaign to scatter, eliminate or seduce the minds that created them, since there is no value beyond salvage or scrap in stealing them."

"How many of your Order survived the attack?"

"I don't know." Ethan collapsed back, letting the pillow catch his head. He looked dejected. "When I regained consciousness it was dark. I saw ten, perhaps fifteen, near me lying dead or unconscious. I ran, thinking I might be the last one alive. I can tell you that we had grown to three-hundred-seventy-three brothers and sisters. Word spread fast and those with ideas and plans for machines and systems came forward to take the vow and join us."

Ethan showed signs of exhaustion. "Now I can only assume that most of my brothers and sisters are dead, the machines destroyed and Theocratic Minds looted." A deep, quivering sigh came out, as if there might be a sob caught in his throat.

Dame Fortune's staff tapped rhythmically as she entered. All eyes turned.

As she appeared Annie said, "Ethan Turlock, I'd like you to meet Dame Fortune, the Oracle of Blister Knob." She smiled. "We call her Dame."

"Ya don't need to be introducin' young Ethan to me. But I be diddly-damn glad to meet ya, boy."

Annie snickered at Ethan's shock at her appearance and gruff manner. She figured he couldn't understand such consensus of calm over Dame's speech habits. Probably has heard lots of men, young *and* old, using far worse profanity, but this from an old woman, the one known and revered as The Oracle of Blister Knob?

Haltingly, Ethan said, "N-nice to meet you, too ... I think."

"I be supposin' you have Annie all caught up on da Order and da attack by now."

That didn't do anything to change his expression. "Yes. But how di—"

"What'd I tell ya?" Annie said with a chuckle, "Like I said, it's phenomenal what an old blind woman can see."

Dame Fortune waved her staff toward Annie. "Don't you be callin' me old."

"Oops." Annie mockingly put a hand over her mouth. "I forgot. We're the same age."

"What're you talking about," Ethan asked.

"Never mind," Annie said then patted him on the stomach. "It's a private joke."

"Jokin' aside, child, Ethan be da beginnin' of your journey."

"Am I going somewhere?"

"Maybe. But dat not what I be talkin' 'bout. I be referrin' to da direction of things to come." She brought up an arthritically gnarled index finger and tapped her temple. "A way o' thinkin' dat be puttin' you on a path to change da world."

Ethan looked to Annie, eyebrows aloft. "Wow, that's quite an endorsement of your worth." He dropped a leg over the side of the bed and turned to sit up. "You say I'm supposed to play a role in it?"

"You betcha."

"And just how am I to do that?"

"I only be tellin' you one more thing; stay close to dis girl and, Annie, you stay close to Ethan. Talk. Get to be knowin' one another from da soul out. Dats all I be sayin' 'bout dat." She left the room, her staff lightly pecking the floor all the way out the front door.

"I don't understand."

"Don't try," Annie said. "Just believe and love her."

Glory took Jake's hand and pulled. "Come on, let's let them do as Dame says and get to know one another." She suddenly stopped and looked back. "Oh, and be sure to tell Ethan about your talents." She cast her eyes on Ethan. "That fifteen-year-old girl you're sitting next to is *amazing*. Make her tell you how. Don't let her hide behind shyness. She's blessed beyond us mere mortals."

Annie blushed. "Go on you two, get out of here."

***

Annie and Ethan filled three days with long walks, talking. As Dame said, Annie formed a vision of the near future led by finding the remaining brothers and sisters of Theocratic Minds and re-establishing the Order. It also spawned an idea that included Glory's dream of creating a corporation and, maybe, let it serve as the protectorate of the Order. With such an extreme vow of benevolence, the Order needed defenders so they might work without fear.

Bruises on Ethan's face had begun to fade and the swelling was much reduced. He told her that he was beginning to feel like his old self again. She was giving him all the time he needed to get to know her and had to force remaining quiet long enough for him to process information. She had the strongest desire to chatter nonstop when around him—clearly an offshoot of infatuation. She caught herself visually exploring his face often.

Sauntering up the trail toward Blister Knob, he attempted making sense of Annie and the people she called family. "So, you're very human, like me or anyone else, huh?"

"Yep."

"But you possess advanced abilities physically and mentally, all because you're descended from genetically manufactured humans two centuries ago. Is that about it?"

She pushed out her lower lip and her eyes drifted upward. "So I've been told. And, yes, that about covers it."

"What kinds of things can you do?"

Casually kicking up dried leaves along the path she said, "Things like run fast, jump high, and my hand-eye coordination is better than most. Plus, I'm pretty good at figuring out things. You know, like puzzles and math problems ... stuff like that." She came to a halt and pointed to a particular tree across the river. "See that mockingbird on that lowest hanging limb?"

Ethan stepped behind her and sighted along her outstretched arm to the end of her pointing finger then beyond. "I don't see a bird."

125

"I do. That's something else; I have advanced vision. I can also tell you that I know the bird is building a nest because it has a blade of grass in its beak." She walked on, shuffling through the leaves on the ground. "It's not that big of a deal, though."

"Not that big of a deal! I suppose that's something else you're blessed with."

She stopped and turned. "Huh?"

"Superior modesty."

"Oh hush." She slapped his arm. "Let's talk about fun things, like my new clothes." She twirled around. "What do you think of them; pretty nice, huh? They were a gift for my fifteenth birthday from Dame. Like 'em?"

"Sure. You look really—"

A mountain lion leaped from a stout low hanging branch of an oak tree and confronted them. It growled then snarled.

"Run!" Ethan yelled.

The big cat tensed, preparing to pounce.

Before Ethan took a step, Annie grabbed his hand and yanked him to a standstill. "Don't move," she whispered from the corner of her mouth. "That's a good way to get mauled, idiot. Your face hasn't even healed yet and, now, you're inviting a lion to tear flesh from it."

Ethan tugged against her hold. She held fast and smiled. It clearly shocked him that he couldn't wrench from her grasp. Her calm finally penetrated his terror.

Still holding his wrist, she turned to the cat and said evenly, "I told you once before that such behavior is not nice." She clucked her tongue. "Frankly big fella, I won't tolerate it." She squatted and pulled Ethan down to kneel beside her. "It appears as though you're hungry and on the prowl again." As she spoke, she surreptitiously picked up a stone slightly smaller than her fist. With the same hand, she waggled a disciplinary finger at the beast. "Uh-uh. I see you looking at this guy beside me. I don't have an extra one this time and this turkey is mine."

"Turkey?"

"Hush, this is between the lion and me. It doesn't concern you ... unless it eats you, of course."

Ethan again tried to pull away from her grasp.

She just smiled and kept a tight hold on him.

She focused on the cat. "You can't have him or any part of him." She shrugged. "Sorry, big fella."

"You're bow. Use your bow," Ethan whispered in nervous vibrato.

"Don't be silly. I'd no more kill him because he's hungry than I'd kill you when you get hungry."

"But what if—"

She squeezed his wrist.

The pain distorted his mouth and quieted him.

Facing the lion, she offered her friendliest smile. "Well, here we are. Once again you've put me in a quandary, a really awkward situation; how can we settle this so that no one gets hurt?"

The cat snarled, baring teeth and went into a crouch. His shoulder muscles flexed.

"Annie!"

With speed that neither Ethan nor the mountain lion could react to, she hurled the stone and hit the animal squarely between the eyes with a crack, causing it to collapse back on its haunch. It sprang back up but teetered and angled sideways. Vision skewed, it took a couple of steps then swiped at a tree with extended claws. Then all its ominous sounds and actions disappeared as it trotted up over the hill.

"What the heck just happened," Ethan asked.

"Nothing really. It just mistook you for a turkey."

"A what?"

"You know, one of those big black birds with a red waddle—"

"I know what a turkey is."

"Then why'd you ask?"

"Why'd I ask? Are you nuts?"

"I don't think so, but you might need a second opinion on that." She enjoyed toying with him but figured she'd better let him off. "Look, I just had to let my friend, the mountain lion, know that you were *my* turkey and he couldn't have you."

"Thanks, I guess."

He looked really cute when confused, except for that silly beard, of course. She made no effort to explain it further.

***

Throughout dinner Annie remained quiet and reflective, mulling conversations she and Ethan had had over the previous three days. She came to believe her destiny was indeed taking shape just as Dame Fortune had said. A plan came together.

Interrupting a buzz of conversations, she cleared her throat and readied to speak. "Excuse me. If y'all will stop talking for a minute, I need to say something."

Jake perched his chin on his palm. With his other hand, he offered her the floor. "What's on your mind, Little One?"

"Ethan and I are leaving."

His head snapped up off his hand. "What?"

The others seemed no less shocked—except Dame.

Jake's attention was no longer casual. "To go where and do what?"

"Now that I'm certain I have everyone's attention let me throw some ideas out." She looked first to Glory. "Do you still have designs on starting a corporation?"

"Well ... yes."

"Good." She turned to Ethan. "And you, do you still plan on searching out survivors of Theocratic Minds and gathering them together again into the Monastic Order?"

His head bobbed in affirmation. "You know I do."

"Excellent." She rose and walked around to stand behind Jake. And you, my friend, my savior, my father, and the glue that holds us together," she said as she wrapped her arms around his neck and put her cheek to his, "How would you like to oversee the construction of a corporate stockade with Theocratic Minds as its centerpiece? That could be part of your legacy." She kissed his cheek. "I, of course, will be the better part."

He puffed his cheeks, held it then let it all out. "That'd be some undertaking." He sandwiched her clenched hands around his neck between his. "It'd be a challenge."

"You're up to it," she said pressing her cheek into his.

Dame wiped bits of pan-seared fish from the corners of her mouth. Annie noticed the old woman's nonchalance. All the while she laid out proposals, Dame grinned and continued eating.

"I don't suppose I need to be asking or telling you anything, dear ol' Dame."

"Oh baby. I be so diddly dang proud o' you, child. My vision of dis moment not supposed to be happenin' for another week. Your mind be sharpenin' like a fine razor."

Annie straightened and clapped her hands. "Okay, here's the plan. Ethan will guide me back to Theocratic Minds; it's not far, about halfway to Stalwart down the river, fifteen miles give or take, then roughly a mile west of the river. Surviving brothers and sisters are probably living out in the weather, too scared to return to the compound, even if it's still standing. With winter coming, ability to survive will plummet. So, the sooner we leave the better our chances will be to find them and guide them to relative safety. Hopefully, we'll find a large number still alive."

"But, Annie," Jake asked, "what if Stalwart comes back in force? You're just one person; granted, an extraordinary person, but you could still be overwhelmed."

"Then we must outsmart them. Think about it; we'll have the smartest group of minds in the known world in one place at the same time. There must be many defensive things we can do that doesn't involve bloody battle."

Ethan became excited. "She's right. Why didn't we at the Order think of that before we were overrun?"

"All of you thought only about how to save the world from itself. That's a good thing. I don't want you ever feeling it necessary to think any other way. I'll put my mind to that task and only come to y'all for assistance and, maybe, the occasional idea."

Dame Fortune clapped her hands in glee. "I be lovin' this conversation."

Little Eva leaped from her chair, ran around the table and clutched Annie's leg. "You're not leavin' us, are ya?" She looked up at Annie with those cute, pleading Asian eyes.

"Eva Louise," Lana scolded, "Annie has a mission that may save a lot of lives. You want her to do what she can, don't you?"

Eva pouted then pressed her head into Annie's hip and nodded.

Annie squatted in front of the young child and took a second to admire the beauty of her delicate features as she ran a hand over the child's silken black hair. "Look at it this way, Punkin, you'll be joining Ethan, all his friends and me real soon." She looked around the table. "You all will." She pulled the youngster into an embrace. "I betcha by the time the bluebonnets bloom in the spring, someone in a brown robe will be knocking on your door and asking you to pack your things."

Eva sniffed. "Promise?"

She pushed the child back. "On my honor," she replied with her hand over her heart then kissed the youngster on the forehead.

Glory scooted her chair back and rose. "Okay then, we should get busy and pack food and lots of warm things to wear. Freezing temperatures are only days away."

Dame Fortune gave her nose a knowing tap. "I been tannin' doe skins since August. You two be needin' dem for beddin' and blankets."

Jake sat quietly, contributing nothing to the conversation.

"You okay with all this?" Annie said.

His head bobbled and he waved her off. "Sure. I'm just turning into a sentimental old fool. I'm already missing you."

"I always been knowin' you to be a fool, Jake Henderson," Dame Fortune said, "But bein' a sentimental one ... well, dat be okay."

CHAPTER SIXTEEN
PICKING UP THE PIECES

Frigid blustery north winds raked the northern territories of the former state of Texas. An Arctic front swept through in the pre-dawn hours. Annie and Ethan were on the trail at daybreak. The journey to Theocratic Minds was underway. Plummeting temperatures and drying air left Annie's face brittle. Fingers numbed by cold, she wrapped her doeskin tighter at the neck, pulling it snug against her shoulders.

As the sun fought its way higher in the sky, the north wind eventually settled. Although the air remained cold, radiant warmth from the sun in a cloudless sky felt good. Walking south, the shoulder wrap blocked most of the chilled wind. A cold bite lingered into the afternoon but calmness and sunshine made it tolerable. She and Ethan resumed the quest to know one another better. Through occasional chattering teeth, conversations began anew.

Late afternoon, tired and in need of rest, talk turned from personal inquiries to searching for a place to relax. A suitable site came into view.

Annie shucked her backpack and dropped it next to a rusted metal dome protruding from the damp earth just up an embankment next to the river. She ran a hand over the time-roughened metal, covering her palm with orange rust. She said, while dusting it from her hand, "What do you think this thing is?"

"Not is, was. They called them cars. You're looking at the top of it. Possibly there's more to it beneath the surface, non-ferrous metals especially. I suspect you're looking at the only part of the body that hasn't rusted totally away."

She pressed on it. Her finger easily penetrated and crumbled paper-thin material that she assumed had once been solid steel sheeting. "What was it used for?"

"It had four wheels, a machine that powered at least two of the wheels and people sat in it. It transported them places, taking them anywhere they wanted to go."

"Really?"

"Sure. Haven't you noticed the black gravel sometimes visible on this trail we're walking?"

"Yeah. So?"

"It used to be totally covered by it, a smooth surface for cars to roll on very fast."

"You mean people didn't have to walk or ride animals or in wagons?"

Ethan smiled. "Not if they didn't want to." He pressed a finger against his lip. "Think of it this way; if scientists two centuries ago manufactured the basic human building blocks that you descended from, then how easy do you think it would have been to create something like a car?"

She shrugged shoulders. "Makes sense, I suppose. I remember Jake telling me stories about such things when I first met him. But I was very young and my head was screwed up. I didn't listen very well." She looked back at the rusting lump. "I wonder what it must have been like to ride in something like that? Wonderful, I bet."

"I hope someday I'll be able to show you. If we can't make it happen and another couple of centuries pass, give or take, it'll go the way of legends. You're a great example of what I'm talking about. You have evidence of a car's existence right there next to you, yet it's like a whimsical fantasy. Can you imagine the arguments in the future when someone insists these things had existed without the advantage of hard evidence?"

"Good explanation."

"Some will believe, most won't; it'll pass as bedtime stories for children or demonic black magic that religious zealots will avoid talking about. They won't understand the science behind such things. Since they won't understand, then," he shrugged and gave a look of mock disbelief, "it must be the *devil's* doing, right?"

"I think I've just had a glimpse at how smart you are ... about some things, mind you."

"Was that a compliment or—"

She slapped a hand over his mouth and put a finger to her lips. She turned an ear to the trail.

Voices grew stronger beyond a bend in the path not far ahead.

She grabbed Ethan's hand and her backpack and slid down the short drop-off, pulling him off his feet to the river's edge. She crabbed sideways into a tangle of vines, waving for Ethan to join her. Preparing for any eventuality, she removed the red cloth that bound long, sandy blonde hair back in a ponytail, gathering it then retying the strip. She then raised her head just high enough to see the trail above them.

From around the curve in the path walked a young woman. She had on the heavy brown robe of Theocratic Minds, like Ethan wore, dotted in leaves and dead grass. She apparently had been lying on the ground—maybe hiding, maybe sleeping. Four Stalwart suppliers followed closely, taunting her.

"Please leave me alone," she begged. "You've ravaged my home and killed my friends. What do I have left to give, my soul?" Despondent, the girl no longer feared them. It was obvious the four men knew that but chose to be entertained at her expense.

Ethan put his lips to Annie's ear. "That's Nina. We have to help her." He came up on his knees.

She yanked him down and put a finger to her lips, offering a frown and negative headshake.

His face drew down. He whispered, "Can't you razzle dazzle 'em, run circles around 'em. throw rocks or something?"

Her mouth stiffened into a thin straight line. She pinched his earlobe between thumb and forefinger until in pained him and pulled it close.

He grimaced.

"Don't be an idiot," she whispered. "I'd rather face that mountain lion than four adult men because I'd be forced to kill or be killed. If they wanted to harm her, it would've already happened. Why would I pick a fight if they haven't hurt the girl and probably won't? For common sense's sake, hush and don't move."

As she pushed her body higher to see better, her booted foot touched something farther down the embankment within the random mesh of vines. It was a human skeleton. Vines laced through the mouth and eye sockets of the skull. It conjured a vision from years ago of an old man she and Jake met on the trail. The remnant of that straw hat and the cane fishing pole was all she needed to see to realize the remains were his. It appeared the old man had been fishing and died where he sat. *I hope he went peacefully.*

After a time, back up on the footpath, and many crude remarks later, including a lewd threat to take the girl's robe, the Stalwart men lost interest in the mean-spirited game and moved on.

Ethan turned to Annie. "Think it's safe now?"

Her eyes were full of tears but nodded for him to go on.

"What's the matter?"

"Just go to Nina. Let her know we're here. I need a moment alone."

"Annie, what's wrong?" He then saw the object of her gaze. "It's just bones. People die and go unburied all the time."

"*Just go,*" she snapped. I'll explain it when you bring your friend back." She watched Ethan grudgingly trot up the trail before turning her attention back to the skeleton. She removed the remaining end of the cane pole from the fleshless clutch of the fingers. "I'll respect your wishes," she said to the bones, then sniffed. "I don't see your copper pan or knife. I guess they were stolen, but I'll keep this piece of your pole as a reminder of your kindness that day long ago. I hope you died knowing that you weren't forgotten."

Ethan reappeared followed closely by the robed girl. "Annie, I'd like you to meet Nina."

Annie smiled. "Sorry you have to see me this way. Not exactly a good first impression, I know."

"It's nice to meet you," Nina said, "And don't worry about that. I've cried so much the past couple of days that I'm out of tears."

Ethan pointed to the bones. "Did you know that person, Annie?"

"Yeah."

"He must have been special. How long did you know him?"

"A few hours about five years ago."

"A few hours! You've got to be kidding."

Annie rose. As she rubbed dirt from the short length of bamboo and broke rotted twigs from it. "If it hadn't been for this gentleman, Jake and I might have gone very hungry that day. He also told us about the Oracle of Blister Knob, so it's likely I'd never have met Dame Fortune if we hadn't happened upon him. And if we hadn't, we wouldn't have built that cabin; Glory may not have found us. And, Ethan Turlock, this old gentleman affected you as well. He may have saved your life."

"How could that be? I never met the guy."

"Doesn't matter. All of those things led to the evening you fell unconscious against our door. Simply put, without the help of this man, my family and I may never have built that cabin. Do you realize what that means?"

"I guess not."

"If Jake and I hadn't met this man, you could have died that night lying in the woods where a cabin should've been."

"It's amazing how you connected all those events," Nina said.

"Not really," Annie said. "Human existence requires connections. Everything we ever say or do reverberates into the future affecting the lives of people we've never met and may never know."

Annie faced the river. "I believe my time on this earth is tied to this truth."

"You sure don't think and talk like a fifteen year old girl."

She grinned. "I've been told I have good genes ... whatever that means."

"She's right," Nina said to Ethan. "It's something I need to remember. Not only good deeds but evil ones live on, too. It doesn't matter if a person is in a corporation, an independent consumer, a member of a monastic order or just an old man fishing, we're all connected."

Annie accepted Ethan's hand. She climbed up onto the trail to join them. "She took Nina's hand in a friendly way. "I apologize for not having said it sooner, but I am pleased to meet you." She looked to Ethan. "Well, friend, one accounted for and three-hundred-seventy-one to go. Let's eat."

"Good idea." Ethan flipped open the top of his knapsack. "Afterwards," he said, withdrawing bread, venison jerky and a turnip while looking around in the bag, "we'll veer west. This is a good place to leave the river trail and head that way. We might make Theocratic Minds shortly after dark. I hope there's something left to get back to."

***

A harvest moon had risen. The three stood fifty yards out from the compound. After a quick survey of the grounds Annie understood why it'd been easily overrun; no enclosure of any kind, just a cluster of loosely organized buildings—no design thought given to security. It obviously had not been a consideration. Add in a vow of absolute non-violence and the outcome could have been predicted.

Annie shook her head, disbelieving an entire colony of mechanical geniuses hadn't considered their own safety. "Humph. Well," she sighed, "at least they didn't torch the place. The buildings appear intact." She took the lead. "Let's not hurry. If all the buildings were left standing, Stalwart people may have remained behind, or others could have taken refuge from the cold. Either way, skittish people, or even animals, may be in one or more of the buildings. We might spook someone or something into attacking."

Ethan pointed to a specific place, "See that smallish building off to the left?"

"What about it?"

"That's our Think Tank," Nina offered.

"It'd be a good place to spend the night," Ethan said. "If it hasn't be ransacked, there're divans we can sleep on."

Trotting on the tips of toes, they ran to it and flattened against the outside wall. They listened. The brilliant moon in a cloudless sky made things easier to see. The air quickly chilled again after sunset. They huffed frosty air into the moonlit night. Hearing nothing, Annie waved for them to follow. She glided sideways along the wall.

As he slid along, Ethan asked in a whisper, "Where're all the bodies?"

"I don't know," Nina said. "I ran around and over many of them trying to get away that night."

Annie reached the front door. It was ajar. She removed the bow from her shoulder, then strung and nocked an arrow. She adjusted her backpack. "Wait here." She craned her head around the jamb and examined the interior. Moonlight streamed through un-shuttered windows. It was only one room. A quick scan of the interior relieved her. Raising her voice slightly, she said, "Come on. There's no one here."

She closed the door behind Ethan, the last one in, and barricaded it with a divan. She could sleep on that one, get some sleep and guard the door at the same time. When she began shuttering and bolting windows, it darkened rapidly. Holding the final shutter, she hesitated. "You think I should leave one open for light?"

Ethan looked to the ceiling then to the wall. "I don't think so. They didn't destroy the lamp."

"What lamp?"

"See that petcock mounted to the wall with a metal tube running through the wall outside and the other end up to this hanging lamp over our heads?"

"Petcock? You mean that thing shaped like a butterfly?"

"Yeah. It attaches to a methane tank outside. It's a flammable gas. There may be some still under pressure." He pulled the counter-weighted lamp down to eye level. "Turn it just a little. I'll listen and determine if there's gas left in it."

She put her hand on the valve and cranked it around. The lamp hissed.

"Too much! Turn it off."

Nina snickered.

She reversed it and yanked her hands away as though bitten. She froze. "What happened?"

"Like I said, the gas is under pressure." He pulled a piece of flint and steel from inside his robe. "Let's try this again. Turn the valve ever so slightly." He struck the tools together, sparking it over the orifice, and a small blue flame popped to life. "Turn it up a little more." He glanced back. "I do mean *a little*." The room flooded with comforting amber light. "That's good. Leave it right there." He grinned. "If I'd lit it and you cranked the valve like you did the first time, it would have burned the hair off my head."

"Sorry."

"No harm done. How do like that for light?"

Amazed, Annie turned full circle noticing how well everything had illuminated. "It's marvelous, much better than candles." She suddenly realized it shined like a beacon through the one open window and hurried to bolt shutters.

"If you think this is miraculous then Nina and I have our jobs cut out for us educating you to what had been true technologically in the past— and can be again. By the way, don't get too excited about this lamp. It's just burning off accumulated gas from the digester. It hasn't been maintained. And, now, it's too cold outside for methane production. The light will probably go out shortly."

Nina yawned. "It's nice, if only for a few minutes." She stretched, lifting her hands toward the ceiling. "It'll be fun showing Annie what Theocratic Minds is all about." She smacked then licked her lips. "I hope there's something left to show her." She shuffled heavy-headed to one of the upholstered divans. She sat, then wilted over and curled on her side.

"I don't mean to be rude but I can't stay awake a moment longer." Even as she spoke, the words trailed and became incomprehensible. She drifted off—asleep seconds later. Her breathing leveled out and became even.

"She's exhausted." Annie glanced at Ethan. "I agree with her apprehension about the condition of things; there won't be much left, I'm afraid." She unfurled one of the doeskins and covered the girl barely older than she. "I bet she's only had a few hours' sleep since the attack."

Annie stood for a moment looking down at her new friend. "What's her last name?"

"Masters … Nina Masters." He looked back at Annie. "Come to think of it, I don't know your last name."

"I don't say it aloud, and won't ever." Melancholy shaded her tone.

"That's an odd answer."

"It's more than a name. It's the first ten years of my life. I hold that time so dear that it's painful when I recall it. I can't forget and don't want to. I owe my mother that much. But I can't bear reminders every hour of every day of that life. It's my worst weakness. I love too much and I care too much. I can't stop it, but I'm working to control it. I have to learn to let sad things go. Hesitation at the wrong time could get me killed, friends and family, too. That's why it's more than just a name to me. Can you understand?"

"I think I do." He smiled. "I think I'm getting a glimpse at just how smart you are … about some things, mind you."

Her face brightened. "Well played. I deserved that one." She backhanded him on the arm. "Let's just say my last name is Henderson. I don't think Jake would mind if I shared his."

"Judging by what I saw, I think he'd be touched to tears."

"I think so, too." She snapped straight and walked across the room to break a powerful sentimental spell. "That's enough of that. Let's talk about Nina. What's her story?"

"Intelligent and good hearted. She turns twenty this month. She thinks her parents are alive and living far to the south. They're members of a corporation called Wellworth. Nina believed it was losing control of its shareholders. A strike seemed imminent, which usually means sides chosen, battle lines drawn and people killed. She couldn't convince her parents to break away from their comfort zone and join her, even though that so-called *comfort zone* has probably crumbled. So, she set out on her own and stumbled upon Theocratic Minds. I'm not as confident as she is about her parents."

"My birthday is in November, too … sort of." She yawned, then turned back to Nina, stepped over and tucked the doeskin tight around her. "Nina Masters and I will be great friends." With the lightest touch, she affectionately stroked Nina's upper arm. The young woman had a short boyish cut of fine brown hair to just below her ears, face overly thin with a straight nose and a dusting of pale freckles over it. She had a slight overbite and appeared younger than twenty, more like a young teen.

"You and I had better get some sleep, too."

Ethan stretched tall. "You don't have to tell me twice."

Annie slept through the night in a dreamless slumber. Nine hours later she woke. It felt like the flutter of an eyelid since snuggling under the doeskin on the divan. She looked across the room and saw Ethan was gone. She snapped a glance at the divan Nina had been on. She wasn't there. *They shouldn't be running willy-nilly around here without protection.*

She leaped up reaching for her backpack. She changed her mind and snatched up only the bow and quiver. She threw open the door and rushed outside to find them sitting on the porch watching the sunrise, both wrapped in a single doeskin, sitting on a small bench.

"Don't ever leave again without telling me where you're going! You scared me."

Ethan's shoulders bounced in a quick shrug. "Sorry; didn't mean to upset you."

Nina snuggled closer to him. "We came out here so we wouldn't disturb you."

"We were reminiscing. It's scary contemplating who of our friends that might be dead. It's hard not knowing."

"Oh. I, uh, just didn't know where y'all had gone and I got worried."

"I appreciate the concern," Nina said, then gestured to the sun breaking the plane of the eastern horizon. "Isn't that magnificent?"

Annie's anxiety melted away. "Look at all those colors. It's sure worth a look." She made a cursory scan of the area. "Speaking of looking, now that we're all up, I want to see what this place is all about, starting with the contraption that makes gas for the lamp. But let's be quiet. We still don't know who we might come across."

Ethan rose. "Follow me." He walked to the corner of the building then around to the side. He gestured toward two tanks boxed in by a short wooden fence that had been insulated by a deep packing of straw, a hefty tube connecting the two tanks. Then a smaller tube extended from the second tank through the wall into the building. He pointed to the larger tank. "That's the digester. We mix a tea of excrement, human and animal, and then pour it in. When kept warm it produces methane gas."

"I assume it's not the kind of tea you drink. Right?"

"Oh, yuck!" Nina shuddered then chuckled. "I don't want to hang around the troll that would."

"The tea," Ethan said, being patient with Annie, also enjoying being able to teach, "turns waste into a free-flowing liquid. In an oxygen-free environment and, staying very warm, a bacterium creates a flammable gas under pressure in the second tank. That's methane. We have these small units on all the buildings, but the smaller units are not efficient once the weather gets cold because of how warm the digester must be to produce the gas. In the winter, we have one large digester heated by a wood fire, but its use is limited to powering a small internal combustion engine that turns a long driveshaft into a shop that powers woodworking tools: stuff like saws, drills, presses, etc. I don't need to see it to know it has been destroyed or stripped for salvage."

"You mentioned animal waste," Annie said. "You keep animals?"

"We did. But I'm sure they've all been taken. We had pigs, chickens, sheep, cows and ducks. You'll see the various pens and enclosures as we walk through."

"Show me what else you did."

"Have you noticed the walls of all our cabins," Nina asked.

"They're smooth."

Nina nodded. "We have a saw mill powered by a steam engine."

"Not have, had," Ethan said, staring in that direction. "It's all been destroyed."

As they walked, Annie stepped in close beside him and draped an arm over his shoulders. "Don't let it get you down. Put it in perspective and look at each thing, one at a time, as a small problem that needs to be taken care of." She gave his braided beard a playful tug. "We can get this place back to what it was, but first we have to locate survivors."

"Maybe you're right."

"Maybe? What the heck do you mean 'maybe'?" She smacked him on the arm.

"Okay, okay. You're absolutely correct. Better?"

She rolled her eyes playfully. "Much."

Annie searched from building to building. Ethan and Nina followed. No one else was around. All the machinery had indeed been destroyed— hacked up with axes, useable parts stolen. But all the buildings had been spared. It was odd they didn't burn it all, a blessing she chose not to question. It was a head-start on resurrection. More importantly, there would've been insufficient time to build shelter before winter winds drove temperatures to frigid levels and kept them there for weeks at a time. She'd already had a taste of winter on the trip from Blister Knob and it'd only get colder.

Arriving at the end of the cluster of buildings, disturbed earth near a tree line a hundred yards away up a gentle incline came into view. It looked to be a crude graveyard, all fresh, numbering eighty-two. "Now, the search is for two-hundred-eighty-nine," she muttered, then said boldly, "Look, I know this is sad but there's a positive here; survivors are somewhere close. Someone had to have buried all these people. Stalwart invaders wouldn't have taken the time to do it."

Ethan cupped his mouth and yelled to the tree line, "I'm Ethan Turlock. If there are survivors of Theocratic Minds, please come out."

They waited and listened. No response.

"Come on, Annie," Ethan said, "I'll show you the water well that we drilled and the field that it irrigates."

They hiked a short distance in the opposite direction from the tree line and saw that the water well pump had been vandalized. Even the two-acre truck patch of corn, peas, tomatoes and squash had been ransacked then destroyed. For some reason, the cotton patch had been left unharmed. Nina sighed. "The corn and peas had dried and we were going to pick all of it and store it for winter." Then she became emotional. "Why ... why can't they leave us in peace?" She dropped to her knees.

"Because you threaten them," Annie said. "Total control is all they know. Without that, they're nothing. Simply put, you scare them." She tucked her hands under Nina's arms and pulled her to her feet.

Nina let out a sardonic laugh. "Look at me. I don't weigh a hundred pounds, robe and all, and you're telling me I scare *them*?"

Annie eyed Nina head to toe and noticed how deceptively slight built she indeed was. The heavy brown robe that extended to her knees concealed a gaunt creature, stick-like legs exposed beneath it and sunken cheeks were strong visible evidence. Even in the morning sun, the young woman's hair had no sheen, almost as if there were a dusty haze over it. Nina couldn't have been much over five feet tall, a solid eight inches shorter than she.

"It's your intelligence. Theocratic Minds is perceived as a direct assault on their ability to keep shareholders. What y'all were accomplishing, just by its nature, encouraged independent consumers to shun shareholder status. If you succeed, their world will crumble without Theocratic Minds forcing its will on anyone. They don't care about any of you individually. But, as a group, you're a force to be reckoned with. If you hadn't been alone, those four men harassing you on the trail would've killed you. To them, you were a wing without a bird. That's why I want to set up a protectorate to allow your ideas to flourish without worry. Without you're fear of them, they'll have nothing."

"Look!" Ethan said, pointing toward the tree line.

Annie turned while reaching across to her opposite shoulder to remove the bow. From the thicket of scrub oak and cedar trees, a host of robed individuals began appearing, like ants from a mound, led by a man well over six feet tall in his mid-thirties and bald.

"It's Henry!" said Ethan and Nina simultaneously. Both trotted in his direction.

Annie held back, gauging potential threats that might crop up — like Stalwart suppliers in hiding that could be forcing the group out as decoys. But, she saw nothing except jubilant faces — except on Henry's big moon face.

She slowly advanced. The late morning autumn sun shined into her eyes. The air held crisp freshness. As she tilted her head and shielded her eyes for the best possible view of the large man, she made a move to follow her friends.

Ethan and Nina slipped into the crowd behind Henry.

"Stop right there," he ordered. "Lay your bow and quiver on the ground."

She did as he ordered, placing the weapon at her feet. "I'm glad to see that so many of your members are okay. What's the number of survivors?"

"That's not important. Who are you? Why are you with Nina and Ethan?" Tall and defiant, he stood unmoving between her and the group. His arms remained tightly crossed over a massive chest.

"My name is Annie Henderson. Last week, Ethan stumbled upon my family's cabin about fifteen miles north of here. He was injured, exhausted and hungry. Once we had him healed on his feet, it was agreed that I'd accompany him back here and assess the likelihood of building some type of protectorate for Theocratic Minds."

"And just how does a young girl go about protecting such a large group of people?"

"You and your family of creative minds use your intelligence to build machines and systems for the betterment of all, whereas my creativity is channeled in another direction."

"Sorry. I can't take the chance that you aren't trying to set us up for another attack." He held out a large square palm. "Hand over your weapon."

"Oh, Henry … that is your name, right?"

He nodded. "The weapon! Now!"

"I'm sorry. I can't do that."

Apparently Ethan noticed the developing confrontation and alerted Nina. They emerged from the crowd and went back. A group of brown robed people followed them down the treeless gentle slope, creating a semi-circle. "Remember your vow, Henry," Ethan said.

Never taking his eyes off Annie he said in a terse voice, "I broke my vow the night we were attacked. I saved lives but it took a cedar fence post applied to Stalwart suppliers' heads to make it happen, the only persuasion they understood."

Ethan advanced. "That's okay, Henry. We can — "

"Stay back!" the big man thundered. "I've taken it upon myself to protect Theocratic Minds against evil connivance from people like her. I'll not be living by that vow ever again."

He moved on Annie.

"You don't understand," said Nina.

"Well enough, I'd say."

Annie finally broke her silence. "Don't worry about me, guys. Being fifteen and a girl I've always known there'd be situations in which I'd have to prove myself. I'm sure this won't be the last."

"I'll be taking that bow now," Henry said reaching for it.

With lightning speed, Annie slapped the back of his big hand then waved a cautionary finger. "Uh, uh, uh, big guy, I wouldn't do that if I were you."

He swung a disciplinary backhand at her face.

Still smiling, she ducked. His big arm whooshed over the top of her head. "Come on, let's not play this game. I want to help and be your friend."

"Henry! Stop!" Ethan shouted.

Annie waved him off. "Don't worry, Ethan, he's not going to hurt me."

"I'm worried about him not you."

Annie snickered. "Oh."

Now angry, Henry balled a fist and swung it in a wide arc at Annie's face.

She simply bent her knees and leaned away from it. His knuckles whizzed by, a fraction of an inch from the end of her nose.

Straightening, she popped the big man on the forehead with the heel of her hand so fast he couldn't avoid it and with such force his head snapped back.

His eyelids fluttered as he stumbled backward.

Annie pleaded, "Come on, Henry, let's not do this anymore."

Refusing to give up, he charged.

Employing an elementary maneuver, Annie sidestepped, hooking a foot around his left ankle.

Like Goliath with a stone between the eyes, he fell. His face went into a grass clump. He turned his head, spitting grass and dirt.

Annie fell on top of him with the point of her knee in his neck.

He went still.

"I know you won't believe me, but I can break your neck quite easily. But I don't even want to bruise you, much less kill you." She removed her knee from his neck, leaned over and kissed the top of his bald head. "Please, Henry, let's be friends. I could really use your help."

Nina knelt beside Henry and bent until her face was in his at ground level. "Well, big man, do you believe her now?"

He rolled over and Annie gave him a hand up. "I guess I have to," he said to Nina.

Still defiant, he looked to Annie. "But, you'd better be working on our behalf or someday you may *have* to break my neck. I won't let you or anyone else hurt these people ever again. They're my family."

"Got it." She threw her arms around his big waist and laid her head against his broad chest. "It's so nice to meet you, Henry."

CHAPTER SEVENTEEN
WINTER WONDERLAND NIGHTMARE

Annie's presence emboldened Henry to convince residents to come out of the woods and move back into the dormitories of the Monastic Order—the first step and only way to survive the coming winter.

November segued into December, with warm days scarce. Long term comfort and security began by getting ready for the cold months upon them. Judging by deteriorating conditions, it appeared severe winter cold would be the rule rather than the exception; certainly no time to be wandering in the woods regardless how safe it seemed.

A member of the Order noticed that of the six underground grain silos only five had been raided and emptied. One had been overlooked, having been built isolated from the clustered five. The round silo, sectioned into three triangular storage shafts, was each filled to capacity with corn, wheat and millet. Carefully reserving seed portions and supplementing with wild meats and foraged root vegetables, it should provide food for the nearly three hundred people during the cold months to come.

On yet another snowy morning, Annie sat by the fire next to Nina. They shared a short stool designed for one person. Annie shoulder-nudged Nina. "Where's Ethan?" They warmed their hands, held out to crackling flames in the stone fireplace of the two-story communal dormitory. "He's been absent a lot lately."

"He's been ... busy."

Annie cast a sidelong glance at her friend. "Why so secretive?"

Nina offered a Cheshire cat grin. "Me, secretive? Humph!" She feigned offense and turned up her nose.

"Uh-huh, you. What's going on?"

Others began gathering in the room but stood away; all looking pleasant enough but guarded, as Nina did.

All at once, the group began forming a tightening circle around her.

"Okay, y'all are acting really strange and, frankly, a little scary."

"Stop behaving like someone is about to attack you," came a voice from behind the circle of people. Ethan appeared from between two of them holding something wrapped in a rag. "We wanted it to be a surprise."

"What?"

"This." He held out the item rolled in an oil-soaked cloth.

"What is it?"

He huffed. "Just open it."

She regarded the offering. "Does it bite?"

Daniel Lance Wright

"Quit asking silly questions."

From where she sat, Annie reached and took it from Ethan. She held it in both hands and looked at it as if it were an injured bird. It smelled of bees wax and oil.

"Open it," Nina said.

Shortly, the small group turned into a larger one of brown robed men and women of all ages.

Annie scanned the circle of people. "What have y'all been up to?" she muttered as she fondled the wrapped item in her hands. Uncertain what to expect, she carefully unrolled the rag to reveal a tooled leather scabbard encasing a knife. The leather boasted a deeply tooled cursive "A" centered with vines and flowers running from it in both directions. It was stained to a dark brown and smelled of new leather.

Ethan snorted smugly. "I got tired of you always borrowing my knife to skin animals or whittle wood."

Annie pulled the knife from its sheath. The polished handle glowed — well-cured red mesquite root had been expertly carved to fit a hand but the end left in a natural curly gnarl. A six-inch blade glistened like a silvery jewel curving slightly to its thorn-sharp tip, complete with blood groove and brass slip guard. Her lip quivered. "You did this for me?"

Ethan fanned his arms wide. "We all agreed that you deserved it for putting us back together."

Henry, who'd been standing to the side with that permanent scowl and arms crossed over his big chest, said, "And don't even be thinkin' about throwin' that thing at me. Got that, little girl?"

Annie laughed through watery eyes. "The only things I'll be throwin' at you are kisses."

"Come spring," Nina said, "some of the girls and I will make you a change of clothes from real cloth of cotton and wool ... once the loom has been rebuilt, of course."

"Don't you like the outfit Dame Fortune, the Oracle of Blister Knob made for me?" She looked down at her furry rabbit vest over the loose linen-like shirt tucked into doeskin pants, the legs stuffed inside tall leather boots as usual.

"Sure I do. The look is very ... practical. But, don't you want something a little girlier you could wear once in a while? We have to wear these itchy old robes all the time as part of our vow, but I don't see any reason you should wear the same thing all the time. If I can't dress myself up then I'll dress you up."

The girls and women among the gathering murmured agreement.

As she continued looking up into the faces of the crowd, Annie suddenly felt small and naked. She pulled her knees together and crossed her arms over her breasts. "I suppose that'd be okay. I'm not accustomed

146

to this much attention."

Ethan stepped to her side. "From what I've seen, you'd better get used to it because you'll be the center of it most of the time. For what it's worth," He rocked his head back and forth shyly, "I think you're beautiful just the way you are."

Annie's cheeks turned radiant rose. She beamed affection for the young man with the shoulder length auburn hair and braided beard and then pressed a cheek against the back of his hand. "Thank you."

Still baffled by it all, she turned to the crowd at large. "But, all this consideration is undeserved. All I've done is help y'all move back into the dormitories."

Nina nodded. "Right. Like Ethan said, you put us back together. That may seem like nothing to you, but we couldn't get it done before you came." She playfully backhanded Annie on the arm. "And, girl, that's *somethin'*."

***

Hard winter weather persisted for weeks—sometimes snow, sometimes ice, but always cold. February came and yet another blast raced down, bringing an ice storm that broke limbs from trees. Others sagged to the ground.

Annie woke to a world coated in ice, creating an awesome silvery wonderland. It was calm. An urge welled fast to be outside enjoying nature's ice sculptures. She scampered down the stairs to see the big man.

"Hey, Henry, care to join me on a hunting expedition to the river?"

The big man stood, back to the fireplace, warming his derrière. His eyes drifted to the ceiling then snapped back. "Sure. Why not?" He stepped to the corner of the room and retrieved a five-foot spear with a long iron tip sporting multiple barbs—a design intended only for hunting. It was for penetrating flesh, then remaining stuck to slow a wounded animal's retreat and make plenty of noise dragged through underbrush.

Ethan sat at a table tinkering with salvaged parts of aluminum and copper, disassembling and cataloguing them.

"How about you, Master Turlock? Care to tag along?"

Without looking up, he grinned. "Master, huh?"

"Better'n *hey you*, don't you think?"

He chuckled. "Thanks, but no. I need to finish this, then join the brothers in a trip to that disintegrating power plant west of here. There're plenty of useable things to be salvaged. We need to get ready to rebuild machinery as soon as the weather breaks."

Annie skipped to his side then snatched his hand up and tugged.

"Aw, come on. You need to get out and do something that requires less brainpower for a while. You never know, we might find more things to laugh about. Whaddaya say?"

Ethan finally looked up. "I don't know Annie. I really need to get this done."

She tossed a thumb over her shoulder toward Henry. "Besides, ol' Henry over there has a big problem just smiling; I need someone with a sense of humor to come with us."

Henry's permanent scowl deepened. "Don't expect that to change any time soon."

"Ya see?" She giggled. "Even he admits it. I think Henry's genetically incapable of enjoying himself." She pushed her lip out then whined, "Come on. Please." She dropped his hand then clapped. "Tell you what. When we get back I'll help you finish that."

Ethan's stare went deadpan. He tugged at the braids of his sparse beard then let out a deep sigh. "Oh, okay, just don't forget you promised to help."

Annie came to attention and crossed her heart. "I always keep my promises," she said in a solemn tone. Then her face metamorphosed into a big grin. "Especially for you."

Henry rolled his eyes. "I think I'm getting queasy. Let's go before I lose the bulgur I had for breakfast."

Although the morning air remained far below freezing, it was calm—not a whisper of moving air. Nonetheless, the cold stung her face and carried a metallic smell. The walk down the well-traveled path near the Brazos River seemed to take no time at all as they marveled at nature's various ice formations within the flora. It was mid-morning and low-hanging clouds evened the light. There were no shadows and Annie's hearing sharpened beyond her already well-above-average range in the calmness and insulating effect of the low clouds.

She stopped walking. "Shh. Y'all hear that?"

Henry and Ethan canted and twisted their heads, but offered only apologetic headshakes and shrugs.

She kept a finger to her lips and whispered, "There are people walking the trail toward us." She glanced about. "Come on."

She led the two men up the hill away from the river where there was less ice, hopefully reducing noise they'd make searching for a hiding place. They stood behind a cluster of denuded Staghorn Sumac bushes, providing just enough cover to break their outline, but preferable to chancing noisy crackling ice that coated denser brush.

Annie noticed when the sound of a conversation in subdued tones finally became audible to Ethan and Henry—they reacted with silent expressions.

Four men and two women came into view. They weren't mere travelers but Stalwart suppliers. The men were clean-shaven and the women's hair brushed and bound, likely hunting for things to steal.

Henry leaned over, placing his lips near Annie's ear. "Is there reason we need to be concerned?"

She glanced at her new knife strapped to her waist then clutched the string of the bow over her shoulder. "Let's not tempt them to take what little we do have if we can avoid it." She looked across to see Ethan's neutral expression. It seemed the presence of those people didn't trouble him in the slightest—an odd twist on how she knew him to be.

The six walked in to plain view a few feet below them but acted unobservant, engrossed in conversation about things concerning Stalwart. It appeared as though they might walk on by.

Annie began to breathe easier but then ice crunched to her right.

She looked across Henry to Ethan. He had pushed a thumb-size sapling and the ice encrustation fell to the ground. In the calm quietness, it might as well have been thunder.

All six people drew their blades and held them at the ready.

Henry clutched his spear with both hands and prepared to advance.

Annie grabbed his wrist. "No, Henry, no violence if we can help it." She glared at Ethan with a disappointed frown meant only for him. She then focused on the six people below them on the trail. She put on a happy face. "What do y'all think about this ice? Beautiful, isn't it?" she called out.

A leader emerged, one of the men. He stepped forward. "Yes it is." The obligatory smiles stretched rubicund cheeks.

"Y'all just passin' through?"

"In a manner of speaking."

"Where ya heading?"

"Here and there."

"Okay," Annie said with a drawl. "You're already here so where is there?" She chuckled, hoping to draw out a semblance of humor. But she saw no change, just those idiotic smiles. *Maybe I can defuse this yet.* She stepped from behind the bushes and sauntered down to the trail. "Where're y'all from?" She held out a friendly hand to the leader.

He looked at the hand but refused it. "So, you're the one," he said.

Annie went rigid and studied the man. "Have we met?"

"No." His fingers worked over the grip of his long knife, clutching it tighter.

"I don't understand. 'I'm the one' ... what? I don't know any of you." She tilted her head. "Do I?"

"Never mind. It's unimportant. We're from a corporation called Stalwart. Ever hear of it?"

"Sure have. Tell me about it. It sounds like a fascinating place."

"It's good you want to know because that's what we do; we travel the countryside explaining to people we meet how important corpocracy is for the future of mankind. Corporations, like Stalwart, will be the salvation of the world's problems. We advise folks to join us in the good fight. Will you?"

"It's awfully nice of you to invite us," she said, "but I choose to remain an independent consumer." She gestured to Ethan and Henry. "So do my friends." She noticed Henry coming from behind the bushes and walking her direction. Ethan remained unmoving, watching.

"That's certainly your choice," the man said. "Now, we must negotiate for payment of the valuable information we shared."

The other three men encircled her. The two women stepped in nearer the leader. The fake smiles suddenly became sinister.

"As you can see," Annie told them, "we have nothing to offer. But we strive to be good humanitarians. So, if you care to hang around, we plan to hunt along the river and, if we kill more than we can carry, we'd be happy to share it with you in exchange for that wonderful information. Deal?"

Again she held out a friendly hand. Again, it was shunned. Waiting for his reply, she noted positions, especially the man behind her and the two at her sides, barely within peripheral vision. Any threatening move made would begin with the leader whom she faced.

The leader's grin widened. "You're only fifteen years old, aren't you?"

"How do you know that?"

"Not important. I must insist you hand over that knife, the bow and quiver of arrows and, of course, I need the big man's spear."

Annie sighed. "I was so hoping we might become friends."

"Oh, we'll stay friendly, but first you have to hand over the items."

"That's what I mean. It ain't gonna happen ... *friend*."

She noticed his knife hand had gone extra tight on the grip and had begun to raise it to attack height. With incomprehensible speed, she jammed fingers into both his eyes.

Before he could grab for them or make a sound from the pain, she sent flying elbows left then right, incapacitating the two men at her sides—then ducked, just as a saber whizzed over her head from behind.

Straightening, she kicked backwards and connected with the assailant's knee. He went down.

Henry joined the fray, battling both women. He held his own until they began to move farther apart, dividing his attention. One of the women was skilled with the blade. His attention focused mostly on her.

The leader regained limited vision and lunged, wailing maniacally, his bayonet high over his head, bent on a downward killing swing into the top of Annie's head. She pulled her knife and whipped it adroitly into the fleshy part of his right bicep, embedding it. He howled and dropped his weapon.

She looked and saw one of the women, now fully out of Henry's field of vision, prepared for a killing hack across his neck.

Unable to do anything else, she shrugged the bow off her shoulder, strung and arrow and let it fly with blurring speed, pointing it at the woman's upper torso.

The arrow's force sent it through her neck sticking into the frozen ground behind her.

The woman went motionless, dropped the knife, teetered sideways … then crumpled.

Fighting stopped.

Annie shook all over, realizing she'd killed the woman. There had not been enough time for a more calculated, debilitating but not mortal strike.

One of the men she'd elbowed regained full consciousness and saw what had happened. He yelled, "Emily!" He stumbled to his feet then fell to his knees beside the woman's limp body. "You've killed her! You've killed my wife!"

"I—I'm sorry." She began to cry. "She would've killed my friend if I hadn't stopped her."

"This wasn't the way it was supposed to be!" he sobbed and shouted. "This is not what Stalwart promised!"

"Shut up!" The leader shouted, then grimaced from the pain in his arm. "Get up and let's get out of here."

He turned to Annie. With no hint of the Stalwart smile, he ground clenched teeth and spewed, "This isn't over." He grabbed the grieving man by the collar with his uninjured arm and pulled him up. "Come on." The third man, holding his head, joined the surviving woman and fell in behind them.

"Annie's remorse turned to anger. "You're right. It's not over, you ignorant man!" Her voice clicked up an octave. "Go back and tell whomever it is that runs that disgusting corporation that Theocratic Minds is no longer a *defenseless* Order!"

The five Stalwart suppliers made no effort to respond.

Annie shouted to their backs, "They're a peace loving people but no longer without protection! Go on! Go back and tell 'em that!"

As she spoke, they moved on, eventually disappearing down the trail. Annie went back to the woman lying dead. She fell at her side, lifted her head and cried. "Why did you make me do this? Why is the world this way? Why?" For a time, she hugged the lifeless woman's head, rocked and sobbed, filled with remorse … she could do nothing else.

Henry and Ethan stood back and let her have this time.

Finally, through watery eyes, she looked up at Henry. "We must give her a proper burial."

"We have no tools, Annie," he said with uncharacteristic softness.

"Then I'll claw it out of the frozen earth with my bare hands!"

Ethan joined Henry. "You couldn't help what happened. It was a reaction to a situation, not a choice with time to consider options. You did the right thing."

She looked up at Henry. "It's not a choice I would've made. You know that, don't you?"

Henry obviously found her level of compassion difficult to comprehend. "I do now," he said.

"Those are good people," she said. "They're just forced into a life they have no control over. They're surviving the only way they know how. They may be roaming the countryside stealing, but they're imprisoned, nonetheless. I will empower them to make real choices without sacrificing family if it's the last thing I do in this life." She hugged the dead woman, pressed her forehead into hers and sobbed. "I will! I will!"

Then a curious question crossed her grieving mind: What did that guy mean when he said 'you're the one.' And how did he know my age?

"Stay with me, child. Don't be flyin' off now. I be needin' your mind."

Annie began walking in the direction of the voice.

"Stay right there. Don't you be goin' nowhere."

Annie only hesitated, then continued at a slow pace. She didn't know what was happening to her, but was eager to find out.

"Ya hear me, girl? I need ya to stop, or your own diddly damn thoughts will whisk ya off to … well, God may know where—I don't."

Finally, Annie heeded the command and stopped, confused by the disembodied voice and surroundings. She stood alone in a sunless meadow, yet it was drenched in light. The ambient air was not cool, not warm. Grass and flowers came up to her knees but lacked their customary fragrance. Looking at her feet, she wiggled her toes wondering where she'd left her boots. *Where am I?* Now that she realized she had no clue where she was, how could she know where she was going? She remained where the voice commanded. Besides, there was comforting familiarity in the voice and it filled her with peace, at ease with it all—just curious.

At considerable distance, a lady took shape from the air and approached. As the dark-skinned woman came fully into view, it was Dame Fortune—but not as Annie knew her. Still, she was certain. This person had black hair and the clear eyes of a sighted woman—a lovely young lady who could pass for Nubian royalty. She strode with the gait of a teenager, almost prancing, and didn't stop until she stood before Annie.

"Dame Fortune? Is that you?"

"It be for a fact, child."

"I don't understand. Where am I and how did you get here? Why do you look like that?"

"I be joinin' you in your dream, girl." She threw a sweeping gesture. "This place be a concoction of your mind 'cuz you grow weary of winter but my appearance be under my control. I see no flippin' reason to be old, blind and ugly … even if it is *your* dream."

"Now that sounds more like the Dame I know and love. Why are you coming to me in a dream? Is something wrong?"

"Not yet. But it be goin' dat way. I be comin' with a warnin', girl; be careful, a traitor lives among you within the Order. Blister Knob is about to feel the bite of that person's treachery. I best not be revealin' more dan dat. No need to explain. You already be knowin' why I can't say more. We'll see you soon … sooner dan we thought."

"But, Dame, who—who is i—" She woke in mid-sentence, the troubling revelation resounding in her ears. Throwing off the heavy quilt, she sat on the bed's edge. She shivered as feet touched the cold wooden floor—hard proof the dream had ended.

Protecting Theocratic Minds had just become complicated beyond expectations. Difficulties as yet unrealized lay in a murky future—a mystery to be solved. Her mind raced. To single out a person bent on disloyalty to Theocratic Minds troubled her. Where do I even start? There'll be no satisfaction when I do discover whom it might be; I love them all.

She forced her head away from sentimentality to a pragmatic view of what needed to be done. The logistical improbability of interrogating over two hundred people had to be worked out. No matter which tack she decided on, it would be a daunting task, a mystery not quickly solved. The mature brothers and sisters would surely be offended, scrutinized by a fifteen-year-old girl that way.

Pushing off from the bed, she shuffled on cold-stiffened legs through her bedroom. Rubbing warmth into her upper arms, she stopped at the window and opened one side of the small double-shutters.

The ice storm of the previous week may have been the crowning weather extreme of this winter but also maybe the last for this season. Even so, nights remained chilly. In the clear and calm of the darkest hours before dawn a herd of eight deer scavenged acorns beneath a broad old oak tree just beyond the wood shop. Annie breathed in freshness and exhaled a frosty puff of white.

The peaceful moment ended when she wondered: why would anyone want to give up his or her own kind? What's to be gained?

She trusted Dame and harbored no doubt her friend spoke the truth no matter how much she wanted to disbelieve. Foreboding weighted her heart as she stared into a sky of twinkling stars and the aroma of cedar wafted up on a chilled breeze. She asked questions of the night but, at the moment, only one mattered. "Why?" she breathed.

***

"You're awfully quiet. Something wrong?" Nina inquired of Annie as they prepared a trap baited with corn to catch wild chickens for domestication.

Annie straightened, centering the quiver of arrows on her back and the bow she carried over a shoulder. She sighed and considered glossing an answer to avoid the truth but, after a long pause, "I just have a lot on my mind," was all she could think to say and her statement was stilted at that.

"For someone so young, you take on too many burdens of the Order." Nina dropped the coiled cord in her hand and sat on a lush patch of soft green grass just now breaking through the dead brown blades of the previous season. "To listen to you speak, it's easy to forget how young you are. You don't talk or even sound like a fifteen-year-old." Nina looked at her for a moment with unasked questions in her eyes. "Oh well, why don't you come sit? Enjoy some of this day. It's spring, Annie." She gestured to the landscape sloping away to the river in the distance from the base of the rocky escarpment she sat atop. "Just look at that magnificent view."

Nina looked at the bird droppings beneath the cluster of cedar bushes where Annie worked to get live traps situated. "Those chickens can wait a few minutes." She picked a grape hyacinth growing next to where she sat and held it out. "Smell this. It's sweet and fruity. It should remind you of all that's good with the world, not just the bad. You worry too much."

Annie finally felt as though she had cause to smile. Only then did it occur to her that she'd been ignoring Nina all morning, mind-mired in the muck of a problem. She took the purplish-blue flower and held it to her nose. "Umm, wonderful," she muttered. "I apologize for ignoring you. Forgive me?"

"Of course."

Annie sat next to her friend and took a long thoughtful look into the distance toward the river. "You're right. It is a gorgeous day and that is a beautiful view." The words fell flat.

"What's troubling you so?"

Annie's jaw muscles worked as she had to force her mouth to remain shut. Should she share what she knew, or keep it bottled up and deal with it in silence? To say nothing or even lie about it, then move on, seemed like the prudent approach, but not to her liking. She hated feeling isolated and left to deal with the issue of a traitor alone. "Nina, you and Ethan are my best friends. We talk about a lot of things, funny things, sad things even embarrassing things. But I hold information that'd tear the Order apart if it got out before I could determine where the truth of it lies."

Nina sidled closer. "What is it?"

Annie pressed her lips tight and filled her cheeks with air until her face reddened. She held it and then exhaled in a huff. "All right, I have to tell someone or I'll explode." She pushed a rigid finger to within inches of Nina's nose. "I must have your solemn promise that you'll say nothing to anyone, not Henry, not even Ethan. Can you promise that?"

"I'm honored that you're considering sharing something so sensitive with me. I keep my promises. I hope you've noticed." She held up her right hand. "I swear this to you, Annie, I'll keep your secrets and speak only the truth, even at the high price of hurt feelings if that's what it takes." Her eyes drifted away to again gaze across the landscape. "Now, you must swear to me that you'll always remember I'm your friend and would never do anything to harm you."

"How could I forget that? A simple yes would've been good enough." Was it hurt feelings she detected for questioning Nina's loyalty?

"I know. But you have to understand the depth of my commitment."

Annie explained the dream involving Dame Fortune and why she believed it to be credible before offering the shocking disclosure. "There's a traitor within the Order, Nina. Someone at Theocratic Minds may be subverting our efforts even as we sit here."

"Who? Why?"

"I don't know. But now you see why I've been distracted."

"I'll keep my eyes and ears open. It could be I've overlooked odd behavior that might be significant. I promise I'll discuss each with you as they occur." she again made eye contact, "and only with you."

"Just knowing I'm not in this alone is a relief, but don't draw attention. If someone is willing to betray us, that person may also be capable of inflicting great harm. Until we determine the motivation behind the betrayal it should be treated as lethal. I couldn't bear it if something happened to you over something I told you."

Nina stood and presented her back to Annie. "Don't worry about me. And, for goodness sake, don't get mushy." She glanced back. "Come on, we have chickens to trap."

***

"Do you think Annie believed the dream?" Jake asked Dame. "If it were me, I'd probably dismiss it," he said with a shrug.

"But dat's da difference 'tween you an' her, ya see. You be a fool. Annie girl be smart. Dat girl got a mind so diddly dang sharp … ooh-wee!" She poked the ground between her knees with the staff as those whitened blind eyes appeared to watch something magnificent. Then Dame offered a long affirmative nod. "She be believin' it, all right. No doubt inside me 'bout dat, man."

"I'm sure you're right."

Dame sat next to him; beyond her were Glory, Lana and little Eva Louise. The other two women and the girl crouched beside the rock Dame sat on. The five huddled together. Piled on the ground were minimal possessions in bags and knapsacks. They hunkered down within a thicket of bushy cedar trees up the hill above their cabin.

"Speaking of being right, have you been able to divine a better timetable of what's coming?" he said.

"Very soon. I be seein' darkness rollin' over our homes like an evil fog. We must be stayin' here 'til it passes."

Two hours passed. Eva wanted to romp and play as any five-year-old would, too young to understand what might become of them should they be discovered. "Please Momma let me play."

Lana ran a hand over the girl's straight ebony hair. Innocent young Oriental eyes fixed on her mother with a pleading stare. "Sorry, Sweetie, I can't do that. If—"

"Shh!" Jake hissed.

"There it is!" a male voice shouted from the trail down the hill near the river. A man appeared from around the bend in the path and stood looking up toward the two structures. "Come on," the man ordered.

Coming into view behind the man were eleven more, all clean-cut and carrying the familiar twenty-four inch broad blade knives of Stalwart suppliers. But something was different: they wore menacing faces—not a smile among them.

The leader walked to the big cabin first. He didn't knock, just kicked open the door then went in followed by four others. Shortly, the leader came out and shouted to the others, "No one's here."

At Dame Fortune's dugout the scenario repeated.

"They knew we were coming," one said.

Eva whimpered.

Lana pulled the child into her lap and whispered into the little girl's ear, "If we stay quiet and don't move they'll never know we're here. When they're gone, I'll let you run and play all you want. But you've got to be quiet and still for now." She placed a light finger on the girl's lips.

Eva edged closer and leaned against her mother.

Glory, sitting on the other side of the youngster, petted the top of the child's head.

The youngster looked up.

Glory winked and smiled at her.

The men ransacked the cabins, dragging out furniture, clothing, cookware, quilts and numerous other items, piling them in a central location. Then Jake heard the leader shout, "Burn it all! Leave them nothing to come back to."

Jake took a final longing look at the cabin, remembering the blisters and blood that went into building it. It was more than shelter. It symbolized family and home, a legacy he struggled for five years to create. "They can't do that." His jaws clenched.

Dame groped until she found his hand and squeezed it. "I be knowin' what's on your mind. It be dat old Jake Henderson fear of bein' forgotten. But you be da one doin' da forgettin'; four people next to ya and one sweet youngun farther down da road wouldn't be together if it not be for you, man. You be da glue. Remember dat. It be you bindin' dis family together."

Dame's words didn't free him. The Jake of years ago re-emerged. His head sank into a mental mess, hating this world in which wickedness won every time. He wanted to bolt, to get away, to outrun fears and responsibility like he used to.

The dugout and the cabin sent licking flames skyward. Natural oils in the cedar logs accelerated destruction. Forced to sit and watch a cherished lifestyle disappear, his energy leached away. Suddenly feeling ancient, even the desire to escape vanished. He withered, deflated and defeated.

How could Dame say he was the glue that held a family together? Annie was the one—a fifteen-year-young girl that fought to protect them and friends. And it was the old lady who guided them away from harm. What did he do? What did he contribute, other than cowering in a thicket watching their homes burn?

Jake swung to the opposite extreme. An urge seized him to charge down the hill screaming, killing as many as he could before they did the same to him. It suddenly seemed doable. He flinched, seconds away from following through.

"You be keepin' it together, man," Dame said in a stern tone. "Keep a lid on dat anger. All dis happenin' da way it should. You not be seein' it but Dame do. Annie be smart for sure, but she be needin' you to guide her. Right now she be thinkin' with that blatherin' heart o' hers not her head. Even if da cabins hadn't been set to blazin', it be time to head south to help Annie anyhow."

"You disappoint me," said Glory. "After all we've been through how could you underestimate what we have? Jake Henderson, we're family. You're telling yourself the worst lie of all if you believe your legacy is that bonfire down there." She flung a dismissive gesture toward the blazing cabins. "That pile of burning sticks means nothing. I don't know what I'd do if you should fall apart." She crossed her arms over her breasts and pouted. "If you believe you're worthless then Dame is right; you are a dang fool."

"But Glory—"

"You're my rock, our rock. As long as we have one another, we can conquer the world because we're family." Glory's dark skin and large, enchanting, exotic eyes glowed with love. Even as their lives were taking a dramatic turn, she exuded satisfaction with their lot in the world.

"I couldn't have said it better," Lana said. "Uncle Jake, you," she looked at each one, "all of you are the bravest and sanest people I've ever known."

"*Uncle* Jake?" he said.

"Yeah, of course, to Eva and me."

A short time later, the cabins lay in smoldering ruins, the men gone. Eva crawled across her mother's lap, stepped around Dame, and stood eye to eye with Jake who was still down on his knees. She hugged his neck. "I love you, Uncle Jake." Finally, it was the affectionate wisdom of a five-year-old that turned his head and put his breaking heart back together.

"As always, Glory, you're right. We have to stick together and I have to keep my head screwed on straight." Embarrassed, he sprang to his feet, dusted his pants and meandered away.

***

Work at the Order progressed nicely. Everyone worked at assigned tasks, a beehive of activity. The exquisite early spring weather, sunny and mild, was infectious—putting extra snap into everyone's step as machines and mechanical systems were methodically put back into working order. There was plenty left to be done but, it became clear that before next winter, it would be as it was before the Stalwart decimation, maybe better.

Annie sought a traitor, walking the grounds of Theocratic Minds but accomplishing little. Long lingering looks became common place, searching for that one person displaying deviant behavior. She hated it. The pain of suspicion became physical. Queasiness trailed each distrustful glance.

Nina caught up to her. "Annie, have you noticed how much time Ethan has been spending at that deserted power plant?"

"No. Many of the brothers and sisters are with him. They've all been spending lots of time there. He's overseeing the salvage operation. Surely you don't suspect him?"

"I don't suspect anyone. I'm just keeping my promise to point out behavior that's out of the ordinary."

"I'm sorry."

"It's okay," she said, then in stealthier tone, "But notice when all the brothers and sisters have returned, he's always late, sometimes a half hour or more. What is he doing for that time? He never brings more stuff back. He's always empty handed, just late."

"This is why I need you." Annie embraced her. "I love both y'all so much that I automatically ruled Ethan out. I still refuse to believe it, but you've asked a question that needs an answer."

Henry approached. "The main methane digester is complete and as soon as we make enough manure tea then we'll have a constant heat source to fire our steam engine to turn the main drive shafts powering our tools. The machine and woodworking shops will be running again soon. Having them will speed the reconstruction of the water well and we'll be able to get back to work on the electric generator, too."

"Since I don't have a clue what you're talking about, I'll assume that's a good thing," Annie said.

"Oh yes, very good."

"Tell me, Henry, you've been spending considerable time at that deserted power plant, haven't you?"

"Certainly, it's rich with copper wire, aluminum and even some galvanized steel that hasn't rusted away yet."

"Have you paid much attention to Ethan?"

"How do you mean?"

"Does he stay with the group at all times?"

"Mostly, I suppose."

"Mostly? Does he disappear occasionally?"

"Sure. He'll disappear from my sight. But that doesn't mean he's gone, just out of sight. Where're ya goin' with this, Annie?"

"Just working on an idea to set up a defensive system here at Theocratic Minds and I'm asking everyone about their habits during the day."

"Good for you. Good luck with it." Henry began walking away, saying over his shoulder, "I'm glad you're here. I don't have to do all the worrying anymore."

"Don't get too cozy, big guy. I still need you."

He waved and kept walking.

"Henry's another one I'm developing deep feelings for. He's gruff but he cares."

"He's a good man," Nina said. "I promised to help cook dinner in our dormitory. I'd better get back."

After sunset the brothers and sisters in Ethan's salvage detail returned to the compound, each carrying pieces and parts. Loaded carts were piled high with structural steel and pipe. Annie noticed Ethan was indeed not among them. She sat on the porch of the dormitory nearest the back side of the compound and watched, waiting.

Eventually, light of day dimming fast, he appeared over the hill walking down toward the compound. Just as Nina had said, he carried nothing. She rose and walked up the hill to meet him.

"Hey, Annie. What's up?"

"Nothing. You're just so all-fired busy most of the time I never have a chance to see my best friend. That's all. I thought I'd come walk you back."

"I'm flattered … and exhausted."

"I bet you are. Find lots of good things today?"

"Almost every day."

Walking abreast, Annie kept her eyes on her feet, unable to ask the questions while looking at him. "Why didn't you come back with the others? How come you're almost always later than they are?"

Ethan stopped. "I take a final look at the dig sites and spend time cataloguing then taking a few minutes to plan how to begin the next day." He withdrew a roll of papers and showed her an inventory list. "Why the questions?"

She merely repeated the spiel she'd offered Henry. "Just working on a protection plan and asking questions of everyone's whereabouts during the day."

He didn't appear convinced, tugging at the braid of his beard. "Okay." He moved on. "I'm tired and hungry." He picked up the pace and split off, clearly not wanting to walk any farther with her.

She felt awful. He saw through the lie. He'd just been interrogated and obviously knew it. But she couldn't deny that his eagerness to end the conversation was itself suspicious. She became conflicted. Another sleepless night loomed.

The sun rose on another day. Annie dressed, hoisted the quiver over her shoulder and grasped her bow. She had to get out and away from the compound for a time, distancing herself from the task of seeking out a traitor. As she strolled with no particular place to go, she fingered the mesquite wood handle of the knife strapped to her hip that Ethan had made for her.

A quarter mile later an odd feeling came over her. Shielding eyes from the sun, she surveyed the countryside. Her gaze moved with calculated precision across topsoil so thin that rocks broke the surface often, scattered cedar bushes interspersed by occasional scrub oak thickets and prickly pear cactus patches—things commonplace. She sensed a presence and searched for something not so ordinary.

Then came an excited juvenile screech and then, "Annie!"

She spun a quarter turn. Eva Louise raced to her, stumbling over the rock-strewn ground. "Punkin!" she shouted and trotted to meet the child, noticing Jake and Glory walking side by side followed by Lana holding Dame Fortune's hand.

Eva dove into Annie's arms. They laughed and twirled in a circle, the girl's legs flagging out. Annie smothered the child in kisses. "How is it that you saw me before I saw you?"

"It's because I wanted to real, real bad."

"You're so big. I can barely hold you off the ground." She pulled her head back to take a good look.

Eva's eyes moistened.

"Is something wrong?"

With pouty face the youngster said, "No. I'm just glad to see you. I've missed you so much."

Annie squeezed her tight. "Me too, Punkin, me too."

Eva looked at the red cloth that Annie now chose to wear as a headband, all the way around the top of her head. She stroked Annie's sandy blonde hair that now hung plank-straight to her waist. "Your hair, it's so long."

"I can't seem to find the time to do anything about it."

"I can find the time," Glory called out.

Annie dropped Eva and trotted to meet Glory, taking her hand while grabbing Jake's in the other. "Just saying I'm glad y'all are here doesn't even touch how I'm feeling."

Jake's jaw slackened. "You've grown another couple of inches. My gosh, you're eye-to-eye with me. You have to be nearly six feet tall. I can't believe it, it's only been six months."

Annie patted his chest. "Maybe you've shrunk. Thought about that?"

"That's my Annabelle." He pulled her into an embrace and whispered into her ear, "I didn't realize how much I'd miss you until you were gone." He kneaded the flesh of her arms. "Are these muscles ... on my little Annabelle?"

"Maybe. But decidedly feminine, don't you think?" She pecked him on the cheek then looked to Lana and Dame Fortune. She kissed the back of Lana's hand then turned to Dame Fortune. "That dream; it was real, right?"

Dame Fortune cackled. "I told you she be really gall-durn smart, didn't I?" she said to Jake.

"Yeah, Dame, you did. But I knew that."

"Annie girl, I want so diddly dang bad to be tellin' you more but I can't. I just be addin' dat she not be a bad person just desperate, da one dat be givin' up information."

"She? The traitor is a woman?"

Dame tossed a hand into the air and tapped the staff to her forehead. "Well, I'll be a flippin' green toad. I just be sayin' more dan I should and not even be realizin' it."

Annie's mind spun out a dizzying array of incompatible thoughts. She turned away to get her head in order when she detected movement within a cedar grove about a hundred yards out. She focused on the spot where the movement occurred, then saw it again. She said evenly, "We need to be heading back to the compound right now."

"Why?" Jake said.

"I love you Jake, but shut up and don't waste time asking questions. Follow me." She'd walked no more than a few feet when every thicket and cedar grove capable of hiding a human came alive with forms moving within them.

She glanced back at Jake. "Can't you see that?" she asked, nodding in the direction she looked.

Jake looked there and elsewhere. "See what?"

"Never mind, just walk faster."

A quickened pace became impossible, hindered by Lana guiding Dame Fortune over uneven rocky ground.

Annie took the bow from her shoulder and withdrew an arrow from the quiver at her back. She strung it.

"What is it you're seeing," Jake asked.

"Just do as da girl say," Dame Fortune said. "What will be will be. And dere be no debatin' dat."

A shrill whistle went up from some distance. From behind trees, shrubs and thickets, men began appearing from hiding—lots of men.

Annie turned in a full circle to see machete and club-wielding men surrounding them. She didn't count but assumed more than twenty tightened a circle around them. "Stand your ground!" Annie shouted, "Or I'll take you down one by one."

Jake put a hand on her arm. "You can't take them all. There's too many." He looked to Dame. "Right?"

The old lady stood straight and didn't answer, even appearing defiant.

"Come on, Dame. Help us. She can't take them all. Or can she?"

The old lady said nothing.

"You only have ten arrows," Glory told her. "Even if everyone hits its mark, those guys will still kill us."

Men advanced, weapons in every hand held ready to attack.

"Everyone lie flat on the ground." She glanced to the gawking faces. "Do it now! I need unobstructed vision. We won't be talking our way out of this one."

She shouted to the nearest assailant, "Stop right there or lives will be lost! Please do as I ask."

No one stopped.

She pulled two more arrows from her quiver and clenched them in her teeth.

Men began running at them.

Annie drew down on the nearest and aimed for his thigh. The arrow hit and sent him tumbling.

She strung another and let it fly, striking one just above the knee. He went down.

They were close enough to begin raising weapons to attack.

Annie spun in a circle firing arrows with blurring speed. All ten found targets.

Still, an overpowering force of men advanced.

She drew her knife and slashed the wrist of the hand holding the first weapon to descend upon her then another and another until flailing arms and weapons overwhelmed her.

Annie's acute hearing detected the whoosh of a weapon singing in her direction. She whirled around to face it only to have a club connect with the back of her head from the other direction.

She went down incapacitated and groggy.

Fighting stopped.

Jake crawled to her and threw his body over hers. "Get away from her! Don't hit her anymore!"

It was as if they'd suddenly lost interest in Annie. They ran to Lana and ripped Eva from her arms. "No! Lana screamed. "She's just a baby!"

The uninjured attackers helped those struck by arrows. They retreated. Eva held both arms fully extended over the kidnapper's shoulder sobbing, "Momma! Momma!"

Lana shrieked and then began running to catch the kidnappers but Glory snagged her arm as she went by, wrapping her up so she couldn't chase after them. "Not now. We'll organize and go get her when we're prepared. You couldn't do anything if you caught them, other than get yourself killed."

Dame Fortune held her staff in front of her toward the retreating gang and shouted in a booming voice, "Da game has begun and y'all be too stupid to know it!" She pointed the staff toward Annie who now had regained full-consciousness. "You just transformed a young teenager into da savior of da human race." She let out a howling sardonic laugh. "I sure be thankin' ya for dat!" Then she muttered, "And it all be for da love of a child."

Annie pushed Jake away and stumbled to her feet with pursuit on her mind. Still unstable, she ran a short distance but tripped and nearly fell.

Jake ran after her. "Stop! You're not thinking straight."

He caught up to her as she struggled to regain balance. He held her back. "Take us to Theocratic Minds and let's put a plan together first."

Annie stared at him through swimming eyes then finally nodded. "You're right. That'd be best."

Dame turned to face the late morning sun. A smile appeared as she muttered, "Idiot men. Dey totally be underestimatin' my Annie girl." She dropped her head. "Now, I pray Annie don't be underestimatin' dat connivin' Tam fella."

CHAPTER NINETEEN
A SAD REVELATION

"I won't allow it!" Jake paced to and fro, fast and erratic.

Sitting before him, Annie slumped, massaging a knot on the back of her head. She looked up without sitting up and calmly said, "Jake, from what I've been told, Stalwart is more of a military fort than a run-of-the-mill corporation. I may have been young but I remember the walls surrounding that place when we left Glory and Myrna there." She sat upright and locked onto his stare. "What's the alternative, gather our small but mighty band of warriors, storm the gate and then execute a full frontal assault with shouted demands and harsh language?"

"Don't make light of this!"

She sighed then wilted over again. "It wasn't my intent."

"You just fought twenty, or so, of them," he said, still pacing near her, "How long do you think the battle will last with twice, or three times that number?"

"You're assuming I'll confront them like that again. I had no choice this morning. I fought them the way I had to. Next time I'll have alternatives and it'd be to everyone's advantage if I put more energy into outwitting those thugs than shooting them full of arrows."

She looked Lana's way, rose and approached her. Lana wept face down into her hands. Annie stroked her finely textured brown hair. Soothing the young mother, she said, "Our best hope for rescuing Eva from that ego-maniac, Tam, is a silent one-person operation." She snapped her fingers. "In and out. From what I've heard about the man, he's arrogant. He won't expect a lone teenage girl to walk in and take Eva. Of course there could be complications. That means I have to stay focused. I can't worry about situations y'all might have gotten into if you're with me. Sorry Jake, but you'd be a dangerous distraction." She swept the room with a finger and added, "That goes for all of you."

She stepped over to Jake and held his hands. "You know as well as I do that unhindered I'll move faster and more decisively if my head is not bogged down worrying about y'all." She kissed his hand. "I can do it. I'm sure of it. If I don't want them to see me they won't. You know that."

"I've witnessed that first hand," Glory said. She moved to Jake's side and threaded her arm through his. "She was much younger and slower then, too."

Glory's recited memory seeded his recollection of a ten-year-old girl snatching knapsacks from easy view by Stalwart suppliers, without ever having been seen or heard. He softened, his objections losing merit.

Annie said nothing more. It was clear by her calm that she detected acquiescence in his changing face.

Still, he didn't want her going alone. Eyes darted as the wheels of his mind spun, but finally he heaved a sigh and his shoulders slumped. "You might be right, Glory."

"'Might be'?" Annie's jaw went slack. Feigning surprise elicited Jake's eye roll.

Despite the ill-timed attempt at humor, he smiled. "My judgment could be tainted, I suppose."

"'Could be'?"

"Be careful. Don't make me re-think it."

She stood, kissed him on the forehead and pressed her cheek into his. "Your argument just makes me love you more."

"I haven't seen you in over half a year and now it's only for a matter of hours? It's unfair."

Dame tapped the floor with her staff. "He be comin' 'round, Annie girl, just a wee bit slower between dem cute ears dan you an' me, das all."

"Now that that's settled," Annie said, "I think I'll ask Henry to oversee making plenty of arrows and small throwing knives. I won't be looking for trouble, but I must be well prepared this time if I should stumble upon it." She took a decisive step toward the door then stopped. Her whole body appeared to deflate. "But first, I have to talk to Ethan. I have groveling to do."

Watching her leave the dormitory, Jake couldn't separate sadness from admiration for the fifteen-year-old girl taking on the burdens of so many at such a tender age.

***

Annie leaped the two steps to the ground from the porch and ran the well-trodden path near the dormitory, kicking up dust as she did. The sun shone brightly in a near cloudless sky. Wildflowers scented the air. Now that she'd convinced Jake, she focused on Ethan. She wouldn't be able to function if she left without apologizing to her best friend for the accusatory questions she had been obligated to ask.

Annie had no intention of waiting for him to return from a day of salvage work at the old power plant. She jogged through the Theocratic Minds compound on her way to the excavation site.

Nina stepped from the door of the machine shop holding two new buckets fashioned from recovered sheet metal as Annie ran by. "What's the rush? Where ya goin'?"

Slowing, she said, "I have to apologize to Ethan."

"Can I tag along?"

"Sure, but hurry, I have to get this done."

"Go on. I'll catch up."

Annie hit her stride and covered the mile in a hurry then stopped to catch her breath. Standing a ways out, she studied the remnants of an electrical generating plant. But most of what she saw was unrecognizable—just heaps of twisted rusting metal, no longer even hinting its original purpose. Had Ethan not told her what it had been, she wouldn't have known.

Walking toward a group clustered around something, she saw Ethan looking across a shallow but broad hole. In it, a group of brothers and sisters dug around an object the size of Dame Fortune's washtub. The casing of the contraption had rusted away in places and the workers had broken even more of it to reveal dull red strands of fine wire that appeared to be covered in green powder and wrapped many times.

Ethan noticed her but only glanced. "Hi."

"Hi. What's that thing?"

He flipped a finger in the direction of the object. "Those red strands are copper windings. It's the remains of an electric motor."

"A what?"

He sighed melodramatically. "I'll explain it later." He still refused to look her in the eye.

Annie remained quiet for a moment digging for courage. Finally, she burst out with, "I need to talk to you."

Keeping his eyes on his work he said, "I've been right here all day. Okay?" He glanced again but his eyes never connected with hers. "I have witnesses. Now, would you please go bother someone else? I have work to do."

"I've come to apologize."

"Oh?" He continued jotting something on an unfurled roll of paper.

"I'm sorry for questioning your honesty and integrity. Forgive me?"

Still facing away, "Why the change of heart?"

Nina arrived and came trotting up to them. "Whew." She wiped beading perspiration from her face. "That's quite a jog."

Ethan's eyes swept right past Annie and landed on Nina. "If y'all came expecting a picnic lunch, I hope you brought food."

Becoming annoyed, Annie moved to within arm's reach and pulled his shoulder around so he had to face her. "Come on, Ethan, look at me. I won't leave until you've accepted my apology."

He slowly looked to the hand clutching his shoulder. "Gonna beat me up? You're certainly capable. You'll have me bleeding and unconscious in a matter of seconds."

"Stop being an idiot. I don't know how many ways there are to say it or how many times I need to, but I'll say I'm sorry a thousand times in a thousand ways if that's what it takes." She let her head dangle. "I couldn't handle it if I walked away from here and you hadn't forgiven me."

Without expression, "I suppose that, in time, I'll get over it."

"What's going on," Nina asked.

Annie huffed and tore her eyes away from Ethan. "I found out the traitor is a woman."

"Traitor?" Ethan blurted, snapping his head up to pay full attention for the first time.

"Yeah," Annie said. "I suppose it doesn't matter that you know, now that I've discovered it's a woman."

Nina's eyes grew large. "How'd you discover that?"

"Dame Fortune told me."

"Another dream?"

"No. She, Jake, Glory, Lana, and her little daughter Eva Louise were coming to Theocratic Minds this morning. I met them about a quarter mile out. It was coincidence that I did. A couple of days ago our homes at Blister Knob were destroyed by Stalwart suppliers."

"Destroyed? I—I don't understand."

Annie sighed. "I don't either. I don't understand anything about what's going on, or why. When Jake and the others appeared and we came together, a conversation had barely begun when Stalwart suppliers attacked in large numbers out of the woods. There were too many of them. I managed to take half of them down, but was overwhelmed and," she winced, her head yanking down in a bob of mental pain, "they kidnapped Eva." Annie squeezed her eyes shut. "I can still see the terror on Punkin's face when she reached for me over that kidnapper's shoulder. I'd been clubbed and couldn't catch them." She glared in Nina's direction with a sudden defiant burst and sternly announced, "I may not understand what's going on, but I *will* find out and I *will* get Eva back. I'll leave it to their deity to help anyone standing in my way."

Nina's breath hitched.

"I bet she's frightened out of her little mind right now. She's so young …" Annie's voice trailed off, punctuated with a whimper of grief.

"Kidnapped? A little girl?" Nina muttered, her face going blank as her head sagged forward.

Annie slammed a fist into her palm, aggravated all over again at her failed attempt to save the child. "I won't fail twice. I'm going after her … and, this time, on my terms."

Annie stepped away to give reeling anger time to cool. "I assume that Fiam Lee Tam fella, the CEO of Stalwart, found out Eva was his daughter. The traitor, whomever she is, pointed the way to Blister Knob and then told Stalwart spies they'd likely head for Theocratic Minds. I have no doubt of that. But what I don't understand, among other things, is why they waited until I met them on the trail to attack."

Nina shook her head. "That's impossible. They wouldn'—"

"They wouldn't … *what?*" Surprised by the odd outburst, Annie took measured steps toward her friend. "Why are you acting strange?"

Nina's face screwed down. She sniveled, then burst into sobs. She whirled around and sprinted toward a cliff overlooking a tributary that flowed into the Brazos River.

"Wait!" Annie shouted. "Talk to me."

Nina kept running.

Ethan suddenly lost annoyance with Annie, the salvage operation and note taking. His attention went to Nina's receding form racing up the gentle slope. "What in the world has gotten into her?"

"I don't know."

Ethan rolled up the papers and shoved them into his robe. He walked in the direction Nina ran. "I'd better check on her."

Annie jogged to catch up. "Not without me."

Ethan quickened his pace.

Annie wondered what was on his mind—if he considered only Nina's unusual behavior or if he thought about her. Although forced into an adult way of acting and talking, she had trouble, at times, inadvertently allowing adolescent thinking to invade more adult-like pragmatism. In this way, she was still very much a teenager. When it came to relationships, her head followed her heart. Loyalty to Nina and concern over Ethan's aloofness split her focus.

Lately, close proximity to him had begun creating physical changes she didn't understand. She questioned love for a friend and love for a life partner. Were the two different? Annie continued maturing unnaturally fast but, in this area, development remained age specific and, maybe, somewhat retarded. Whether friendly or romantic, relationships remained a mystery. *Someday I have to talk to Glory about this tingling I get when I'm around Ethan.*

"There she is," Ethan said, barely under a shout.

Annie abandoned Ethan's profile to see Nina standing precariously close to a sheer rock cliff, not terribly high, thirty feet perhaps, but enough to do great damage if she slipped and fell. "Nina, get away from the edge!"

Tears flowed from puffy eyes down reddened cheeks. "Don't come any closer! I've messed up really bad."

Annie stopped. "What are you talking about?"

"They promised no one would be harmed. They said they were only concerned about machines and stopping construction of them. They told me they wanted to consult the Oracle of Blister Knob about what to do. I didn't see any harm in it and told them where she lived and that your friends were there with her. Oh Annie, it's all my fault! I abused your trust. I gave them information then denied it to your face."

"Why would you do that?"

"My parents survived the hostile takeover of Wellworth and traveled north to find me but found Stalwart first. When a traveler told me they were there, I went to see them. Mister Tam said they were too old to be of service to the corpocracy and that I needed to provide information about Theocratic Minds as payment for their cottage and food." She stepped back.

"Stop! Don't move!" Ethan looked sideways. "I'm sure Annie will agree that you did what you thought was best for your family. Any one of us would have."

"Of course," Annie said. "I'll get Eva back and those cabins they burned don't matter. Jake and the rest of my family had planned on moving to Theocratic Minds anyway. The torching of the cabins only changed the timing. That's not a big thing ... nor important ... at all."

"You—you've sh-shown me kind—kindness. And I ... I repaid ... with betrayal," she blubbered out between sobs.

"You're our friend," Ethan said. "We'll work through this together."

"He's right. I'll bring your parents back with me when I go after Eva. They can live with us at Theocratic Minds. Don't do anything foolish."

"Foolish? You think atonement is unwise?" She pulled the cord that bound the brown robe, dropping it off her shoulders. She stood naked looking skyward. "If there is a God that hasn't totally abandoned the human race then I want to meet that deity naked and humble, begging forgiveness for a life poorly lived." She, again, inched backward, heels now off the edge.

"Don't!" Annie yelled.

Ethan began running.

"I love you both." She leaned back and allowed gravity to take over.

Before Ethan could get there Annie passed him. When he arrived, she was leaning over the edge, looking down onto the top of a short dead tree. Nina's impaled body dangled, twitching, skewered on a stout, upright branch, its splintered-sharp end protruding out of her chest. A few seconds later the twitching stopped; she was gone.

Annie threw her head back, pumped a fist to the sky and railed, "The world shouldn't be this way! A person shouldn't be forced to betray friends and die just so her family might have food and shelter!" She sank to her knees then fell over onto her side still looking over the edge. Tears flowed and dripped onto the lifeless form of a lost friend.

Ethan knelt beside her. "My bruised ego should never have come between us. It is I that owe you an apology. I'm sorry." He sat and pulled her head onto his lap. "I acted childish." He kissed the top of her head.

"I've loved you from the moment I awoke in your house and saw your face. I'm sorry that it took Nina's death for me to finally find the words."

He, too, cried.

CHAPTER TWENTY
IN NEED OF A HELPING HAND

Annie scanned the star-filled sky, dots converging to create the Milky Way. She sighed, wishing she felt as serene as the twinkling celestial blanket appeared. Advanced vision paid huge dividends on nights like this; even in starlight, little escaped her sight. She stood at the top of a rise looking down the slope less than a hundred yards to the compound known as Stalwart. It was early evening. Lights glowed from most of the visible windows within the walls. *That place gives me the creeps.*

She rechecked armaments. On a belt over her shoulder and across her chest, fifteen eight-inch throwing knives had been affixed, all plain and flat but ground to perfect balance, meant only to fly true and stick the mark. Henry had also fashioned razor-sharp six-point throwing disks. In Annie's hands, these innocuous appearing little things were formidable weapons that could embed in bone with no great thought given to finessing the throw. She carried ten. Henry wanted her to have more but ran out of time. She took what he had. At her back hung the quiver jammed with thirty cedar-shaft arrows tipped with hair-splitting steel points. And, of course, a weapon that meant more to her than the sum of its varied uses, the knife Ethan made.

She fondled its mesquite wood handle thinking of the handsome young man with a not-so-handsome braided beard that had darkened and was now in need of a few more braids. She longed to be at his side. *It'd be nice to have someone to talk to.* It was a silly notion. *Nah.*

She began loping down the well-graded road toward the stockade high on her toes, eyes sweeping the area as she ran. With such sensitive sight she had the advantage, capable of spotting trouble before it saw her.

Concentration narrowed to the task before her, rescuing Eva and finding the Masters, Nina's parents. She had to figure a way to get the elderly couple out, too.

She passed row after row of vegetables in the large garden left and right of the well-trodden approach to the gate. An elevated irrigation sluice trough gurgled lazily nearby, fed by a small wind-powered waterwheel at the river's edge.

Arriving at the wall, she moved laterally along it away from the main gate hoping to scale it without rope or ladder. The native white stone had been mortared into neat straight rows but varied sizes created the occasional protrusion. She searched for one the right height. *There it is!*

Three feet off the ground a stone stuck out—just about right to leap onto then spring higher from there. She calculated the wall to be no more than fifteen feet high. A running start, one foot on the protruding rock and a leap from there should put her within easy reach of the top.

She backed into a row of knee-high corn twenty feet from the wall. She blew warm breath into her cupped palms, rubbed them on her breeches, and then breathed deep, all the while rocking to and fro. *One ... two ... and three ...*

In an extraordinary blast of speed, she sprinted and hit the stone with her right foot and with only the muscles of a single leg sprang skyward. The leap surprised even her, as her body was catapulted straight up, needing only a little guidance with her hands to alight feet-first atop the wall.

Wow! I'm getting good at this stuff.

She adjusted the belt of knives, her quiver, and then re-secured the bow over her shoulder as she examined the stockade interior. Just as Glory had said, it was neat—too neat. The orderliness was unappealing— even disconcerting. Only a dangerous obsessive compulsive could demand such radical cleanliness.

She had no reason to doubt Glory's opinion that Tam was treacherous. Despite how he might present himself, he'd have her killed if he saw fit. This had to remain top-of-mind at all times, keeping natural affection under control and not suckered by charismatic charm. That weakness could get her killed. She used the memory of her mother's murder at the hand of Hiram Baker to give her a hardened focus on the job to be done.

Annie had no way of knowing where Nina's parents were but believed Eva had to be in the main house. That structure stood out. It faced the front with a strange stone spire centered between it and the massive oak gate. The elderly couple could be dealt with after rescuing Eva.

She climbed half-way down the wall then dropped, landing quiet and buoyant. She ran in bursts from one hiding place to the next.

She made it to the main house and peeped through windows on one side of it, working toward the back. Finally, she walked alongside the outside wall craning her neck around to look inside the last one. An oil lamp illuminated the room in a soft golden glow. It was a bedroom.

A small dark-haired man, almost feminine in appearance and manner, sat beside Eva. It appeared he consoled the child. The youngster whimpered, shying from his touch.

Is that Tam? He looks Asian, like Eva. It must be.

It shocked her to see that Tam was not a large warrior type—was delicate. By the stories she'd heard he should have been an ugly monster and huge. She figured she was at least a head taller.

Tam stroked Eva's hair, brushed her cheek with the backs of his fingers then rubbed tiny circles on her thigh—an inappropriate touch. It had nothing to do with concern for the child. Annie was repulsed. Her face went tight while gnashing teeth.

He turned to the window and smiled.

She jerked her head out of sight. *He acts like he heard me. But how? I didn't make any noise. Did I?*

Tam said in raised voice from the other side of the glass, "I'm pleased you're finally here, Annie Henderson. I'll meet you at the front door."

Finally here? She stared into the darkness wondering if confronting him in such a casual way was better than simply breaking the window, snatching Eva off the bed and running with her into the night. A civilized approach appealed to her.

She reasoned, if I grab Punkin and run, saving the Masters will be almost impossible.

Seeing no further need for quiet anonymity she walked to the front door arriving at the same time he opened it. "Miss Henderson," he said holding out a hand with a warm smile.

His cordial manner confused her.

Glory warned of it and to not be seduced by it. "That little man is evil to the core and what you'll see is a mask," she'd said. As mature as Annie had grown to be, she retained ideas of the way things should be, associating evil people with lack of hygiene and ugliness—in appearance and of character, like Hiram Baker. Even the breath of this refined man smelled sweet.

Without good reason she extended her hand to meet his. "How'd you know I was outside your window?" She examined him—so short that she saw right over the top of his head.

"I have been blessed with a wonderful ability—born with it, actually. I know you think you were quiet but I heard you."

"If that's so, then ..." She shook her head, realizing she was being drawn in by charm. "That's not important. I've come to take Eva home."

"Eva? Is that the girl's name?"

"Yes. I've come to take her back to her mother, Lana."

"Ah yes, sweet Lana. How is she?"

"Distraught. You had her daughter kidnapped, remember?"

"Correction, *our* daughter, and it was not a kidnapping; I merely retrieved the child."

"Eva has one parent, Lana. What you repeatedly did to her does not make you a parent, but a criminal."

"You're quite articulate for such a young woman. It's admirable how you present your case, but I urge you to remember where you are and to whom you speak. If I choose to keep Eva, I will. If I choose to keep you, I'll do that, too."

"Glory was right. You are an arrogant little man."

"Glory ... yes. Now there was a magnificent woman. I wish I'd had my time with her. She still owes me, you know. I will collect what is due me ... someday quite soon, I wager." A smile came up as he obviously thought about Glory. He closed his eyes, dancing his tongue across his lips as if catching the aroma of something enticing then tasting its sweetness. The trance broke. "Your boldness fascinates me. How old are you—sixteen, seventeen perhaps?"

"I'm fifteen. But thanks for thinking so. I'll take that as a compliment." A teenage gleam of pride escaped. She shook it off and forced renewed focus. She began walking toward the door beside the fireplace heading for the back bedroom. "You bore me. I'm taking Eva home."

Tam smiled. "That zeal, that fire—exactly what I'm looking for."

Annie stopped and turned. "What you're looking for ... what're you talking about?"

"It was not the child I was after. It was you."

"Me? Why?"

"You've become somewhat legendary in your young life. Stalwart suppliers are spreading word fast of your capabilities. I sought *you* young lady, not the child. Eva just happened to be an easy way to get you here. Otherwise, I feared you would've disabled my entire force if they tried to bring you all the way here, even if they should get you bound initially. I told them to go after the young girl. I knew you'd come for her. As it turned out, twenty-six men had a problem getting it done. On top of that, as I understand it, you did an admirable job fending them off without any preparation whatsoever." He clasped his hands together and with excited flare held them to his mouth. "I hear that you rendered over half of them helpless. You're so much more than I'd hoped for. It seems that your genetics have not diluted in the slightest over two centuries."

Annie spit air and said dismissively, "You're a lunatic." She began walking.

With speed that astounded even her, he shoved her into the wall and moved to stand between her and the door to the back hall leading to the bedrooms. "There's something I suppose I should share with you. I'm like you."

"You're nothing like me." She pushed him aside. "Get out of my way."

"Think not?"

Before she could react, he plucked one of her eyelashes and presented it to her in his open palm.

She slapped a hand over her eye, but too late. "The quickness of your hand, how did you acquire that?"

"I didn't acquire it, child. Like I've already told you, I was born with it."

"Did you descend from genetically manufactured humans, too?"

He was pleased, raised one eyebrow. "Indeed."

"That means you don't want to harm me anymore than I want to harm you. Does that explain why you're always sending others to do your dirty work?"

He chuckled. "Not quite." He placed a finger to his lips and looked to a point beyond her. "Ah, to have been alive during the time of the genetic experimentation you and I descend from would have been phenomenal. I'd loved to have been there."

"Sure. I would have, too. The difference is that you would've sought ways to profit by it and I would've done everything in my power to prevent it. It wasn't right or ethical and the result was the creation of people who weren't quite human. Are you so blinded by an appetite for power that you can't see how freakish we are?"

"Freaks?" He smiled and placed a soft hand upon her shoulder. "Oh, child, such sweet naiveté; we may be aberrations of nature, but not freaks. I think it is you that cannot see well; people of our prowess can own this planet."

"I don't disagree, and that scares me. That's too much control in too few hands. I've heard the stories; that's the same way the world got into this mess we're in now." She shrugged his hand off her shoulder. "If we came from the same line, how is it that you're not concerned about the sanctity of life, as I am?"

"It baffles me, too, but, I assume that, genetically speaking of course, my congenital affliction and love are quite close cousins; you're bent one way, I the other. Or, it could be that each descending line has become genetically altered in different ways. Caring for others has nothing to do with my motivation. I've been blessed with over-the-top lust, materially, sexually, etcetera, etcetera. I can't control it. I don't want to. I enjoy it. Opportunities abound within these walls. But that's enough about recreational choices. I suggest that you not test me. You'll not win a confrontation, I assure you."

"Then you're more hare-brained than I thought. If you believe you'll be having your way with me then you're out of your mind."

Tam eyed her from head to toe.

"Stop looking at me like that … you—you pervert!"

"As much as I'd enjoy it, that is not my plan. I already have a young gentleman selected as your mate. You'll like him. He's young, good-looking and terribly aggressive. He'll challenge anyone over almost anything then attack and kill without hesitation or remorse. I want your child to share that characteristic amended by your inherited talents. It's possible, you know."

"You're out of your mind. That's not gonna happen." With as much speed as she could summon, Annie ran past him down the hall and turned into the bedroom where she'd seen Eva. A hand grabbed her long blonde hair before she breached the room's threshold and yanked. Her head slammed the opposite wall of the hallway.

Tam stood over her. "Yes, dear, it *is* going to happen."

Dazed, she heard noise then saw men converge over her. They tied her hands behind her then bound them to her feet, pulling her heels to meet her hands in back. She glanced and saw Eva curled on the bed crying, reaching in her direction. Once again, she'd been put in a situation that she could do nothing for the child. Even after all the warnings she still had underestimated Tam. Groping hands stripped her of weaponry.

In that overly familiar way, Tam said, "After you've mated, dear, how about I have you back for dinner? You are truly fascinating, much more mature than your years. Long discussions would be most enjoyable."

Just the thought of spending time with that monster was disgusting. She forced down bile that rose in her throat as she was dragged away.

***

"What's the matter, Dame? Why so agitated?" asked Jake, watching her pace, tapping her cedar staff on the floor with more force than necessary.

Small guttural moans escaped intermittently. "Da girl must sleep and she must do it soon."

"Annie?"

"It's da only way I be gettin' a message to her." She sent out searching hands and fanned the air until she found Jake. She clutched wadded fistfuls of his shirt. Tears glistened over widened blind white eyes. "Our little Annie girl be in big danger, Jake Henderson."

"Has she been hurt?"

She didn't speak, despair frozen on her face.

He fidgeted. "You'll not be standing quiet this time!" He placed hands on each side of her face and shook her head. "Tell me what you know, hag! Tell me now!" He hissed through clenched teeth, "So help me I'll twist your head right off your shoulders."

Glory came to her defense. "Jake, calm down."

Instead of struggling and trying to push him away, Dame pulled him into an embrace. "Dis time, friend, I be tellin' ya everthin' and be tellin' ya true. It only be doze times I foresee a good outcome that I don't speak of it 'cuz it might change it for da worse. Dis time—" She began to cry, streaming tears glistening over her black cheeks.

Jake pushed her away. "What? Spit it out. Get it said, woman!"

"Dis time I saw our little Annie girl lyin' in a spreadin' pool of her own blood."

"How?"

"She be in dere control as we speak, bound and locked away. If we do nothin' den she'll discover an advantage and get herself free 'cuz she's so flippin' smart, ya know. But it be sparkin' a fight with dat devil, Tam. It's a fight she'll not win 'cuz she be goin' against him unarmed."

Glory wrung her hands. "What can we do?"

"Das why I hope exhaustion be takin' da girl down soon, otherwise I can't be in her mind. I be needin' her relaxed and receptive. All we need to do is be havin' her not act until we can get dere and find her weapons. Dat be her edge." The old lady turned on leaden legs. "I must be gettin' off to m'self now, alone."

She shuffled from the room as Jake, Glory and Lana huddled together; the unspoken consensus obvious: Annie's fate lay in the hands of an old white-haired blind woman.

"It gonna be a long damn night," Dame Fortune muttered as she disappeared through the door.

***

Annie grunted and strained. "If I believed in such things, you malicious midget, then you'd have to be the fabled Satan." She tugged at the rope that bound hands to legs behind her but never took eyes from Tam looking down at her. It was an odd admiring look she saw. He stood on the other side of the expanded metal door of the cell she'd been locked in.

Tam remained serene and pleasant. "Sweet child, don't you realize the devil *does* exist? But it's not a spirit that twirls a jagged claw in our brains to make us do wrong; it's the blackness in our hearts. It resides in you just as it does in me."

Still struggling to free her hands, voice dripping with contempt, she said, "Then it consumed your heart long ago."

"I don't need to read your mind to see that your hate for me grows. That is the blackness I speak of, the devil within you. In a confrontation you'd do everything possible to avoid killing me, but at this moment the thought of me lying dead comforts you. That, dear, is Satan at work." He laced his fingers together behind his back and shook his head. "Don't you see, child, you want me dead so much right now that it leaves a rancid taste in your mouth. At this moment, you don't want justice, you want revenge."

Annie ceased trying to free herself and went still, lying on her side on the cold uneven stone floor. In that moment she realized that Tam's quickness was not confined to physical competency. Sharpness of mind, tactically and philosophically was also advanced. She couldn't outfight him and, now, outwitting him seemed remote. She calmed, struggling served his purpose not hers. "You seem to hold insight into my mind. Now, let me explore you. Has your heart grown totally black over the years or is there a spark of humanity still in you?"

"Humanity? Is it mercy you're referring to?"

"I may not be as smart as you but I have enough intelligence to realize that taking Eva is impossible and escape futile for us both. Therefore, there is no advantage in attempting it. Why not loosen this rope so that I might at least sleep tonight."

His smile broadened. He chortled arrogantly. "You're playing me. That's so novel. If your mind against me settles, wonderful philosophical discussions could be in the offing. You speak as an intellectually advanced adult, not a teenager. You're a magnificent creature."

"Play you? Maybe. But only to the extent I'd rather have free arms and legs because sleep upon this stone floor will be difficult enough. And, I wish you wouldn't speak of and treat me like a prized breeding mare. You say you admire my intelligence, yet you're treating me like some thoroughbred livestock. If it is my ultimate disrespect you desire, then that is certainly the way to get it."

Tam placed a contemplative finger to his lips. "Then let's have a small test of trustworthiness. Will you guarantee that no attempt to escape will be made if I grant you this wish for the night?"

Annie's mind whirled with the right and wrong of such a promise to a man she was certain she could not trust. But, to have free hands and legs might put her in a better situation tomorrow. After all, his requirement was only for the night. "That's an easy agreement to make and one I'll promise to keep. In this life we have little to share other than our word thanks to people like you. My promise is sacred. I don't offer it lightly." Even as she made the pledge and spoke the words to seal the agreement, the vow to rescue Eva and help Nina's parents obtain their freedom remained solid.

"Eloquently stated. I appreciate such articulacy ... so much so I think you've earned the right to blankets, too."

She drew a contrived smile. *You arrogant little man!* "Thank you Mister Tam. It's a kindness I did not expect."

As Tam stood watch, a Stalwart supplier untied the rope that bound her and another supplier tossed into the cell a couple of blankets. "Tomorrow, Annie Henderson, I'll introduce you to a man I'm sure you'll come to know well." In a benevolent fatherly way as if he offered her the world, he added, "You'll know him better than you've known any man in your young life."

It took everything she had to remain neutral. He finally left and she released a held breath.

Since I'll not be going anywhere tonight, sleep does sound good.

***

"Where you be, child?" Desperation tainted the question.

From the darkness a picture formed. Annie saw herself standing between massive stone pillars, arms splayed and chained to them. The stone columns supported nothing but seemed to be a dividing line, a gateway perhaps, separating a darkened dead world behind her and a light-filled garden in front. She wore a long white layered dress of flowing sheer cloth; so white it was like a source of radiance unto itself except for a strip of black at its bottom. But the black wasn't a color, instead, more of a shadow, or maybe a stain. It rose overtaking the white in a slow measured way, drawing down luminescence of the fabric as it went. Rattling chains held her. She yanked at them but stood helpless against massive links. Each time she looked down, the black had moved higher and continued moving up the lacy trim. The dress reacted to a breeze she couldn't feel, as did her long hair. She couldn't say what the encroaching shadow meant but somehow knew it shouldn't be allowed to cover her. She fought against the clanking chains.

"Don't fret, child, Dame is here."

Annie figured out quicker than before that Dame Fortune had invaded her dream. The ghoulish nightmare lost its bite. "Dame, I've failed Lana and Nina. Now I'm failing promises of purity for myself," she said, as she again glanced to see the shadow rising.

"I be tellin' ya true, child, you cannot be gettin' away from Tam alive. Don't be tryin' it, not yet. Help be on its way. Da vision I see for you does not be endin' good. You must be goin' against your nature and stay put. Ya hear me, do not be escapin'. You won't be gettin' far if you do."

As Dame spoke, she materialized. As before, the old lady came as a beautiful young raven-skinned woman of sight walking toward her. This time she didn't stop at a respectful distance. She kept walking until her perfect ebony face came within scant inches of Annie's. She kissed each of Annie's eyes. "Dis information will free you but only if you follow da rules of it." Dame clutched the chain locked to Annie's left arm and then the one to the right; with apparent ease, she pulled the columns until they fell into crumbling heaps of stone. "I be freein' your mind to play Tam's game. It be da only way to defeat him. Your family be comin' to help ... be comin' to help ... be comin' to help ..."

Annie's eyes opened to near-absolute darkness save for a few stars visible through a small window beyond her cell. *I won't let the blackness win, Dame. I promise.*

With that she drifted off with ease and, this time, the sleep was dreamless.

***

"Get down Lana!" Jake hissed. "In case you've forgotten, it's a sunny afternoon."

She dropped back onto her haunches fast. "Sorry. I just want Eva back."

"I know you're impatient, but we have to be cautious or we'll find ourselves locked up next to Annie. That'll accomplish nothing."

Glory squeezed Lana's hand. "I miss Eva, too. But let's give ourselves every advantage to get both of them out of there." She turned to Jake. "What do you think Dame meant when she told us we'd be getting help from an unexpected source?"

Jake, still studying the layout of Stalwart, said, "Not sure, but it's a good sign when she refuses to offer specifics. That means she's seen a less-than-disastrous outcome."

Glory sighed. "I suppose it's time to put the plan into action."

The comment broke Jake's strategic planning spell. "Look, you don't have to offer yourself as bait, neither of you." His eyes darted between them.

"Try not to worry. We have no choice but to play to his weakness. You have to proceed as if we've successfully diverted Tam's attention. It's the only way. Locate and retrieve Annie's weapons and get them to her. Lana and I will buy you time. Tam is such a creature of habit, he won't try anything even if he accepts our offer until the sun reaches the tip of the obelisk; that's his preferred time to get evening activities underway and it always begins with dinner. We just have to make the meal last longer than usual."

"I don't like the idea of that maniac touching you."

"He won't have a chance."

"I know Tam," Lana said, "And I think he'll be salivating at the mere thought of having us both."

Jake grimaced. "That's what bothers me. If I fail—"

"*Stop it, Jake.*" Glory pinched his chin between thumb and forefinger and yanked his face so his eyes could be nowhere else but on hers. "Don't talk like that. Don't even *think it.*"

His tight face eased. "That's certainly strong incentive to get my part right."

182

Glory backhanded him on the arm. "Yeah, well, remember you said it. I'm counting on exactly that."

"Ditto," Lana said. "I'd vomit if forced to follow through."

"Okay," Jake said, "Let's go over it one more time. You two knock on the gate and ask to speak to Tam then present your offer to him directly. In the meantime, I'll circle to the back of the stockade to that garbage door you told me about. With luck, I'll be on the inside by dark and head for the building with the holding cells. Are you positive of its location?"

"I'm sure," Lana said.

"Good. That's probably where I'll find Annie. I just hope I can locate her weapons or that she knows where they are. Either way, I'll remain aware that time is of the essence for you two."

Glory held a distracting stare on him.

"What?"

"Oh, just thinkin' how wonderful you are."

"I, uh … I don't—"

She covered his mouth with fingertips. "Don't respond. I just felt compelled to let you know what I think." She turned to Lana and tossed a thumb in Jake's direction. "I remember the shy, filthy, overly suspicious man that he was. Quite a difference, I'd say."

"You got a good one, all right."

"Stop talking about me like I'm a ripe melon. We have a job to do. Stay focused."

"Sorry." She turned to Lana, "Think it's time?"

"Let me put it this way; I'm sure Eva would like to go home."

Both women rose into full view and walked in the direction of the Stalwart gate. If anyone should be looking, there'd be no turning back.

Jake wanted to stop them, still wishing for a better way. They'd discussed it part of last night and most of the day today while traveling from Theocratic Minds. All ideas kept coming back to Glory and Lana baiting Tam. Sitting on his heels, rubbing sweaty palms on his thighs, he hunkered down and waited for his turn to move.

***

We can do this. I know we can. Glory rolled the motivation over in her mind as she and Lana approached the imposing cross-buck gate that required the lives of several large oak trees for construction. She stopped and looked at the long rows of vegetables on both sides of the road that ended at that gate.

"What's the matter," Lana asked.

"Just remembering that this is where I met Hiram Baker. I know I shouldn't speak ill of the dead, but I can only imagine how many lives have been spared because he's gone."

Lana nodded. "Annie was only ten. To this day, it doesn't seem possible a girl that young did what she did."

Glory considered Lana, how she'd matured into a beautiful woman. Honey blonde hair that flowed over her shoulders as a teenager had darkened to brown with a healthy sheen, her features and figure had seasoned favorably. No longer rail thin, Lana's curves created voluptuousness that Tam would seize upon. It worried her. Lana remained psychologically ill-equipped to handle advances from Tam with calm confidence, given their history. Just the thought of the man terrified her.

Glory pursed her lips and stiffened with resolve. "It's time."

Crouching in a cedar thicket growing from fissures in broad flat rocks, Jake watched Glory and Lana disappear behind the closing gate of Stalwart. The compound was at the end of a gentle descent beginning where he waited. An uneasy flutter tickled his stomach. Urgency to get his part of the plan right had begun to pressurize. He'd only get one shot at it. The love of his life and a young woman he'd taken responsibility for were to offer themselves as barter for the release of young Eva. To offer Tam what he wanted was the only way to distract him, play to his weakness, while Jake did his part. Consummation of the offer was never part of the plan.

The sun's rays flowed down over him. It should have been welcomed warmth, but not today. Dread pushed sweat through his skin. The temperature, as mild as it was, swiftly became unbearable. The pungent aroma of cedar had itself become a distraction. Everything his senses perceived vied for attention. Focus suffered. It was time to get on with it before Tam had a chance to figure out the deception. Lives were ruined or lost when that man's intentions were forced, yet he grew richer and more powerful. Now was no time to be unraveling mentally. *The plan, think only of the plan.*

Jake mapped a route down and around the corporate enclosure. He glanced about repeatedly. Twitching with anticipation, courage finally caught up. He bolted, angling left to a large oak tree and flattening behind it. He looked around the barky girth and saw the next stop a short sprint ahead—corn standing knee-high in long straight rows.

That should put me within fifty feet of the wall.

He breathed in confidence and again dashed.

He stumbled and tripped, falling to his knees halfway to the outside cornrow.

In rapid shots, he looked right then left searching for anyone that might have seen the clumsiness.

Still kneeling, he heard voices to his right coming from the same approach road that Glory and Lana took to the main gate. Two men appeared from around a clump of bushes but they hadn't noticed him. They strolled in a straight line down the path toward the entrance.

Jake forced slow and shallow breathing, assuming they could hear him. He wilted over onto his stomach, keeping the two in sight. At this distance, two, maybe two-hundred-twenty-five feet, it was impossible to discern what was said but the tone seemed light and amiable.

The bright rust-colored shirt Glory and Lana had collaborated on and made for him suddenly seemed to glow in high contrast to surrounding spring vegetation. He cringed, becoming as small as possible. The two kept walking, eventually disappearing from sight at the other end of the cornrows about fifty yards away.

Sweat streamed in rivulets and stung his eyes. Blowing out a held breath, he sprang to his feet, started jogging and then fell onto his stomach in the relative safety of a thick stand of cornstalks that appeared ready for another growth spurt under the spring sun.

After a moment lying flat and motionless, he lifted his head above the plants. He scanned all directions for movement. Seeing none, he leaped up and ran the final distance to the end of the front compound wall.

There it turned ninety-degrees then straight to the rear of the huge enclosure. Along that line he saw the garbage wagon as Glory had described it, next to a small gated passageway. The only other access ways into the compound would be over the top the wall or through the front gate, neither feasible.

He ran the final distance to the wagon piled high with rotting food scraps, dropped down and sat, leaning against the outside wheel to catch his breath. The stench made easy breathing difficult.

As he calmed, he twisted around and looked beyond the wagon wheel to the low wide set of doors, all the while swatting insects swarming his face.

How am I supposed to push a slide bolt mounted on the inside of those doors?

It never had occurred to them to address the locking mechanism on the garbage portal. Planning had focused on what to do once inside. He wondered if getting in without detection was even possible.

Now what?

It'd be dark in a couple of hours. The caw of a passing crow between him and the setting sun struck him as a mock the dilemma.

***

A guard lounged on a three-legged stool. "They told me you were some kind of super human. If that's true, why haven't you tried to get out of here?"

His legs were extended and crossed at the ankles while he rested the back of his head in his locked fingers leaning against the opposite wall from the jail cell. Like all Stalwart residents, this man was clean shaven, hair neatly groomed and that idiotic compulsory smile disgraced his countenance. The hair was dusty red and wavy, bunching in curls at the back of his head, and his face was covered in freckles subdued by a deep tan. He dressed neatly; dark brown shirt tucked into canvas pants over oiled leather boots. He was a big man, well over six feet. There was something hopeful in his eyes that Annie noticed; she believed kindness.

Sitting, back against the wall, she lifted her head from the points of her raised knees. "I gave my word that I wouldn't try to escape as long as I was not bound during the night, that's why." She omitted that the promise had nothing to do with Tam, or her own comfort, but everything to do with a vow made to Dame Fortune in the dream vision. Still, to make a promise to anyone carried considerable weight. "I don't know the creed you people live by around here but, with so little trust in the world, I consider my word a tangible asset, extremely precious. I never offer it lightly."

She gazed into the man's eyes. That softer look was still there, the one she interpreted as compassion. He didn't appear threatened, maybe even bored—the perfect opportunity to find out more about these people and why they were so overbearing and larcenous.

"All well and good," he said, "But your word doesn't get your friend back or put food in your mouth." The smile remained but the rest of his face appeared perplexed. "From where I sit, your word is accomplishing nothing but keeping your butt fixed upon a hard stone floor under guard in a jail cell."

"So it would seem." She considered her next words carefully. "You have questions about me but no more so than what rattles around my brain about you."

"Ask anything you like," he said. "I have no place to go. For this day, you are my task. I'll be here as long as you remain there."

"First of all, please stop smiling? A smile without warmth is nothing but a smirk. There is no hint of good will behind it. It's so obvious and silly looking."

"I've done it long enough that it's an unconscious act—just one of Mister Tam's rules if we want to stay in Stalwart."

"And just why is that?"

"What?"

"Why do want to stay? Is your life so wonderful that you'll blindly follow stupid rules like that?"

The pointed question succeeded in forcing the smile away. He sat up and draped his arms over his knees. "You're too young to understand."

"Try me. I may be fifteen but I'm analytical. I assure you that I'm old enough to accept logic ... provided, of course, you're capable of making sense of it for me. But even if I understand what you say there's no guarantee I'll agree."

"Fifteen, huh? I figured you to be older, closer to my age."

"And that would be?"

"Middle-age, twenty-six."

"Do you have family?"

"Yes, a wife and two very young children, girls, four and six. And that's also the answer to your abrasive question about following stupid rules. My family lives well here. I think it's worth the price of admission to take the corpocratic oath, smile blankly and chant a ridiculous reaffirmation every morning."

"Can't you see that it doesn't stop there? Suppliers take what is not theirs to take, destroying people's lives to secure those comforts."

"We don't steal. We offer valuable information about the corpocracy and how the future of mankind depends on a flourishing corporate world run by intelligent CEOs to protect and provide. As suppliers, we negotiate with independent consumers. It's fair barter, not theft."

"Pffft. Do you even know what 'negotiate' means?"

"Sure. It's exchange of value for goods and/or services."

Her eyebrows lifted, surprised by his answer. "That's the barter, the final deal, the end result of negotiation. A true negotiation is coming to terms and then *both* parties agreeing on the outcome. If the will of one party is forced without agreement by the other then it's theft, pure and simple."

"That's not what we were told."

"Let me set up a scenario," she said coming to her feet, "Let's say you, as a supplier, negotiate and take property. As you merrily begin walking back to Stalwart, like a cat with a mouse clenched in its jaws to lay at the feet of its master, full of good feelings about a job well done when people suddenly and unexpectedly pop out of the woods," she stopped and raised a punctuating finger into the air, "oh, and by the way, they're heavily armed and aggressive. We can't forget that. Once they have you surrounded, they tell you the corpocracy is lunacy and only idiots believe in it. In return for that valuable information everything you're carrying is taken from you. It's done against your wishes because, *in your opinion*, that information is worthless. Now what do you think of that? Is that a fair negotiation?"

The man rose to his feet. "I've never thought about it that way."

"Of course not. Tam manipulated you and everyone else here into believing one way, his way. For all his faults, Tam is a master at molding people's beliefs. He can be quite charming, and therein lays his strength. Everyone living in Stalwart is more than willing to accept anything they're told in exchange for a clean, comfortable cottage and plenty of food. To question it would be an irreversible ticket to excommunication. Is his way good? Yes and no. Is his way bad? Yes and no. The point is, my friend, there are many sides and opinions on everything. But to force one's will upon another is absolutely wrong, regardless of good intent. Always remember, value is determined by the individual, no one else.

Even food is practically worthless to someone with a full belly. But that same person a day later will see a good meal as extremely valuable. The priority list for surviving in today's world is always changing and, thus, value."

The man's mind clearly reeled. He paced in front of Annie's cell.

She stood at the expanded metal door, fingers hung from the diamond gaps and watched, pondering how to use this opening window of opportunity.

"This is not the only way to provide for your family," she continued. "You're assuming no one outside Stalwart's perceived protection can be trusted. You've been taught to believe that, and it's simply not true. You're looking at one person that'll gladly help, expecting nothing in return except your trust and friendship. More importantly, Theocratic Minds, the monastic order north of here that Tam wants destroyed is attempting to rebuild technology and wants only a peaceful co-existence while they put it all together. Their plan is to give it to the world, not sell it. Tam is threatened by that. He wants them eliminated. He'll lose control if it flourishes. That scares him."

He stopped pacing. "You have a way of making sense of things, like Mister Tam. At the same time you've confused me."

She smiled, figuring it might be best to change the tempo of the conversation. "What's your name?"

"Horace McCann but my friends call me Corky. I hate the name Horace."

"Okay, Corky, let me simplify it for you; no matter what you choose to believe, I support your right to believe it; just don't harm anyone unless it's defending your life or that of another. Okay?"

Corky scratched his head. "You can't be just fifteen years old."

"Oh, but I am."

"How do you do it? How do see things so clearly?"

"Caring for others over self is how it begins. Try it. Once you do, it'll become natural to you, like that stupid smile. You'll find that, soon, all your smiles will be real and warm. It's wonderfully addictive. Decision making becomes easy and good things come back to you in great volume."

His eyes drifted to the exposed rafters overhead and remained there as he considered all he'd been told. His eyes came down to meet hers. He smiled—this time sincerely. "Want to play checkers?"

"Sure. I have nowhere to go."

***

Tentatively, Glory said, "Do we have a deal, Mister Tam?"

189

"The idea is intriguing." He paced away.

"I'll not mince words, the offer was meant to be enticing. That precious child you're holding needs her mother. To us, this arrangement is acceptable under these extreme circumstances. We possess nothing to exchange that you'd be interested in, aside from ourselves."

"And, you say you are willing, too," he asked Lana.

Lana's eyes sank to the floor. "If that's what it takes to get my daughter back, then … yes."

He clucked his tongue. "Such a cold, disembodied response, I'm disappointed."

"Did you expect an enchanted flutter of eyelashes," Glory cried out. "This is not to be considered barter. It's ransom payment."

Tam's gaze shifted to Glory. A smile came up. "Point made. I suppose it might be presumptuous to expect honest sensuality out of a business arrangement."

His gaze held on Glory. "I wish you hadn't bolted like a skittish rabbit when you were here before. But I understand the trauma you suffered and that you likely distrusted everyone in Stalwart after Baker's attack.

Glory ignored the musing. "We'll do this thing for you but, in return, we get Eva Louise and are allowed to leave Stalwart unrestricted. Deal?"

"We'd be so good together, you and I. You're strong and sensible. I like that." Fanning his arms wide he said, "I'd offer you a vested interest in Stalwart if you'd willingly choose to stay with me. Think about it, Glory, all you see outside that door could be yours. All I ask in return is your devotion." His charismatic charm had the power to tempt and soften a cold heart.

Glory forced her expression to remain neutral and stay with the plan. She said nothing, resisting his wiles, realizing the last one to speak would be the loser. She drew her shoulders into a questioning shrug to let him know it was his turn to accept or reject. Underneath that measured response brewed discontent that threatened calm. She hoped he wouldn't see through it to notice the sniveling coward that, for the tiniest slice of a second, considered temptation.

He closed his eyes and drew a long breath. "I can't let this opportunity pass."

Glory glanced at Lana. The younger woman refused to look up, disgusted even though it was never intended to actually happen. Glory stepped sideways, scooped up Lana's hand and squeezed it.

"Now," he said, "go down the hall to the bathroom and bathe. Lana, you know the way. Show Glory where things are kept. Perfumed oils are on the shelf and extra robes are hanging on hooks."

Glory stiffened in shock, disbelieving that she and Lana had miscalculated how soon he'd demand imbursement. "Would it be possible to have dinner first? I don't think my growling stomach would add anything pleasant to intimacy."

"Again with the pragmatism; I like your style." Head tilting, he thought about the request. "I think I'd like a hot dinner and a glass of wine, too." His eyes sparkled with desire. "Since our time together is short, I want a sublime experience. A full stomach and the glow of wine in your cheeks will add to the pleasure."

"Now, Lana and I can bathe knowing that good food and wine will follow. Then, Mister Tam, we … rather, our bodies will be yours." She walked past him and smiled but it wasn't even a good Stalwart version as a vivid image of a passionate embrace with this man lit up her mind. She shuddered; the image ghastly and disgusting. And, now, it seemed as though it might happen. All the while, Glory presented Tam the face of calm.

Where are you, Jake?

***

Jake sat impatiently next to the garbage wagon wheel swatting flies. No better plan had come to him on how to get inside. So focused on the goal of getting to the other side of that wall, he'd forgotten the rotting rancid garbage just above his head. Half an hour had passed and the sun sank low in the western sky.

He visualized Glory and Lana forced into sordid servitude. A whine escaped his constricting airway because he didn't know what else to do. He looked up the wall and wondered what he might use to get over it.

He heard a commotion on the other side of the door.

He left his hiding place and ran to the wall next to the short wide double doors, slamming his back into it.

Someone worked the latch bolt and, by the sound, struggled with it.

Finally, a grating sound indicated it had been pulled free.

The door pulled inward.

He held his breath and waited.

A middle-aged woman pushing a two-wheeled car came into view.

He wanted to avoid a confrontation. Seeing that she came alone, he quietly slid sideways and then backed through the open passageway, watching her the whole time. He then turned and scoped his surroundings.

He looked back and saw the woman mindlessly heaping pea hulls onto the garbage wagon. She paid no attention to anything else, looking neither right nor left, clearly just blankly going about the task.

If he did happen to be noticed, it wouldn't be by that woman. He saw another cart similar to the one the woman used not far away—just big enough to crouch behind. After sprinting the few feet to it, he took a second to get his bearings, remembering what Lana told him about the location of the building that housed the holding cells.

The woman was coming back through the low garbage portal.

He squatted behind the cart.

She appeared zombie-like. Jake wondered if so much as a single thought was in the woman's head. She pushed the squeaky-wheeled contraption down the gravel path away from his hiding place, the crunch of gravel constant beneath the spoked wheels.

He resumed inspecting the compound layout. From where he hunched, he observed he was on the gravel path at the end of multiple rows of cottages. Behind him only a couple of rows remained and behind them the back wall. In front of him he saw all the rest. Per Lana's instructions, he noted the second pathway back from, and parallel to, the front wall. The jail, he'd been told, was somewhere up that row.

A smattering of people went about daily chores. He wondered how to make it to that second row without being noticed. Pristine neatness loomed cold and uninviting. It occurred to him the style of dress of the men might be neater and cleaner than what he wore, otherwise not so different. And Glory had just insisted on him shaving last night, too.

Maybe if I smile like they do, I'll blend in and they won't notice me.

Jake practiced smiling then came out of hiding and strolled toward that second row of cottages. He passed a woman, "Good afternoon," he said in a joyful burst.

The woman's face never flickered, just continued smiling stupidly and staring straight ahead. She didn't acknowledge him at all. He walked on but spoke to no one else. It seemed to be the way it was done. They're certainly an unfriendly lot.

Coming to the second row of cottages from the front wall, he turned left up the path and began searching for the building used as a jail. He came upon a stone building different from the cottages, but in line with them. It was no wider but twice as deep with no windows on the front.

He noticed the obelisk over the top of and beyond the front row of cottages situated between the building he had been told was Tam's residence and the front gate. He wondered if Tam kept Annie's weapons in his house or had them stored in the jail—something he wouldn't know until he got inside and freed Annie. He wasn't sure about it even then. A twinge of fear stuttered his step—the weapons may have been destroyed. If so, what then?

Glancing again at the stone obelisk near the front gate, he saw that the bottom edge of the sun touched its tip. Time ran out—no choice now but to ignore downside possibilities and race headlong to the heart of the

Annie's World: Jake's Legacy

matter and, hopefully, stay alive in the process.

The entire operation hinged on freeing Annie. If not, he'd be dead. Glory and Lana would likely be raped and killed once Tam realized their complicity in the plan and Annie might die, too. Until this moment, Jake had not thought about the enormity of what rode on what he did in the next few seconds. Becoming infuriated by fears that did the Devil's dance in his head, he pounded his forehead with the heel of his hand.

Stop over-thinking and just get it done!

"Go ahead, jump me," said Annie.

Corky, the guard, studied the pieces on the checkerboard and pulled his brow down, yet still smiled. "You dog you. You've set me up again."

"You still need to take your jump."

Resigned to it, he grabbed his checker and flew it over Annie's. Before he'd retracted his hand, she reached through the knee-high food pass-through in the door from her cross-legged seat and jumped his last four checkers to end the game.

"Another one?" she said.

"What's the point? We've played, what, six games?"

"So?"

"I haven't won one and probably won't. You've proven your superior intellect. At the same time, you've taken the fun out of checkers."

"I like you, Corky."

"I'd better not say the same about you." He scrunched up his nose. "You know, in case I have to kill you."

She stared straight-faced momentarily then burst into laughter.

He laughed, too.

As the laughter faded, the vow to her dead friend, Nina, crossed her mind. "Corky, do you know the Masters? They're supposed to be residents here."

His eyelids fluttered as he considered the name. "Masters ... Masters," he muttered. "Can't say that I do."

"They're an elderly couple that arrived from the south a few months back."

"Oh, those people. Yeah, I did meet them." His face went sullen. "I'm sorry to say that they passed away a couple of weeks ago."

"Passed away! They couldn't have."

"I'm afraid so." He rose, gathered up checkers and the board to put them away. "Why the interest? Related?"

"No. I promised a friend I'd check on them. That's all." Her voice trailed, but then anger bubbled up. She snorted as she scooted back against the cold stone of the wall, leaning hard against it, suddenly feeling impotent. "Corky, don't you think it's odd that older people at Stalwart pass away with alarming regularity?"

"I haven't thought about it." He opened one side of a freestanding double-door locker and put the game away.

"Maybe you should before your hair turns gray." She put a finger to her lips then pointed it in his direction. "Consider this: what is the average age of people living here?

He closed the locker door but kept his hand on the knob a moment longer than necessary. "Let me think." He faced her. "I'd say that most people here range from newborn up to about fifteen years older than I am." His eyes fixed on a nondescript area of the wall. "Humph." He rubbed the nape of his neck. "That is troubling. I can't think of a single elderly person still alive within Stalwart walls."

Does anyone with gray hair and wrinkled faces stay long?"

The hand massaging his neck moved around and tickled the soft skin beneath his chin as he tried to remember. "Can't say for sure, but I haven't seen any old folks lately." He squared his body to Annie's cell and looked down at her sitting on the floor. "Do you think it's possible that Tam—"

It was clear, he knew the answer already.

"Think about it; it's just too weird. Even among the elderly a few tend to live longer than others." She waggled a finger. "Think about how much effort it took for those people to get here from wherever it was they came from. For heaven's sake, most of those old people were as tough as boot leather. I'm sure the goal wasn't to make it to Stalwart then keel over dead."

He sat on the small three-legged stool in front of her cell as if he were suddenly very tired. "I've never thought about it before."

"I believe this is just one more example of why the awful sterility of this place gives me the creeps." She rose and leaned against the metal wall separating them. "I want you to think about all we've talked about. There's something dangerously fishy going on here that neat cottages and spotless grounds can't hide. What I see is neurotic orderliness, even to the point of maintaining gender balance and within some specific age range. Not only is litter removed from Stalwart on a regular basis, but also people viewed as substandard. It's time you questioned these things. Someday your daughters will be unceremoniously informed that you and your wife passed away."

Corky stared back raking teeth over his lower lip. "You really believe that, don't you?"

"I do."

One of the planks of the wooden porch just beyond the front door squeaked. Before Corky could get to his feet, Jake burst through with a knife in his hand and ran straight at him, bowling him over off the stool.

Annie gasped. "No Jake! Stop!"

Corky pulled the machete from its belt clip on his waist and, with a short chop, hacked the back of Jake's knife hand as they rolled together across the floor.

With a grunt, Jake released the knife. It clanked across the floor and with it went advantage.

Corky, bigger and stronger, rolled over on top of Jake and held the machete blade to his throat.

"Don't hurt him!"

"He would've stabbed me, Annie! What the hell do you expect me to do?"

"Listen to me," she said, "I know this is a strange way to make an introduction but the man you're about to kill is like a father to me. That's Jake Henderson."

"Henderson ... as in Annie Henderson?"

"Yes."

"But if I let him live, Tam will have me killed."

"No he won't."

"What makes you so sure?"

"I won't let it happen."

Corky looked down as he remained on his knees straddling Jake's chest. Slowly, he pulled the big knife away from Jake's throat. "Mister Henderson, I've come to believe and respect that girl. I can't say for sure why, but she seems to know things I've never considered and there's something about her that I just flat-out trust. She's the only reason I didn't run this knife across your Adam's apple and let you bleed out right here." He stood and clipped the machete back onto his belt.

Jake gagged and coughed then rolled over to face Annie. "Are you okay?"

Annie let her head fall then shook it slowly. "I'm okay, but you were about two seconds away from not being okay at all, dead in fact. Meet Horace McCann. But don't call him Horace. He might kill you yet if you call him that. He prefers Corky."

Jake nodded to the man and muttered, "Thanks for, you know, not killing me." Then his attention went right back to Annie. "I had no choice but rush in and hope for the best. Glory and Lana baited Tam with the promise of sex and—"

"Both of them!"

"Yeah. I'm behind schedule and afraid they might have to follow through. Going through with it was never part of the plan. There's no time to waste, we have to get Eva Louise and the women out now."

"Do you see now, Corky, the lengths Tam will go to? The man only thinks about total control and personal gratification in his spotless little world. He's Satan personified. The man is obsessively compulsive and extremely dangerous. Is that what you want to be part of?"

"But my wife and kids; what about them?"

"Once we're all safely out of this waking nightmare, you have my personal guarantee that all four of you will have a place to sleep, plenty of food and friends, real friends, not these cheesy-grinning zombies at Stalwart."

"I'll back her to the hilt on that," Jake said. "Her word is my word. I'll need plenty of help setting up a defensive compound around Theocratic Minds. I know I may not have endeared myself to you but I'm begging, please join us."

Corky's eyes shifted from Annie to Jake then back. He reached into a shirt pocket and retrieved a key. "I must be out of my mind trusting a girl I met just last night and a man that tried to kill me seconds ago."

"Crazy? Maybe, but in a really, really good way; you're just now beginning to see this place for what it is."

He unlocked the cell door.

Annie stepped out and wrapped him in a hug, pinning his arms to his sides. She pressed her cheek onto his shoulder. "You're a special person, Corky McCann. For as long as you and I live, I'll have your back in good times and bad, in battle and in peace. This is my vow to you. And, I've already explained how seriously I take my promises."

"I hate to break up this sentimental moment," Jake said, "But where are your weapons? I love Eva Louise more than words can express. Still, I don't think Glory or Lana care to have another one of Tam's children."

"Corky?"

Corky backed away from her embrace. "First things first," he said reaching for a rag hanging from a peg on the wall. "Wrap that cut on the back of your hand, Mister Henderson. It doesn't look too bad but you need to stop the bleeding."

He then stepped over to the opposite side of the double-door locker from where he stored the checkerboard and opened it.

Annie saw what she entered Stalwart carrying; her bow and quiver crammed to the limit with arrows, ten multi-pointed throwing disks, the shoulder belt loaded with throwing knives and the one weapon that carried its own special light, the scabbard holding the knife Ethan made for her.

As she began affixing it all to her body, she became all business. "Corky, once Jake and I walk out that door, you run as fast as you can to your cottage, get your wife and children and get out of this compound. Make your way down to the river trail and head north. Once we've finished what we came to do, we'll catch up to you."

"But—"

"No buts! Just do it. Get your family out of here." The last item she picked up was the bow. She shouldered it, then again moved in close to him and pulled his face to hers, kissing him on the forehead. "I'll never forget this kindness. I pray our friendship lasts many years. Now go."

Corky trotted to the front door but hesitated. "And you say you're just fifteen?"

"Well … yeah," she said then added with haste, "but I'll be sixteen this fall."

He shook his head as he continued out the door.

Jake took out, too. "Come on, Annie. We don't have a second to waste."

"Hang on, there's something I have to tell you that you need to be aware of."

He stopped, but was antsy to keep moving. "Speak up. What is it?"

"Tam is like me. That's how they managed to overpower me."

His jaw fell slack. "Crap! You mean he could slap me to death with his pinky finger?"

"Without breaking it down specifically, yes."

His shoulders slumped. "Oh no."

"Under no circumstances are you to engage him in a fight. If Corky was a problem, Tam will dispose of you in two beats of your heart and that's only if you get the jump on him. Besides superior speed and strength, his hearing is more acute than mine. On top of that, his weakness is lust, not caring about others. So, he'll not hesitate to kill you like I might him."

"What's your plan?"

"I'll head directly for Eva's bedroom window. You go to the front door. Once you hear the noise I'll surely make, you burst through the door, go left of the fireplace and as fast as you can go down the back hall to a door on the right, next to the last I believe. That should be where Glory and Lana are. By that time Tam will be in Eva's bedroom and I'll keep him busy while you get those two out safely. Then — "

"By yourself?"

"Remember what I told you before; I don't need the distraction of worrying about your safety or anyone else's. Just get Glory and Lana out of there while I take care of Tam."

"Maybe I should — "

"Maybe you should *do what I say.*"

He snapped his head back. "Hey …"

She clenched her teeth and took a moment to breathe. "I suppose this is a problem I'll have, being so young and all, but that's a discussion for another time." She fixed a stern stare on him. "You know that I love you, don't you?"

"Well, yeah, but — "

"Good. Now *shut up and do what I say.*"

"But — "

"*Just hush.* Listen to me; I can handle Tam as long as I'm sure all of you have safely gotten out. No more talk."

They stepped out the door. The sun had begun to set but there was still full light, another hindrance to overcome. Dark would've been preferable. Leading the way in short spurts she ran from cottage to cottage waiting at each stop for Jake to catch up. People were about but mostly women. She saw only a few men.

The last surge of speed brought her to the rear of Tam's house. She moved parallel to the outside wall to the window of the bedroom where she last saw Eva. She turned to Jake as he approached and waved him on to the front door. Stepping lightly, he slipped past her.

Annie craned her neck and saw Eva lying on her side, knees drawn up. The little girl faced her but her eyes were shut. She was crying.

She noticed the girl rubbed her eyes frequently. Each time she did, they were open for a second. The next time she pushed and rolled her balled fists in them, Annie began waving with both arms, trying to capture the child's attention.

Nothing.

Annie watched for a time, but the girl kept her eyes closed. Then Annie noticed a mockingbird alight on the roof next door singing its varied song. During a brief lull in its call, she mimicked one of the sounds with a quick warbling whistle—a sound she'd attempted to teach the youngster while once sitting in the woods together.

Eva's eyes popped open.

Again, Annie waved with both hands.

The child saw her.

Annie put a finger to her lips and frowned.

Confused, Eva stared for a moment then got out of bed and walked to the window.

Annie heard the bedroom floor squeak even from where she stood outside.

***

Glory and Lana wore identical red satin robes and stood in Tam's bedroom waiting. Glory noticed Tam's interest wasn't confined to one on one contact. Artwork in the room bore overly intimate references, every piece. An intricately detailed and highly explicit sculpture stood as a centerpiece on a long narrow table against the wall. Smaller figurines of similar ilk, all unambiguous, surrounded it. Paintings depicting nude forms lined the walls. Lighting was subdued and red, also a favorite color of the drapes, bed canopy and bedspread.

Lana's eyes floated in tears.

"Hold it together, hon," said Glory, breathing the words directly into her friend's ear. She put an arm around Lana's waist just as Tam entered the room. Glory wondered if avoiding this perversion was at all possible now. *Jake, please be on your way.*

"I trust you found the bathroom accommodation satisfactory."

Glory now looked around the room for a different reason; she sought a way out.

Lana whimpered. "I'm sorry, Glory; I can't go through with this … not again, *ever* again."

Tam's pretense of pleasantness vanished. He said with an edge, "Let me explain something about business, Lana. If you fail to live up to your bargain then you'll be in breach of contract. Do you know what that means?"

Head down, Lana sniffed.

"It means that I'll hold both of you in forced compliance for a period of my choosing. In other words, dear, I'll still have my way with both of you but you'll be locked away and not allowed to leave. And *our* daughter will be mine to do with as I see fit. Is that what you want?"

"I should never have come!" Lana wailed. "I'm just making things worse."

"Don't *say that*," Glory scolded. "Your daughter needs you." She tightened the belt on her robe. "Well then, if you can't go through with this, neither will I. If he has his way then it will have to be forced upon us. I'll not submit voluntarily."

Something captured Tam's attention. He cranked his head to the side and listened, holding the pose for only a second when, suddenly, the sound of breaking glass came from across the hall.

***

Annie reached through the window and pulled Eva through, dropping her to the ground. "Run, Punkin! Go as fast as you can." Annie turned and dove through the window into the bedroom, bounding to her feet in time to look back and see something astounding; five-year-old Eva ran dodging and darting with the speed of a frightened rabbit.

Eva inherited the trait. She's like her father.

With no time to consider it further she focused on the closed bedroom door. She slipped a throwing knife from the belt angled across her chest and palmed it.

As her arm reared for a throw, Tam burst through the door.

She let it fly with all the strength she could summon.

He howled as the knife sunk deep into his right shoulder joint, only the handle still showing on his chest.

While looking at the protruding weapon he growled, "You have just become more trouble than you're worth." With no further show of pain he pulled the knife from his shoulder with his left hand and, with the flick of a wrist, sent it sailing back.

The left hand was undoubtedly his non-dominant side. Although it had power and swiftness, the aim was skewed. Annie rolled sideways, leaned away and watched it whoosh by leaving a shallow cut on her cheek.

She heard a human whistle outside then another and another.

An alarm had been sounded and spread throughout the compound. Advantage dwindled fast.

Tam back-stepped to the bedroom door as the sound of many feet came running down the hall. "I have a wound to tend to, then I must dress more appropriately for our next meeting. I needn't worry about you leaving; your hands will be quite full for the next few minutes." In a blink he was gone, replaced by men spilling through the door.

Blood trickled down the side of her face but she had no time to wonder how badly she'd been cut. She turned, dove headfirst through the shattered window, rolled and sprang to her feet outside.

Men closed in from both ends of the narrow alley between buildings.

Knives came flying at her from both directions.

She leaped back, slamming into and flattening against the outside wall of the main house as all but one of the knives sailed past her. That one glanced off her ribs and stuck in her rabbit fur vest.

Without taking time to grimace she pulled it out and sent it right back. It pierced a man's throat. She whimpered, knowing it was a fatal stick.

The others crowding behind him hesitated.

Four to her right kept coming.

She reached into the waist of her leather pants and pulled out two of the spiked disks, one in each hand, hurling them simultaneously. Before the small weapons had arrived at the targets, she withdrew two of the knives and prepared to throw them but hesitated when the thrown disks embedded in the foreheads of two men.

Hesitation became the bigger enemy.

Attackers moved closer.

A flash image of her mother dying in a pool of her own blood as the result of showing mercy overcame her. She ground her teeth together. *Get over it or die.*

A surge of renewed power coursed through her; adrenaline spiked.

With unearthly agility she whipped knives and disks with such ferocity none of the men in either direction had time to react.

As she prepared to throw again, it became came clear that she'd felled fourteen armed men bent on killing her. Others came streaming around the rear corner of the building.

She raced over the pile of injured and dying men to the front and on to the obelisk standing between Tam's house and the front gate. There she had room to fight.

She reassessed armaments. Disks were exhausted and only two of the throwing knives remained. But her quiver of arrows was full and she had her beloved Ethan knife.

She noticed a crowd gathering in a wide circle.

Then she saw something that threatened her focus: six armed men surrounding Jake, Glory and Lana, who sat submissive, huddled on the ground. She didn't see Eva.

Armed men came at her.

She grasped three arrows, placed two between her teeth, strung the other and shot the nearest aggressor.

He tumbled to the ground with the arrow protruding from below his clavicle. She fired the two between her teeth, then two more, all four finding their intended targets.

The attackers slowed and fanned wide.

In a sweep of the eyes, she counted seventeen still on their feet. "Hold your ground," she shouted, "Or, so help me, I'll drop all of you!"

"I don't think you can," one shouted. "Come on, men. She's just a kid." They came at her, all brandishing machetes.

She detected a whoosh of something flying in from her right and turned in time to deflect a small knife with a quick slap of her bow but not before another coming in from the left stuck her in the thigh.

Careening sideways, she dropped to a knee, yanked the knife from her leg with a fleshy slurp and hurled it side-armed into the offender's chest.

With no time to stand, she remained down on one knee. She pulled arrow after arrow and fired them all. Within the span of a scant few seconds, she'd emptied the quiver.

Two remaining men were upon her before she could drop the bow and pull her knife.

Glory shouted, "Run Annie! Get out of there!"

The appeal was quickly followed by a slap of flesh and a groan.

Annie looked and saw a guard standing over Glory. He had backhanded her with a severe blow, knocking her friend into the dirt onto her side.

There'd be no running away. That opportunity vanished with a knife to her thigh leaving a painful wound that'd hamper speed. Blood streamed from it.

She bled from three wounds. Loss of blood would soon impair her. She had to get things under control—*now*.

She ducked just as a machete swished over her head.

She came up lunging and popped the man in the left side of the chest with the heel of her hand so fast and hard it stuttered his heart.

He stumbled backward and fell, holding his chest.

She dropped down and, with bleeding leg extended, whirled in a circle, clipping the other man's legs from beneath him.

By then the one she'd punched was back on his feet, howling in anger with the machete raised high.

As he swung in a wide arc at her head, she pulled the ornate knife from its scabbard and drove it into the man's groin in an upward thrust.

Although it had no power behind it, the downward momentum of the machete gashed her upper arm.

She ignored the sting.

He screeched like a small frightened child.

She pulled the last throwing knife and flicked it sideways at the one she'd tripped, now charging in from the other direction. It flew with a mighty momentum—entirely disappearing into the left side of his chest. He floundered a step, then crashed to the ground with a thud.

She finally had a moment to consider the situation. Lying dead or dying were twenty-eight men.

The screech of the man with his groin gouged by her knife unnerved her.

Her lip quivered. Tears filled her eyes. Remaining on her knees, she let her head fall and wept for lives lost. She then looked skyward and yelled in frustration, "Please! Bring sanity to the world!"

A familiar voice filled her mind. Although unspoken and heard only by her, the source was clear enough. "Bringin' sanity back is what you be doin' now, sweet Annie. Da weight of da world be settin' squarely on your shoulders. Da future of humanity in dis nasty ol' world is yours to mold."

Although Dame Fortune's admonition should've brought to bear an unimaginable burden of responsibility, it had the opposite effect. It was comforting. She drew strength from it, coming to believe that what she did might have a positive impact on the course of future events.

Clapping came from Tam's house.

She looked a last time at the mortally wounded man nearest her, his screams waned and had now transformed into whimpers as life leached away.

She turned to face the sound and, through watery eyes, saw Tam standing dressed in a royal blue satin robe that extended to just above his sandaled feet. Large open sleeves ended below his elbows. He was applauding. "That was magnificent. I didn't think you'd be able to overcome those odds."

"It was needless! I shouldn't have had to do it!" she shouted, then sobbed, her arms hanging limp at her sides; the blood covered knife clutched in her right hand.

"You just did what you had to. Now, I must do the same." He pushed out an arrogant pouty lip. "It saddens me. You and my chosen mate for you would've made splendid offspring. But, alas, you chose to make trouble."

"You egotistical, delusional madman—I chose nothing! All of this is your doing."

"It would appear that we must agree to disagree." Tam pulled a strange looking sword from a sash around his waist. "Now, my friend, as they say in upper echelons of the corporate world, it's time for a win-win." The strange looking sword curved and widened toward its end then blunted.

Annie took note that he used his left hand. The knife she'd stuck in his right shoulder may have helped even the odds somewhat. Still, she was about to go up against a sword with only an ornate hunting knife and wounds that bled profusely. She was also becoming light-headed, blood loss taking a toll.

Tam advanced, confidently resting the sword over his shoulder. "Once I've ended this problem, that would be you, then I'll order my men to execute those other troublemakers that came to your rescue. You've decimated my elite guard and ruined my day. No need for you to ruin my evening, too. Dinner will be ready soon."

Annie came off her knees. She rolled a shoulder upward and wiped the blood trickle on her cheek then swooned. She stumbled sideways, fluttering clear vision into her eyes. She limped, fresh blood flowed from the leg wound with each step. She glanced to the widening blood drenched spot on her shirt over her ribs and checked the gash on her left shoulder that now had her left hand covered in blood and dripping from her fingertips.

In a flash, he was upon her.

She attempted a defensive posture, but too late.

He slapped the knife from her hand with the flat of his sword.

It flew into the flowers around the obelisk. On the backswing he put a shallow cut just above her breasts, meant only to humiliate.

Unsteadily, but with as much speed as possible, she backed away, glancing about looking for anything that might offer advantage.

She became increasingly faint. Blood and sweat streaked her face.

She kept sweeping bodily fluids from her eyes with the back of her blood covered hand, desperately trying to maintain clear vision.

Tam stalked her with a smile.

Then a beautiful sight—Eva hiding behind the obelisk. The innocent features of the child were out of place in this dangerous situation. The youngster had retrieved Annie's knife from the tangle of flowers at its base. The stone spire hid her from Tam's view.

The youngster tossed the knife to Annie.

Tam looked to see from where it came.

Annie caught it and threw it in a single lightning sweep of her bloodied arm.

It entered Tam's midsection with tremendous velocity—burying past the hilt and halfway up the carved mesquite wood handle, stopping only when it stuck in his spine.

The surprise on his face couldn't have been greater, bested by an injured fifteen-year-old girl.

He dropped the sword and pulled the knife from his abdomen.

He tried advancing aggressively, holding the bloodied knife in one hand and the sword in the other.

He teetered and fell, made a final pathetic attempt to get up. Instead, he caved in, and flopped face first to the ground.

Annie pulled the knife from his grasp and fell to her knees at his side. "Why, Mister Tam? It didn't have to be this way?"

His eyes swam. Death stalked. "It's my nature. I could no more fight who I am than you can."

He gasped and drew a loud spastic breath. He clutched her arm and fought to lift his head, desperate to get the words out. "P—Please, Annie Henderson, don't hate me." After another breath, he went limp, and lifelessly still.

With those words, Annie realized he did care but, even in his final moments, his concern remained distorted. He cared more about what people would think of him after he was gone.

The gathered crowd closed in.

The armed men guarding Jake, Glory and Lana dropped their weapons.

It was over. Adrenaline drained away. She keeled over onto her side then rolled onto her back.

Eva dropped down next to her and cried. "Don't go, Annie. Please don't go."

The last thing Annie remembered as she drifted off unconscious was thinking what a beautiful child her li'l Punkin was.

Annie stood some distance from the cluster of buildings called Theocratic Minds. She took in the view, heretofore ignorant that a panorama was possible from this distance or angle. But there it was, spread before her. A tingling rush raced from her toes through the top of her head. She viewed this place as home and was overjoyed to be back. It warmed her.

Never having given it much consideration before, she noticed ordinary things beyond everyday perspective—sprawling cedar bushes, natural heady aroma perfuming the air, prickly pear cacti with brilliant yellow blossoms scattered randomly over clusters of them, and scrub oaks—gnarled and strong in artful ways. She gave it all an appreciative look, a smile and a nod.

Then it occurred to her, she stood in this place without Jake, Glory, Lana and Eva Louise. She looked about.

Where are they?

She took note of other things that should be part of this experience but weren't—no pain, no bloodstains, and no people, anywhere. Deep feelings of joy and peace remained, but questions circled. *I want to share this moment with my family. Where are they?*

"They be damn busy takin' care o' you, child." Dame Fortune's voice sounded as if the old lady was next to her but, instead, stood at a great distance.

"This can't be a dream, I didn't go to sleep. The last thing I remember is passing out. Did—did I die?"

In an instant, the enchanting, youthful black woman that Dame Fortune chose to appear as stood directly in front of her. "No, Annie girl," she said with a sympathetic eye slant. "You're unconscious and will stay dat way for a long while but you be in good hands. Dey be workin' to fix your body while I be workin' at moldin' your thoughts."

"Why have you come to me? Couldn't it wait until we could sit and chat in the flesh? Is there another matter of urgency I must confront?"

"It be urgent all right. But ya don't need to be worryin' yourself with deadline pressure. It be a problem of this age and surely be needin' a fix but ya don't need to be concernin' yourself with runnin' out and doin' anythin' soon. Okie dokie?"

"Are you going to tell me about it? Is that why you're here?"

"Oh, child, we be doin' more dan dat. Since we have da time, you bein' unconscious and all, I be showin' not just tellin'."

"What do you mean?"

"I mean, child, ya be getting' da chance to know what flyin' feels like."

"Huh?"

"Take my hand."

Annie wrapped her hand around Dame's extended fingers and kissed her dark, wrinkle-free and supple knuckles, then said with a broad smile, "Have I told you lately how much I love you?"

Dame cackled. "Oh, child, ya be tellin' me in everythin' ya do, in every move ya make. Come on. Let's go flyin'. Dis be my favorite part."

Hearing the gruff voice come out of that beautiful mouth was a strange combination indeed. Annie grinned. "I'm ready."

Together they floated high into the air.

Annie felt a sudden rush course through her. It took her breath. "Oh, wow."

Dame looked at her with a strange glint.

"Why are you looking at me like that?"

"'Cuz you gonna be lovin' dis."

Dame went prone, pulling Annie over to join her in that position then accelerated to warp speed—sweeping over treetops as Annie watched the landscape rise and fall beneath them, changing from heavily wooded country to open plains, crossing rivers, canyons and crumbling remains of villages, towns and cities. "This feels fantastic, Dame, I don't ever want to stop."

"Dis what ya be needin' to repair your broken heart and heal da wounds of battle. Enjoy da velvet brush of wind against your face and just be goin' with it. Da world beneath us will reveal its secrets so you be knowin' more about your place in it."

Distance ticked off in thousands of miles. Appearing on the horizon, she saw a long shoreline. By the time she looked down to check it out, they passed it. She had to look backward to maintain a view of it for a second longer. Ahead, she saw nothing but expansive water.

"Da Pacific Ocean," Dame said.

"I've never seen an ocean. It's huge."

"Man had almost taken all da flippin' fish out of all da oceans. But now dey be teemin' with life again. Dere is good still in dis world; dat's just one small example. You need to see it and know dat ya not be fightin' dis battle alone."

They again came to a long shoreline, now crossing over land. "Where are we now?"

"Asia. Dis once be called China."

Below was a sprawling city unlike any she'd ever seen. It wasn't in decay like in America.

Dame Fortune slowed their speed.

People, hundreds of thousands of people, all looking similar to Tam and Eva Louise, went about daily activities as they flew over them. "Dame, they all look content and happy. And this city is magnificent. Why are they so blessed?"

"Years ago, dese people had help takin' dere lives back from da manipulators in big business. Dey started all over buildin' a society dat served everyone, not just da powerful few."

Once again accelerating, they flew across the broad expanse of an urbanesque environment.

Dame slowed. "See dat old man wit' all da children around him?"

"Who is he?"

"He be just like you, Annie girl, genetically enhanced with da biggest gall-durn heart on dis continent. As a young man, he fought da fight you be just beginnin'. Dis city is da result of all dem good works by dat feller."

"Does he rule over all this?"

"He be rulin' nothin', child. But he be cheerleadin' doze who do."

"Can we do that? Can we start from scratch and make that happen?"

She laughed. "Oh, baby, ya still don't be seein' dat you've already started it. You be da seed of everythin' to come in our part of dis big ol' world."

They sped away veering south.

The terrain below changed rapidly, passing over bodies of water, mountains and deserts.

Again they slowed.

A jungle opened to reveal a cozy clearing in the, otherwise, dense canopy of lush rain forest. People with skin darker than Dame's milled about, armed with spears, bows and knives—weapons she was familiar with. Thatched roof structures were tightly circled around a common yard.

What she called weapons, they used as tools for hunting meat. "Why are you showing me these people?"

"Dis tribe, like hundreds of others in dis part of da world, were never under da influence of big business. Da lives of dese people have gone unchanged for thousands of years because dey live by a simple rule: take from da earth only what is needed. Dis is da lesson to be learned from dese beautiful people." Dame sighed. "Dey are beautiful, aren't dey?"

"Yeah they are." Annie looked to her friend and mentor. "Too bad they don't know you. They might love you as much as I do."

"Oh, dey be knowin' me good all right."

"How can that be? You're in my head. This is not really happening."

"It be happenin', child."

"Really?"

"What you be seein' girl is as it is. And dat be a good thing 'bout simple people. Dey not encumbered by biases. Anytime I choose I can enter dere thoughts. Dey not be questionin' da reality of my presence. Baby, I have friends all over dis world dat would scream in terror if dey knew what I really looked like." She laughed uproariously as the flight gathered speed.

"Where to now?"

Dame Fortune's face tightened. "Now it be necessary, child, to visit a place back in our part of da world dat not be so peaceful and not beautiful at all. Ya need to be seein' it, ya need to know. It's time to leave dis place once called Africa and go home."

They flew northwest at blurring velocity, finally slowing, then coming to a hovering stop.

Annie looked down and around. "Where are we?"

"Ya don't be recognizin' dis place?"

Annie glanced sideways. "It's not every day I fly around the world and I'm certainly not accustomed to looking down on it."

"Funny girl." Dame pointed to a spot off to the left where a river flowed. "Dat be da Brazos River and dat bald patch of earth with two burned out buildings be Blister Knob." She shifted her gaze now pointing to the right at just another crumbling city off in the distance. "And dat place, once upon a time, be called Dallas."

"I've heard of it. But what's so special about it? Crumbling cities are scattered everywhere."

"Special? No, Annie Girl, it not be 'cuz it's special dat we go dere. We go 'cuz it be typical."

"I don't understand."

"I be showin' ya." Again they took off. In an instant they were floating over the carcass of the city.

Annie sighed. "I can only imagine the grandeur of this place a couple of hundred years ago."

Below, children played. Among the rubble of a collapsed building, she saw six youngsters, all preteen. "They seem normal, laughing and playing like they should be."

"Dey be da main reason we're here—dem and all da children in all da cities like dis one."

Dame guided Annie to the ground and touched down as a feather might on a calm day. They watched for a time, unnoticed by the kids, as Dame and Annie were in spiritual formlessness. A girl, ten years old perhaps, said, "I'm hungry. I'm going home. See y'all later." She merrily waved and split from the group, skipping away.

"Come on child, let's follow dat youngun," Dame said.

The girl ran into a hovel where a ragged cloth drape served as a door.

As if gliding on a pad of air, Annie and Dame followed the youngster into the building.

A woman tended an ample cast iron pot over a fire in an open hearth. With a large wooden spoon, she stirred what appeared to be a stew. She seemed happy and smiled at the girl as she came through the doorway. Then her face went stern. "You didn't go into the brickyard district, did you?"

"No ma'am."

"Good girl. See that you don't. Now that your father has brought home a young tender one for dinner," she took a sip of the boiling broth from the spoon and smacked her lips, "I fear the Riley Gang will be skulking about trying to steal our food."

Annie leaned into Dame and whispered into her ear, "Is there a territorial rivalry going on here? Is that what this is about?"

"Yes, but dat's only a tiny part of da story. Watch, listen and learn."

A man with long scraggily hair and a full black beard came through the draped entry. "Let's eat," he said brusquely and sat on a stool next to a rugged plank table.

"You're just in time," the woman said. She waved the young girl to her stool. "Sit down, Lizzy." She took a thick rag and wrapped it around the handle, lifted the pot from the fire and set it in the center of the table. With two wooden spoons, she reached in and pinched a chunk of meat between them and dropped it in front of the girl, who closed her eyes, sniffing the aroma with pleasure, then opened her eyes and exclaimed, "That smells and looks good. I'm so hungry."

"Eat up," her mother said, then smiled.

"They seem like such a normal, happy family," Annie whispered.

"Keep watchin'."

The woman stuck her spoons back into the pot, apparently fishing for a specific cut. She smiled at the man. "I know what your favorite piece is. Aha, here it is." From the pot she lifted out an unmistakable human forearm with the hand and fingers still attached and plopped it on the bare table in front of the man.

"*Oh my God*," Annie hissed.

The man twisted off the hand and began nibbling on the fingers, as if it were the most natural thing in the world.

"I can't believe what I'm seeing," Annie said. "He's so nonchalant. It's just lunch to him." Her lip began quivering. "That's the hand of *a child*."

Dame nodded. "Life as usual for dese poor people not be at all normal to you and me. Dey not be knowin' better, 'cuz its all dey ever knew." Her voice thickened, drenched in sadness. She scooped up Annie's hand. "As dese people leave childhood to become adults dey grow insane and die young. Even da people ya be watchin' now don't be thinkin' straight. Dey be crazy, child, insane don't ya know."

Annie bolted and tried yanking her hand free of the old woman's hold on her. She wanted to fly away, to turn her back on the savagery, but Dame Fortune held fast.

"I know ya want to be runnin' but ya must be knowin' it and for dis old blind woman to just be tellin' ya about it over a cup of tea isn't good enough. Ya have to be seein' it, girl. It has to be an image seared forever in your memory, 'cuz it's you dat's gonna be changin' it." Holding tight to her hand, Dame stood unmoving. She forced Annie to watch.

As the man ate, he said, "Missus Billings caught the sickness. There'll be a community sharing this afternoon. I'll see if I can get a prime cut for us." He smiled at the young girl then tweaked her nose. "That'd be worth a celebration. Don't you think, Lizzy?"

"Yeah, Daddy, that'd be great." She became giddy and giggled.

The woman seemed to be saddened by the news. "Poor Missus Billings? She was such a dear friend." Then she shook it off and brightened. "Oh well, maybe there'll still be a tender cut or two from her by the time you get there."

As Annie watched, the entire scenario became increasingly difficult to believe. She shook her head, dismayed. "Dame, what's the sickness?"

"When people be eatin' one another for many years, da steady diet of human flesh drives people mad. Dey don't be knowin' its source and don't care much either 'cause when someone goes down with da sickness, it be an excuse to harvest dat person for food."

"It's hard to believe. To them, it's so ... every day, so normal. They don't seem to care that what they're sticking in their mouths was once a living, breathing, talking, feeling human like them."

"Like I said, Annie girl; to dem it is normal and dey not be thinkin' straight like you an' me. Still, it be an abomination dat needs fixin'."

"If what I'm seeing is happening in the remnants of every large city, how can I make a difference? I'm just one person."

Dame Fortune pulled Annie's face away from the grotesqueness of that table and what those people did. She took a moment to run her fingers through Annie's long, straight, golden hair and caress her cheeks with the flats of her palms. Dame's sympathetic dark eyes sparkled with youth as they searched every nuance of Annie's features. "It's only da children ya need to be concerned with, Annie ... da children."

"I still don't understand."

Dame dropped her hands onto Annie's shoulders. "It be like da shark. Once dat flippin' fish gets a whiff of blood, it can't think 'bout anythin' else and will go into a frenzy until dat lust be satisfied. A lifetime of cannibalism be like dat shark. Adults can't be helped." Dame stepped away and locked her fingers together at her front. "Oh, dey may seem friendly enough and offer shelter and protection but dey will always be lookin' at you like we looked at dat turkey ya brought home in da autumn of last year. And someday, dey be havin' you for lunch. Dey might even be tellin' one another what a doggone good person you were as dey gnaw da meat from your bones. It's all dey know. Da children are different. Dey still be impressionable and can be taught respect for human life and dere diet can be changed. Dey can be saved and dat's what ya need to be settin' your sights on. Now, do you be understandin'?"

"I think so."

"Ya got to be takin' dem into da country where other food sources can be learned before it's too late for dem to change. Theocratic Minds is a great place for dem to live and learn. But you'll be takin' children from dere parents and dey won't be understandin' at all 'bout dat. You be actually havin' ta convince children to leave dere own parents. It'll be da hardest thing you've ever done. But ya gotta do it. Ya hear me? Ya gotta."

***

The vision disappeared in a dazzling flash of light. Annie opened her eyes. She was no longer standing in the doorway of a Dallas hovel watching people eat people. She was being carried in a heavy cloth sling between two poles running slightly longer than her length. She tilted her head back and looked up at Jake on the right and Corky McCann on the left, each manning a pole. A sharp stinging pain across her upper chest reminded her of multiple wounds. She clumsily traced fingers across her chest, face, leg and ribs to find that all had been bandaged. She took a breath to speak but only managed a moan when injured ribs cut it short.

Jake looked down. He signaled Corky to set her on the ground. They placed the litter on a soft spot of earth. "Hey, Little One, how're you feeling?" He knelt next to her.

Eyes closed, she squirmed. "Like I lost the battle." She opened them and saw Jake's puffy red eyes.

"You had us worried. You lost a lot of blood."

Softly she said, "Oh Jake. I'd never leave you. How selfish would I be if I croaked without telling you goodbye?" She grabbed a fistful of his shirt and pulled him down, kissing his cheek.

"It's not funny."

She smiled, but in a lazy, pain-filled way. "It wasn't meant to be. I was serious."

She then looked at Corky McCann and realized his presence was odd. "I thought I told you to take your family and head north."

Corky grinned and pointed behind her. "Blame Cynthia."

213

"Cynthia?"

"My wife."

That was the unrecognizable woman holding one of the poles at the other end. She looked into the caring face of Cynthia McCann, smiling at her. Cynthia was a plump woman wearing a long dress to her ankles, strawberry blonde hair pulled back into a bun. Her skin was pale with faded freckles. She stood next to Glory and Lana. Behind her were two cute little girls with curly brown hair, freckled faces and the deepest dimples ever.

"She's a good doctor," Corky said. "All those stitches and bandages are her doing."

"In that case, I'm glad you didn't listen to Corky and he didn't listen to me. Thanks, Cynthia." She looked up at Corky. "I bet you can't beat her in checkers, either."

Cynthia's head recoiled. "What?"

"Your husband is not very good at checkers. That's all."

Corky smiled shyly. "She's right."

"What do you know? It took a stranger to fill you in on just how bad you are at that game. I never had the heart to tell you," Cynthia said then chuckled. She smiled at Annie. "Anyone willing to go against Tam deserved all my support, simple as that. I may not have known you but once I heard the story I certainly knew your cause and shared it."

"Tam ... is he dead, or did I dream that?"

Glory came around to stand over her. "You didn't dream it. He's gone."

"When we walked out of Stalwart this morning, a community meeting was underway to elect a council to run the compound," Lana said. "No guarantees, but I believe thievery by so-called suppliers is a thing of the past."

Annie breathed deep then expelled a satisfied sigh. "Good. We need to set up ongoing communication to assure them support during the transition."

From behind Lana's leg stepped Eva Louise. She pouted.

"Hey, Punkin. What's the matter?"

"I thought I lost you."

"Come here, you."

Eva dropped to her knees and Annie, wincing and struggling with pain but determined to not let it stop her, raised her arms enough to pull Eva to her, embrace and smother her miniature face in kisses. "Did you know that you're just like me?"

Eva's eyes grew large. "Really?"

"Yeah, really. You don't think everyone can run as fast as you can, do you?" Annie came up on an elbow and began to roll over.

"Lie down," Jake demanded.

Annie squinted up into his darkened silhouetted face, the sun beaming in over his shoulder. "It's okay. I think I can walk." She sat up. Her head spun. She fell back on her elbows. "Well, maybe not quite yet."

Jake's lip quivered. He signaled Corky and the girls to lift the litter. "You've done what it would've taken a small well-armed militia to accomplish." He quickly turned his head away. "I think we can carry you another mile or two. We owe you at least that much. Relax. We're almost home, Little One, almost home."

Is Jake crying? She wondered.

"Thanks, Henry." Jake wiped sweat from his cheeks and forehead on his long-sleeve shirt.

Henry slapped him on the back. "Let's save a little for tomorrow. We've had a full day."

"It was a good one all right." He looked to the other Brothers of Theocratic Minds who'd toiled alongside him all day. "Thanks to all of you, it has been a good day, indeed," he called out as they walked en masse back to the dormitories.

Henry waved without looking back. "We'll be ready for another one tomorrow, Mister Henderson."

Jake scooped a dipper of water from a sheet metal bucket fashioned out of salvaged scraps from the old power plant. It hung by its wire handle on a stubby tree branch. He savored a drink and then sat on the last cedar log rolled off the flatbed wagon next to the rebuilt sawmill. Hitched to the wagon were two newly acquired horses that had been vital in the heavy work. The Order had begun replenishing its stock of animals. Besides the horses that they had bartered for, they'd found chickens, wild hogs and ducks. All had been penned and were being held for breeding. It'd take a generation, but the fowls and livestock would become domesticated and easier to manage in time.

Things were coming together. A life worth living had finally caught up to Jake. He figured all he had to do was keep working and be patient. In time, this new home would be better than the one at Blister Knob.

He thought about that dark time before Annabelle came into his life. But he'd been a vastly different person and that a different time, dreamlike. He wondered if it actually had happened as remembered.

He saw hope and felt it deep in his bones. He had a wonderful family to thank for that: Annie, sweet Glory, Lana, Eva, Dame, and every resident of Theocratic Minds. In all his life there had never been a deeper peace than now, as he moved into an age considered advanced by the standards of the day—somewhere around fifty, he guessed. He no longer obsessed about that or if anyone would remember him when he died. A better world was in its infancy and he was blessed to have seen, and contributed to, its birth. He looked forward to many more years.

This overly warm late October day waned but the wind picked up and swirled around, now coming in from the north, brushing his face with streamers of fresh cool air. The seasons had begun the push and pull of change. The smell of that fine distinction carried upon the breeze. It felt natural to become reflective at this time, the advent of a new season.

Although the year began fraught with danger and radical changes, it took a blessed turn, thanks to Annabelle's tenacity and natural talents.

Sipping water from the dipper, he watched her play hide and seek with Eva Louise. She looked so childlike, so innocent. She'd turn sixteen next month but right now she ran and laughed with young Eva as if she and the girl were the same age—not a care.

He had yet to come to terms with Annabelle's enigmatic extremes. He watched the girl, now squealing with delight over the shenanigans of a five-year-old. The same youngster who had single-handedly fought a bloody battle—against odds no mere human could possibly confront, let alone overcome and be victorious—all to free them and save Theocratic Minds from future attacks orchestrated by a brutal CEO. She bore scars as proof. He feared her lifetime would be filled with scars: some visible, others psychological. A still-pink scar across her cheek remained as a stark reminder of many important battles yet to be fought. Jake feared that mark and others hidden beneath her clothes were only the beginning. His responsibility as Annabelle's guide into adulthood was still somewhat nebulous. He wanted to believe he protected her from an evil world. That was absurd. She was *his* guardian, destined to be the protector of many she had yet to meet—the liberator of a generation.

Yet, as he watched her play, it was obvious she kept the immeasurable scope of it in the recesses of her mind—beautiful youth. At this moment, she only knew joy and love for a young child, little more than a child herself—a chameleon, whether she indulged in an immature romp with Eva or planning a military operation with the precision of a battle-hardened general. His Annabelle had grown into an enigma of the times in which they lived, better suited to a more advanced age over two hundred years in the past.

He sighed, exhaling disbelief. *Why couldn't she be a normal teenager, giddy one moment and loaded with bad attitude the next?* It seemed cruel that she be cheated out of a childhood, denied simple pleasures enjoyed by others her age—unfair that she be thrown into the unlikely role of savior to a world overrun with insanity. To see her at play now, carefree, provided some small comfort. *I hope she can have and enjoy many more moments like this.*

"You seem deep in thought," Glory said as she approached from behind.

Startled, he looked up. He then settled and smiled. "Deep? Me?" He chuckled and winked. "I doubt that."

"Something is holding your mind hostage. I can see that."

"Oh, I'm not held hostage in what I was thinking about. It's exactly where I wanted my head to be, feeling thankful," his eyes connected with hers, "beginning with you, of course."

She smiled, threaded her arm through his and pulled him close. "Of course."

He caressed her smooth dark cheek with the backs of his fingertips while admiring her exotic beauty. Her tightly curled black hair glistened as it fanned wide from beneath a leather thong across her upper back. "I love you."

"And I you," she said, then kissed him on the lips. She sniffed and grinned. "You need a bath something awful, Mister Henderson."

"You're not going to let me forget a former life I'm not too proud of, are you?"

"That's when I fell in love with you, silly." She chuckled. "I don't think you could've smelled worse back then. Now, whether or not you care to believe it, I enjoy remembering that time. It was special. You were a beacon in a world that Mother and I had just about given up on, a smelly angel. So, prepare yourself for a lifetime of reminders of that stinky former life." She pecked him on the lips once more, sprang to her feet and began walking away. "I'll have you something ready to eat after your bath."

As he ran a respectful hand over the twelve-inch log he sat on, he thought: Tomorrow, you'll be transformed into magnificent boards. He looked to the partially built cedar-planked structures that would become a combination of corporation and protectorate facilities of Theocratic Minds. He wondered about the wisdom of having no wall around it. That choice had been Glory's. She wanted a welcoming sight—a place that visually spoke of home, not a fortress, believing people had suffered enough and would respond favorably to such a sight. It had been Glory's dream and she would be its CEO. Jake respected and abided by her decision. It lacked a name, but Glory wanted to somehow work her mother's name, Myrna, into it. Given time, she'd come up with the perfect name to attract the tired, the poor and the hungry. One day it'd be the best known city-state in these parts. In that, he had no doubt.

A number of the brothers and sisters originally unaccounted for had come back, but refused to reaffirm the vow. Like Henry, they chose to bear arms—many having been injured and some coming close to death in the Stalwart attack last year. They'd be the police for the monastic order and be the first residents of the protectorate under Glory's capable guidance.

A bath beckoned but this rosy feeling was a strong inducement to stay a while longer.

Then came Lana's shrill voice. "Eva, time to come in. Dinner's ready," she called out to the youngster some three hundred feet away. Annabelle chased the girl down, picked her up and twirled her around, kissing her then patting her butt and pushing her toward her mother's voice. "Go on now. We'll play again tomorrow."

Dame Fortune appeared on the wooden plank porch beneath an overhang supported by debarked posts. The brothers and sisters had voted unanimously to give her the small building, known as the think tank, as her new home. Annabelle scampered over to her.

***

As Annie jogged to meet Dame, she noticed Jake sitting on a log grinning at her, his look whimsical and odd. "I wonder what Jake's doing?" she said as she came to stand in front of the old woman.

"Oh, girl, whatsa matter with you, child? Ya be forgettin' I'm blind?"

"Sorry, just thinking out loud."

Slowly, Dame's lips curled into a grin. "But it just so happens I do be knowin' da answer to dat question."

Annie shook her head. "Oh you. You just love messin' with me. Now that you've given it away, care to enlighten me?"

"He be thinkin' dat he be blessed how life turned out for him. You still be his sweet little Annabelle, ya know."

"I know," she said, looking at him fondly.

Dame's smile leveled out. "Annie girl, time is upon us to continue da course set for you, child. I know you be lovin' da tranquility here but dere are many children in need of you, whether dey be knowin' it or not. Dey be needin' da easy peaceful feelin' you be havin' right now. Defeat of Stalwart and dat evil man, Tam, merely stalled da tide. Da waters of ignorance disguised as good intentions be closin' back up as we stand here."

"I suppose tyranny means there are many others like Tam out there and ignorance relates to those man-eaters within the crumbling cities."

"It does for a fact, child."

"Oh Dame," I want the world to be like this …," she fanned both arms and turned a slow, swooning, full three-sixty, "peaceful. Everyone different but working toward the same end."

"It will be someday. But it won't be happenin' on its own. Never forget, child, you be da seed for da change you so badly want. Every day, ya be gettin' stronger—no three men can bring ya down. In time, ya be stronger dan any five men on dis earth. No eagle in da sky can see farther or more clearly dan you. Da speed of your hands and fleetness of your feet continue to mature as your body does. Right now, a mountain lion would barely be able to chase you down. Next year dat same lion couldn't get close enough to sniff your heels. No arrow will be swift enough to ever find its mark on ya unless ya be asleep. And, decisions on which path to take will come to ya at da speed o' lightnin'. Ya be knowin' what is right but hesitation will always be da nemesis." She pecked Annie's temple with a gnarled black finger and brought her voice down. "Da mind knows da way." She then slid the finger down to Annie's chest. "But da heart can obscure da will to make it happen. Always be on guard, girl."

Dame's pragmatism put Annie's mind on the inevitable. "That trip around the world opened my eyes. What I saw disturbs me still." She began the metamorphosis from childlike purity to serious adult contemplations. "I realize that family of cannibals you showed me were only examples of the larger problem, but I'm compelled to consider beginning with them because I can't get that little girl, Lizzy, out of my head. She seemed so sweet and pure, innocent of heart."

"Dat she be for sure." Dame's smile returned. "But da years will steal dat away from her. Da course is set. I don't need ta be tellin' ya nothin'. You know whatcha need to be doin', girl." The old lady tapped Annie's booted foot with the end of her staff. "Now, don't ya think it be time to let Ethan know why you don't wear da knife he made for ya. I know ya been strugglin' with it. And I know he be wonderin'."

"You know, Dame, I might be able to think fast but those thoughts are unique to me. Whereas you not only think fast but also know what everyone else is thinkin' just as quick. Your mind must pull in everyone's thoughts like a tornado sucks in debris."

The old lady cackled, her milky porcelain eyes glistening. "Dat be a fact, child … dat certainly be a fact."

***

Annie stood at the open dormitory door and gazed at Ethan. He sat at a table and worked on a design drawing. A young brother and two of the sisters looked over his shoulder. In subdued tones, he explained to them the principle and function of the proposed machine in the drawing between his hands. He finally noticed Annie across the room and stopped talking.

"Sorry. Didn't mean to interrupt," she said.

"That's okay. It's time to put it away for the day." He rolled up the paper and looked at his cohorts. "We'll continue tomorrow."

As the three walked away, Annie approached and sat across the table from Ethan. "Dame figured it was time I had a talk with you about," she hesitated, "well, about the knife you made for me and why I don't carry it anymore."

"I've wondered about that."

"So Dame told me." She traced the straight line of a gap between the boards on the tabletop with a fingertip and stared at the mindless act as she did.

"Well?"

Her eyes came up to meet his. "This isn't easy for me because I treasure that knife more than words can express."

"Then why don't you carry it?"

"I—I can't."

"That doesn't answer the question."

Unappreciative of his tone, "Look, when I shoot an arrow at a person or throw a spiked disk at someone, I wouldn't dream of ever retrieving those weapons because they all would be stark reminders of the lives they took, that *I* took using those weapons. Even to simply touch those weapons again would cause me to vomit." Again she allowed her eyes to drift away from him. "I'm sorry but the same thing holds true for that knife." Her eyes came back to him. "Ethan, I killed two people with it. Now, when I hold it in my hands, my insides are ripped apart. I want to keep it because it's from you but I can't look upon it anymore."

"Then give it back."

Her face distorted. She began to cry. "I'm so sorry."

He sprang up and moved around to her side of the table. "You don't understand. I don't want it back because I'm angry." He knelt next to her chair and looked up into her anguished face. "It's because I'll make another one, even better this time and it won't even resemble that one."

Her smile expanded to where her lips disappeared into dimples burrowing deep into tear-streaked, rubicund cheeks. "You're my best friend in this whole crazy world, ya know that?" She admired his thick, nearly black hair that hung down covering his ears, the dark sparkling eyes and strong jaw with a braided beard that now hung down over six inches. She reached and toyed with it. "Do you plan on always having this … *thing* on your chin?"

"Don't you like it?"

"No. Should I?"

"You have to admit it's uniquely me."

"And a red waddle on a turkey is unique to that bird, too. But it's not very attractive."

Ethan wrapped his fingers around the braid and held it. "Humph. You certainly have a way of explaining things."

Annie said nothing more but hoped he'd consider changing it. She imagined what he might look like without that nasty thing dangling from his chin and then wondered about the absence of a beard altogether. *I wonder?* The idea of romantic love intrigued her. *I am fifteen going on sixteen after all.* She kissed her finger then placed it on his forehead and shoved his head back playfully. "You're my kind of guy, Ethan Turlock. Don't ever change, except for that beard of course."

***

Jake stood and patted away accumulated heat and moisture from a hard day's work from the seat of his pants, doing his best to disguise the motion as brushing away dirt. This moment of appreciation had run its course. But each day would begin with a renewed sense of it. He, now, believed that.

Movement captured his attention. He saw his Annabelle come bounding out of Ethan's dormitory. He remembered the exact moment that his life changed forever and led to the legacy he so ardently sought. A moment frozen in time when giving a gift of apples to two starving people opened his eyes to compassion he'd not known before—a lesson taught him by a ten-year-old girl. Now the dark world he'd lived in most of his life had been set on a collision course with a new, and far better, destiny.

And it all began with Annabelle and me.

He whistled a tune as he called it a day.

About the Author

A lifelong Texan, Daniel (Danny) Lance Wright is a freelance fiction writer and novelist born in Lubbock, Texas now residing in Clifton, Texas. He lives with Rickie, wife of 42 years, and has two children and three grandchildren.

Daniel has received recognition for writing skills from The Oklahoma Writers Federation in 2005, 2006, 2010 and 2011; from Art Affair in 2008; from Frontiers in Writing in 2004 and 2010; from Writer's Digest in 2008, and the Abilene Writer's Guild in 2004; Canis Latran of Weatherford College in 2011.

Author of:
"Six Years' Worth"/Father's Press/mainstream/print & ebook
"Paradise Flawed"/Dream Books LLC/action-adventure/print & ebook
"Where Are You, Anne Bonny?"/Rogue Phoenix Press/ historical drama/ebook only
"Trouble", short story/CrossTIME Science Fiction Anthology, Vol. IX/print only
"Dancing Away"/ short story/romance/Untreed Reads/ebook only
"Phobia"/Booktrope/2012/suspense-thriller/print & ebook
"Helping Hand For Ethan/Rogue Phoenix Press/2012/young adult/ebook only
"Defining Family"/Whiskey Creek Press/July 2012/young adult/print & ebook
"Annie's World: Jake's Legacy"/ATTM Press/2012/soft science fiction/print & ebook

COMING SOON
"The Last Radiant Heart" (re-release)
"Hackberry Corners, Texas 1934"
"Life, Love, and Lubbock"

Search Daniel Lance Wright on Amazon.com